"Well-plotted . . . Julie[...] P9-BJC-269 loving and sympathetic [...] ed by the L.A. entertain[...] search for clues . . . What a motive, what a resolution, and how clever of Juliet to figure it out." —*Publishers Weekly*

"The Mommy Track mysteries get progressively feistier and wittier . . . *Murder Plays House* is a well-thought-out mystery." —*Midwest Book Review*

"As always, Waldman uses humor to portray the Los Angeles scene while making some serious points about what is really important in life. This thoroughly modern cozy will be popular." —*Booklist*

"Witty Waldman is so endearingly pro-kid that you may run right out and get pregnant and so unsparing about Hollywood sylphs and pro-anorexia websites that you may never diet again." —*Kirkus Reviews*

PRAISE FOR
DEATH GETS A TIME-OUT

"Juliet and her patient husband make an appealing couple—funny clever, and loving (but never mawkish). Waldman has an excellent ear for the snappy comeback, especially when delivered by a five-year-old." —*Publishers Weekly*

"Waldman is at her witty best when dealing with children, carpooling, and first-trimester woes, but is no slouch at explaining the pitfalls of False Memory Syndrome either." —*Kirkus Reviews*

"Think *Chinatown*, but with strollers and morning sickness. Arguably the best of Waldman's mysteries." —*Long Island Press*

continued . . .

MURDER
PLAYS HOUSE

Ayelet Waldman

BERKLEY PRIME CRIME, NEW YORK

THE BERKLEY PUBLISHING GROUP
Published by the Penguin Group
Penguin Group (USA) Inc.
375 Hudson Street, New York, New York 10014, USA
Penguin Group (Canada), 10 Alcorn Avenue, Toronto, Ontario M4V 3B2, Canada
(a division of Pearson Penguin Canada Inc.)
Penguin Books Ltd., 80 Strand, London WC2R 0RL, England
Penguin Group Ireland, 25 St. Stephen's Green, Dublin 2, Ireland (a division of Penguin Books Ltd.)
Penguin Group (Australia), 250 Camberwell Road, Camberwell, Victoria 3124, Australia
(a division of Pearson Australia Group Pty. Ltd.)
Penguin Books India Pvt. Ltd., 11 Community Centre, Panchsheel Park, New Delhi—110 017, India
Penguin Group (NZ), Cnr. Airborne and Rosedale Roads, Albany, Auckland 1310, New Zealand
(a division of Pearson New Zealand Ltd.)
Penguin Books (South Africa) (Pty.) Ltd., 24 Sturdee Avenue, Rosebank, Johannesburg 2196,
South Africa

Penguin Books Ltd., Registered Offices: 80 Strand, London WC2R 0RL, England

This is a work of fiction. Names, characters, places, and incidents either are the product of the author's imagination or are used fictitiously, and any resemblance to actual persons, living or dead, business establishments, events, or locales is entirely coincidental.

MURDER PLAYS HOUSE

A Berkley Prime Crime Book / published by arrangement with the author

PRINTING HISTORY
Berkley Prime Crime hardcover edition / July 2004
Berkley Prime Crime mass-market edition / July 2005

ISBN: 0-425-19869-3

BERKLEY® PRIME CRIME
Berkley Prime Crime Books are published by The Berkley Publishing Group,
a division of Penguin Group (USA) Inc.,
375 Hudson Street, New York, New York 10014.
The name BERKLEY PRIME CRIME and the BERKLEY PRIME CRIME design are trademarks belonging to Penguin Group (USA) Inc.

PRINTED IN THE UNITED STATES OF AMERICA

10 9 8 7 6 5 4 3 2 1

Acknowledgments

MY thanks to Sylvia Brownrigg, Peggy Orenstein, Micheline Marcom, and Susanne Pari, brilliant writers and fine editors all; to Natalee Rosenstein, Esther Strauss, and Rebecca Crowley for taking such good care of me; to Lisa Desimini for such delightful and original covers; to Jan Fogner for details of the real estate business (all errors are my own, of course); to Kathleen Caldwell for her unending support; to Mary Evans, not just a remarkable agent, but a good and loyal friend.

Sophie, Zeke, Ida-Rose and Abraham give me something to write about, and their father makes everything possible.

Berkley Prime Crime Books by Ayelet Waldman

NURSERY CRIMES
THE BIG NAP
DEATH GETS A TIME-OUT
A PLAYDATE WITH DEATH
MURDER PLAYS HOUSE
THE CRADLE ROBBERS

To my girls,
Sophie and Ida-Rose

One

As I huddled in the six inches of bed that my three-and-a-half-year-old son allowed me, I comforted myself with the knowledge that at least I was marginally more comfortable than my husband, who had been reduced to camping out on the floor. We didn't normally permit Isaac to evict us from our bed, but since he'd made his toddler bed uninhabitable with a particularly noxious attack of stomach flu, we'd been forced to let down the drawbridge and allow the barbarian through the gate.

"Are you sure you don't want to sleep on the couch?" I whispered to Peter.

He grunted.

"Honey? Do you want to try the couch?"

"Yeah, right," he muttered.

"It's not *that* wet," I said defensively.

He groaned and rolled over.

It wasn't my fault that the dryer broke down two loads

into laundry day. Perhaps it was shortsighted of me to use the couch as an impromptu drying rack, but how could I have anticipated a night of vomiting and musical beds?

I jumped as Isaac jammed his foot into my stomach, and reached a protective hand around my bulging belly. I patted at the tiny elbow I felt poking up just north of my belly button and murmured to the little girl swimming in the warm dark inside of me. This was likely just the first of many beatings she would suffer at the hands of her older brother.

"Juliet?" Peter said softly.

"Mm?"

"Is he asleep?"

"Like the dead." I heaved myself over so I could see Peter's shadowed form on the floor.

"You win," he said.

"Good," I replied. Then, "I win what?"

"You win. We buy a house. A big house. With lots of beds. At least two for each of us."

I sat up in bed. "Really? Really? Oh sweetie, that is so great. You will not be sorry, I promise. I'll start looking tomorrow. I'll find something with enough room for all of us, and even a special place for your collection."

The truth was, I'd started looking for a house months before, and Peter probably knew it. I had paid little or no attention to his insistence that our entire family could continue to fit comfortably into a two-bedroom apartment, even with the pending arrival of our surprise third child. Peter was just nervous about spending the money on a house. He preferred the flexibility of a month-to-month lease, comforting himself with the notion that if his screenplays ever stopped selling, we could just pack up our children and his twenty cubic feet of vintage action figures still in the original blister packs and move into the trailer next to his mother's. Yeah. Like that would ever happen. While it's possible that there has been born a man both cruel and strong enough to force this particular Jewish American Princess into a double-wide in Cincinnati, Ohio, it is certainly not the sweet, sensitive, grey-eyed guy I married.

Anyway, I knew the moment I saw the double pink line of the pregnancy test that we were going to buy a house, and since then all of Peter's protestations and carefully constructed arguments about mobility and low overhead had had about as much effect on me as flies buzzing around the ears of a hippopotamus. Sure, they were irritating, but did they prevent me from wallowing in the mud of the Los Angeles real estate market? As my six-year-old daughter would say, "I don't *think* so."

I drifted off to a sleep enchanted by dreams of second bathrooms and front-loading washers. Alas, it seemed as if I had only just managed to close my eyes when I was awakened by an insistent whine in my ear.

"Come *on*, Mama. It's seven fourteen! We're going to be late for school." As I had every morning since Ruby's sixth birthday, I cursed my mother for buying my overly conscientious daughter that *Little Mermaid* alarm clock.

I hauled myself out of bed, scooping Isaac up with me, and prodded Peter with one toe. "Bed's all yours, sweetie," I said.

Peter leapt up off the floor and burrowed into the newly vacant bed. I sighed jealously and herded the children back to their room. My husband works at night; he finds the midnight hours most conducive to constructing the tales of mayhem and violence that characterize the particular style of horror movie for which he has become marginally well known. That leaves the morning shift to me, a system that works well, by and large, although on the mornings following nights punctuated by the cries of sleepless children, I sometimes wonder if I'm getting the short end of the stick. Before allowing myself to become awash in a sea of self-pity, I reminded myself that since I barely earn enough with my fledgling investigative practice even to pay a babysitter, it is in my interest to make it possible for my husband to get his work done.

I left Isaac wrapped in a blanket in front of the television set, a sippy cup of cool, sweet tea propped next to him, and a plate of dry toast balanced in his lap. He had strict instructions to wake his dad if he felt sick again. He had already started to nod off when his older sister and I walked out the door.

"Mama, what's in my lunch?" Ruby said as we drove down the block to her school.

"Peanut butter on whole wheat, pretzels, half an apple, and a juice box, of course." I always packed Ruby the identical lunch. She is a picky child, and I'm a lazy mother, and once we figure out something that suits both of us, we stick with it.

She sighed dramatically.

"What?" I said.

"Well, it's just that that's an awful lot of carbs."

I nearly slammed into the car in front of me. "What did you say?"

"You know, carblehydrapes. Like bread and stuff. They make you fat."

"First of all, it's carbo*hydrat*es. Second of all, they do *not* make you fat. And *third of all,* you don't need to worry about that, for heaven's sake. You're only six years old!"

I could feel my daughter's scowl burning into the back of my neck.

"Honey, really. You *don't* need to worry about your weight. You're a perfect little girl."

"Miss Lopez says I'm fat."

Now I really did leap on the brakes. "Your teacher called you fat?" I was very nearly shouting.

"Not just me. All of us. She says there's a eminemic of fatness."

"An epidemic."

"Right. Epinemic. We're all fat. The whole first grade."

I pulled into the drop-off area of her school and turned to look at my child. Her red curls were tamed into two pigtails on either side of her narrow face. She was wearing a thick sweater and jeans, so it was impossible to see the shape of her body, but I knew it better than I knew my own. I knew those knobby knees, the narrow shoulders, the tiny rounded belly. I'd memorized that body the moment it came out of me, and had been watching it ever since. She wasn't fat. On the contrary. She was lengthening out into a skinny gradeschooler who looked less and less like my baby every day.

"Sweetheart, there might be an epidemic of obesity— that means fatness—in the *whole country*. But not you, or your friends. You guys are all perfectly shaped. You don't need to worry about your weight. All you need to worry about is being *healthy*, okay?"

Ruby shook her head, sending her pigtails bobbing. "You worry. You worry all the time about being fat."

"No I don't," I lied, feeling a vicious stab of guilt. I had obviously done exactly what I swore never to do. I had infected my lovely little girl with my own self-loathing. Despite all my promises to myself, I had handed down to her my sickening inability to see in the mirror anything other than my flaws. Was it too late? Was Ruby already doomed to a life of vertical stripes and fat-free chocolate chip cookies?

She unclipped her seatbelt and bounded out the door, dragging her Hello Kitty backpack behind her.

I rolled down my window and shouted, "Don't forget to eat your lunch!"

She didn't bother to reply.

AS I waited in traffic to get on the freeway, I called my partner, Al Hockey. Al and I had worked together at the Federal Public Defender's office, in the days when I imagined that I'd spend the rest of my life representing drug dealers and bank robbers, cruising the streets of Los Angeles looking for witnesses who might have seen my clients anywhere but where the FBI claimed they had been. Back then, I'd been a fan of the leather miniskirt, and thought of child-bearing as little more than an excuse to buy cute maternity suits and garner a little extra sympathy from the female members of my juries. It had never occurred to me that once I had my kids I'd end up shoving all my suits into the back of my closet and spending my days in overalls and leggings, ferrying squealing bundles from Mommy and Me to the park, and back again.

Al had once told me that lawyers like me, the ones who seem to get off on squiring the lowlifes through the system and giving the prosecutors a run for their money, invariably end up growing old on the job. I remember that I felt a flush of pride at his words, but replied that I wasn't getting off on it—rather, I loved being a public defender because I did *justice.* Al had looked up from the evidence we were sifting through and held up a photograph of our client pointing a gun at a terrified bank teller. I'd muttered something about the Constitution protecting the guilty as well as the innocent, and had gone back to preparing my cross-examination.

I had surprised both Al and myself by deciding not only not to spend my life as a public defender, but also to quit work altogether to stay home with my kids. On my last day at the office, I swore to Al that I'd be back someday, but neither of us had imagined that the work I'd return to would be as his partner in a private investigation service run out of his garage in Westminster. Al and I specialize in criminal defense investigations, helping defense attorneys prepare their cases. We interview witnesses, track down alibis, take photos and video of the crime scenes, and do everything we can to help earn our clients the acquittals they may or may not be entitled to. As partnerships go, we have a good one. His years as a detective with the LAPD taught him top-notch investigative skills, as well as the delicate art of witness intimidation, and my criminal defense experience makes it easy for me to anticipate what an attorney will need when trial rolls around. Given the spotty quality of the private defense bar, sometimes I end up crafting the defense from start to finish, even going so far as to give the lawyer an outline for a closing argument.

We work well together, Al and I, even if ours is an unlikely match. I'm a diehard liberal, and Al's, well, Al's something else altogether. I pay my dues to the ACLU, and he pays his to his militia unit. He belongs to a unique band of gun-toting centralized-government-loathers. Although some of their rhetoric is a bit too close to that of the white supremacists seeking to overthrow the U.S. government, Al and his colleagues are an equal-opportunity bunch. They'd have to be. Traditional groups would have tossed Al out as a race-mixer, and despised his children as mongrels. Al's wife, Jeanelle, is African-American. Al's positions are purely political and entirely unracist. He feels that all of us, white, black, brown, and green, are being screwed over by a government concerned with maximizing the wealth of the very few. The difference between Al and normal people who might at least sympathize with that opinion, especially come April 15, is that Al expresses his belief by amassing guns and marching around in the woods with a cabal of similarly committed loonies.

"What have we got going on today?" I asked Al, when he snarled into the phone. Not a morning person, my partner. That's one of the few traits he shares with my husband, although Peter would take issue even with that. He hates to think he has anything in common with Al. Peter just doesn't find the whole libertarian-militia-black-helicopter thing as charming as I do.

"Rats. Rats is what we've got going on," Al said.

"Those rats pay our bills," I reminded him. Al is a notorious despiser of lawyers, preferring to call my fellow members of the bar either "liars" or "scum," and referring to every firm we do business with, somewhat tediously, as "Dewey, Cheetum & Howe."

"Not your kind of rat," he said. "Real rats. Big, fat tree rats, all over the office. My idiot neighbor took down his palm tree, and they've all migrated into my garage."

I felt my stomach heave. "Al," I groaned. My rat phobia probably stems back to the time my mother let me take my kindergarten class gerbil family home for Christmas vacation. I woke up on New Year's Day to find that Penelope, the mother gerbil, had eaten her children. Also the head of Squeakers, her husband. I found her belching over the remains of Squeakers's body. All these years and two children later—while there are certainly days when I sympathize with Penelope's impulse—I still cannot abide rodents. Even rabbits are too whiskery and slithery for my taste. And rats are beyond the pale.

"I'm not coming to work today," I said.

"I figured as much. Anyway, why should you even bother? It's not like we've got any business."

Al isn't a guy inclined to self-pity, which made his woeful tone of voice all the more worrying. Our business *had* been limping along lately. We'd certainly experienced flush moments, but it had been far too long between well-paying gigs. Al's optimism had been less and less apparent, and now I feared it had seeped entirely away.

"When is the exterminator due?" I asked.

"Today, but who knows if he'll be able to do anything. They're everywhere."

"So what do you want to do today? Come up here and work out of my house?"

"No point. Nothing to do. I'm calling this day a loss and heading on over to the shooting range as soon as the rat guy shows up."

"Good idea." Firing a few rounds into a paper mugger was just what Al needed to improve his mood. By tomorrow he'd be chipper again. I hoped.

I decided to take advantage of my newly acquired day off and do some house hunting. I had already gone around with a realtor a few times, in a more or less desultory manner, just to see what was out there, and what our money could buy us. Not as much as I'd hoped, it turned out. Lately, I'd taken to cruising the nicer neighborhoods, more to torture myself with what I couldn't afford than for any other reason. Although there was always the chance that I'd pass a house at the same time an ambulance pulled away, bearing its owner to his final rest, and setting in motion a probate sale.

I pulled into a Coffee Bean & Tea Leaf, bought myself a mocha freeze (promising the baby that this would be the last jolt of caffeine I'd expose her to for at least a week), and pulled out my cell phone.

"Kat Lahidji," my realtor murmured in her slightly breathy voice.

"Hey Kat, it's Juliet."

"Hi! Are you on your way to class?" Kat and I had met at a prenatal yoga class on Montana Boulevard. I liked her despite the fact that she, like every other pregnant woman in that part of greater Los Angeles, didn't even *look* pregnant when seen from the rear. She was in perfect shape, still doing headstands in the sixth month of pregnancy. She had sapphire blue eyes and nearly black hair that she tamed with a collection of silver and turquoise pins and clips and wore swirled into a knot at the nape of her neck. Only her nose kept her from being exquisitely beautiful. It looked like something imagined by Picasso—a combination of a Persian princess's delicate nostrils, and the craggy hook of a Levantine carpet merchant. Kat had once told me that her mother-in-law was on a tireless campaign to convince her to explore the wonders of rhinoplasty.

Kat and I had become friendly, meeting weekly for yoga, and even once or twice for lunch, although Kat never did much more than push her food around her plate. Despite the fact that her food phobia made me feel compelled to double my own consumption in order to compensate, we enjoyed each other's company. We had the same slightly off-beat sense of humor, were plagued by similar insecurities about the state of our careers and the quality of our parenting, and shared a fondness for crappy chick flicks that disgusted our husbands to no end. I had been surprised to find out that Kat was a real estate agent—she seemed entirely too well, *real,* for that dubious profession. She did have the car for it, though. She drove a gold Mercedes Benz with the embarrassing vanity plate, "XPTD OFR." When she had caught me puzzling out the plate's meaning, she had blushed a kind of burnt auburn under her golden skin, and told me that her husband had bought her the car, plates and all, as a present to celebrate her first year's employment in his mother's agency.

"You work for your mother-in-law?" I had asked, shocked.

"Yes," Kat sighed.

"The nose-job lady?"

"The very same."

I had wanted to ask my friend if she was out of her mind. But I had also wanted her to show me some houses, so the question didn't seem particularly appropriate.

Kat responded to my invitation to join me on a morning of house-hunting with her usual professional excitement. "God, do you really want to bother?" she said. "I mean, what's the point? There's nothing but dumps out there."

"There's got to be *something*. I finally got the official go-ahead from Peter; I've graduated from a looky-loo to a spendy-spend."

She sighed heavily. "All right. I'll see what I can scrape up to show you. At least it will get me out of here for a couple of hours."

Kat was a truly dreadful real estate agent. Perhaps she kept her loathing for her job hidden from clients who didn't know her personally, but I doubted it. She lacked the fundamental realtor ability to seem upbeat about even the most roach-infested slum. On the contrary. She had a knack for telling you as you pulled up in front of a house exactly what was wrong with it, why you were sure to hate it, and why she wouldn't let you buy it even were you foolish enough to want it. Her standard comment about every house was, "Who would ever live *here?*" Sometimes she just shuddered in horror and refused even to step out of her car, forcing me to explore on my own. It made for entertaining, if slightly unproductive, house-hunting.

I actually might have considered the first house Kat showed me that day. It was a crumbling Tudor whose prime was surely in the 1920s or 30s, but the kitchen and bathrooms still had the original art tiles, and the master bedroom had a killer view of the Hollywood Hills. It could have worked for us, except for the fact that in the gaggle of young men hanging out on the corner in front of the house I recognized one of my old clients. He'd weaseled his way out of a crack cocaine conviction by ratting out everyone both above and below him in the organization. Given that in the thirty seconds I was watching him, I saw him do two hand-offs of what looked suspiciously like glassine packets, I figured he had resumed his original profession. Either that or he was still working for the DEA, and was just pretending to deal.

"Nice neighborhood," I said to Kat.

She laughed. "My mother-in-law calls it 'transitional.'"

"Transitioning from what to what?"

"Slum to crime scene, apparently," she said. That kept us giggling through the next couple of inappropriate dives.

"Okay, I've got one more house on my list, but there's probably no point. It's not even really on the market," Kat said. We were attempting, with the assistance of another round of frozen coffee drinks, (no reason not to start breaking promises to this baby early—her childhood was most likely destined to be a series of failures on my part, and if Ruby and Isaac were anything to go by, caffeine exposure would surely be the least of her problems) to recover our senses of smell from assault by a 1920s Craftsman bungalow with four bedrooms and forty-two cats.

"I don't think I can stand it, Kat," I said.

"I *told* you they all sucked." She heaved her feet up on the dashboard and wriggled her toes with their violet nails. "My legs are killing me. Look at these veins." She traced her fingers along the mottled blue lumps decorating her calves. Kat was only six months pregnant, a month or so behind me, but already she had a brutal case of varicose veins, the only flaw in her otherwise perfect pregnant persona. I had been spared that particular indignity, but had plenty of others to keep me occupied: ankles swollen to the size of Isaac's Hippity Hop, most notably, and a belly mapped with stretch marks like a page out of the Thomas Guide to the city of Los Angeles. I was desperately hoping the lines would stop at the city limits, and not extend all the way out to the Valley.

"It's kind of nice how your toenail polish matches the veins," I said.

"I paid extra for that. Anyway. One more. I'm sure it's no better than any of the others, but I haven't seen it yet. My mother-in-law asked me to go check up on it for her. Apparently it belongs to the boyfriend of the son of her cousin. Or something. She wants to make sure they've got it in shape to show it. We could just pretend we went, and go catch a movie or something."

My ears perked up. "Gay owner?"

Kat nodded, stirred her straw in her drink without sipping, and held out her hand for my empty cup. "Yup."

"That's terrific!" I said. Gay former owners are the Holy Grail of the West LA real estate market. Who else has the resources, energy, and taste to skillfully and painstakingly decorate every last inch of a house down to the doorknobs and crown moldings? Single women generally lack the first, straight men always suffer from a dire shortage of the third, and straight couples with children definitely have none of the second.

"Movie time?" Kat said, hopefully.

"No. Let's go see the house."

"But it's not even on the market. And it's bound to be hideous."

"Come *on*, Kat! Gay owners! Let's go!"

I wasn't disappointed. We pulled up in front of a large, stucco, Spanish-style house with wrought-iron miniature balconies at every front window, tumbling purple bougainvillea, and a small but impeccably maintained front garden. The house was only about ten or so blocks from our apartment in Hancock Park, in an even nicer neighborhood called Larchmont.

Even Kat looked strapped for something negative to say. Finally, she grumbled, "I'm sure it's out of your price range."

I jumped out of the car and raced up the short front walk. The house was a little close to the street, but the block seemed quiet, at least in the middle of the day. I was already imagining how the neat square of grass would look with Ruby's bike overturned in the middle and Isaac's plastic slide lodged in the flowerbeds.

The front door was of carved oak. In the middle of the broad, time-darkened planks was a knocker in the shape of a gargoyle's head. I grabbed the lolling tongue and rapped once. Kat came up behind me.

"There's a lock box," she said. She reached into her purse, pulled out a keypad, and snapped it onto the box attached to the door handle. Then she punched a few numbers into the keypad, and a little metal door at the bottom of the box slid open. In the box was a security key that looked like it belonged in the ignition of the Space Shuttle rather than in the front door of my dream house. The house I planned to live in until I was an old lady. The house I intended for my children to call 'home' for the rest of their lives. My house. Mine.

"Open it, already," I said.

Kat rolled her eyes at me. "Playing hard to get, are we?"

It was real estate love at first sight. The front door opened into a vaulted entryway with broad circular stairs leading up to the second floor. A heavy Arts and Crafts style chandelier hung from a long chain. It looked like the pictures of the Green & Green mansions I'd seen in books about early Los Angeles architecture.

The living room took up the entire right side of the house. At its center was an enormous fireplace tiled in pale green with a relief of William Morris roses. The walls were painted a honey yellow and glowed from the lights of the ornate wall sconces with hand-blown glass shades that were set at regular intervals around the room. There was a long, rectangular Chinese carpet in rich reds and golds.

"I wonder if they'll leave me the carpet?" I said.

Kat shook her head. "Don't get so excited."

"What?" I said. "This is my house. It's perfect. I'm buying it."

"I'm sure there's, like, a twenty-thousand-dollar pest report. And a brick foundation. Plus, Larchmont is known for car theft because it's so close to Beverly Boulevard. It's a car jacker's fantasy—the lights are all perfectly linked. Anyway, you can't afford it. Let's go get some lunch."

"You're really good at this, you know?"

She just followed me across the hall to the dining room. There was another fireplace in this room, smaller but just as beautiful as the one in the living room. The walls were papered in what had to be vintage floral wallpaper, tangled ivy, and vines dotted with muted roses. I immediately began fantasizing about all the dinner parties we'd give in this room. The fact that we'd never actually given a dinner party, and that my culinary skills are limited to pouring skim milk over cold cereal, interfered not at all with this flight of the imagination.

"Oh my God," Kat said, from behind the swinging doors she'd passed through. I followed her into the most beautiful kitchen I'd ever seen. The centerpiece was a restaurant stove as big as my station wagon. Across from the stove was a gargantuan, stainless steel Sub-Zero. The appliances were professionally sleek, the counters zinc, and there were more cabinets and drawers than in a Williams-Sonoma outlet. One half of the huge space was set up as a sitting room, with a deep, upholstered couch, and a wall unit that I just knew hid a television and stereo system.

I sighed, and turned to Kat. "There's no way I can afford this place."

She rifled through some papers. "There isn't even an asking price yet."

"It's definitely going to be more than I can afford."

"I told you. Should we even bother going upstairs?"

"Why not? I'm already depressed. A little more won't kill me."

There were three small but adorable bedrooms on the second floor, with a shared bath, and a master bedroom that nearly made me start to weep with longing. It was so large that the owner's massive four-poster bed fit into one small corner. There was an entire wall of built-in bookcases, a fireplace, and not one, but two upholstered window seats. But it was the master bathroom that really got to me. It was Zelda Fitzgerald's bathroom. Two oversized pedestal sinks, a built-in Art Deco vanity with dozens of tiny drawers and a three-panel mirror, black and white tiled floor and walls, and the largest claw-foot tub in the known universe. It was so big it could easily fit a family of five. Or a single pregnant woman.

"I hate you," I said to Kat. "Why would you show me this house? I can't afford it, and nothing else will ever seem good enough after this."

She sighed. "I know. It's totally hopeless. Let's go see the guesthouse."

"The guesthouse?"

She began reading from the printout in her hand. "Two room guesthouse with full kitchen and bath, located in garden."

"Guest house like office for Peter, and even office for Al and me so we can escape the rats in Westminster?"

But she was already headed down the stairs.

The guesthouse was as beautifully restored and decorated as the main house. We opened the door into a pretty living room with wainscoted walls and leaded glass windows. However, unlike the main house, which was immaculate to the point of looking almost uninhabited, the guesthouse was clearly lived in. There was a jumble of shoes next to the door—Jimmy Choo slingbacks, Ryka running shoes, and a pair of black clogs with worn soles. The tiny galley kitchen with miniature versions of the main house's lavish appliances was filthy—there were dishes on nearly every surface, and a month's worth of crumbs on the counters.

"Ick," I said.

"Some people," Kat said. "It would have killed the tenant to clean up? The place is probably infested with mice. Or rats. Definitely cockroaches."

One corner of the living room was set up with a long wooden table scarred with rings from glasses and what looked to be cigarette burns. On the table was a brand new Mac with a screen larger than any I'd ever seen. There was also a huge, professional-quality scanner, a color laser printer, a printer designed specifically for digital photographs, and a thick stack of manuals and reference books. I lifted one up—"The Mac Genius's Guide to Web Design.'"

"Check this out," I called. "I bet there's like twenty thousand dollars worth of computer equipment here!"

"Hmm?" Kat said.

There were two large stacks of eight-by-ten photographs on the table. One showed a generic-looking blond woman, her hair teased into a halo around her head, and her lips shiny and bright with gloss. An illegible signature was scrawled across the bottom with black marker. The other stack was of a more peculiar photograph. It was clearly of the same woman, but showed her from the back, with her face turned away from the camera. Her arms were wrapped around her body, her fingers gripping either shoulder. The bones of her spine stuck out like a string of large, irregularly shaped beads along the center of her back. These photographs were also signed with the same indecipherable scribble.

A bulletin board hung crookedly on the wall, and I winced at the hole I was sure the nail had made in the thick, creamy plaster. The board was full of what appeared to be fan mail, much of it in the ornate curliques of young girls' handwriting. I stood up on my tiptoes to read one of the letters, but Kat stopped me.

"Come on," she said. "Don't be so nosy."

I flushed. That's certainly one of my worst qualities. Or best, if you consider my job.

"She must be an actress," I said.

"Probably."

"With a knack for self-promotion. And a really good website."

Kat shrugged, not particularly interested, and led the way

down the small hallway next to the kitchen. We walked into a surprisingly large bedroom, with French doors opening to the garden. Dappled light shining through the windows illuminated the piles of clothes and gave the veneer of dust on every surface a golden luminescence.

"Pig," Kat said.

"Yeah, but it's a gorgeous room anyway, don't you think?"

"Hmm."

"Is that the shower running?" I asked, but Kat had already pulled open the door to the bathroom and begun to scream.

Two

ALICIA Felix's was not the first dead body I'd ever seen, but I think it would take years of experience in crime-scene investigation before one became inured to the sight of a naked woman slumped against the wall of her bathtub, her chest and belly defaced with a scrawl of stab wounds. I reached the bathroom door in time to catch Kat as she tottered backwards. I held my friend up with one arm as I stared at the grim scene in the small, white-tiled room. Kat sagged against me, her face buried in her hands, her chest heaving. I looked at the dead woman for only a moment, but what I saw seared itself into my memory. This was a hideously violent murder. The poor woman's torso had been hacked and torn, nearly shredded. Her wide-open eyes had a milky quality, as though a haze had lowered over them as life seeped away. Her body looked rigid, almost like a grotesque statue, particularly around the neck and jaw. Her skin was mottled; above the flesh was white and waxy, but what I could see of the bottom was purple, the color of a deep bruise. Postmortem lividity, the pooling and settling of the blood in response to gravity. The shower was still running, washing her body with a constant stream, and thus there was very little blood spilled anywhere at all. I could see only the smallest smudge just underneath the woman's shoulders and neck, which were bent to one side by the protruding taps of the shower.

What made the starkest impression on me, however, was not so much what had been done to her, although that was certainly awful, it was rather the *shape* of the woman's body. She was, in a word, emaciated. Her legs were long and horribly thin, withered as if by a wasting disease. Her knees bulged larger than her thighs, contrasting starkly with her skin-draped femur and tibia bones. Her ribs and the gullies between them were clearly visible even despite the stab wounds. Her clavicles stood out from her neck, nearly framing her bony jaw. The only hint of fleshiness about her body was the one breast, the right, that had not been horrifically mutilated. It sat, perfectly round, obviously fake, in the brutalized expanse of her chest.

I slowly backed out of the doorway, pushing Kat behind me. I settled her on the edge of the bed, but then remembered that the room was a crime scene. The whole house was one, and Kat and I had wandered through it freely, stomping across the floors and carpets, handling everything, probably obliterating all signs of the murderer. I grasped Kat more firmly around the shoulders, heaved her off the bed, and together we stumbled out to the courtyard. I sat her down in one of the wrought-iron lounge chairs in the garden. She leaned her head back on the white muslin cushion, her eyes still closed. I don't think she had opened them since she'd first seen the body. I reached into my purse, pulled out my cell phone, and dialed 911. Then I called Al. He asked no questions, just took down the address and hung up the phone.

Kat and I sat in silence while we waited for the police to arrive. A gnarled and lush jasmine vine grew up a trellis nailed to the side of the guesthouse, and the air was redolent with the blossoms' heady fragrance. I closed my eyes and inhaled deeply, relishing the smell, the steady beat of my heart, and the sun warming my flushed cheeks. It felt, for a moment, as if Kat and I were ensconced on a tiny island of sweet-smelling tranquility, the twittering of birds and the steady hum of our breath the only sound that disturbed the silence.

In a few minutes, however, I heard the faint shriek of police sirens, and got up to open the front door to the four uniformed officers that were the first of the hordes that soon invaded; their loud voices, heavy footsteps, and barking radios banishing every trace of that odd moment of serenity.

THE supervising detective seemed a bit taken aback at the sight of two heavily pregnant women rolling around in the middle of his crime scene. In addition to asking us the same long series of questions about who we were, what we were doing there, and what we had seen, that we had already answered for the uniformed officers who arrived first on the scene, and again for the detectives who had shown up fifteen minutes later, he grilled us about how we knew each other, even going so far as to request a description of the prenatal yoga class in which we'd met. I watched him carefully jot down the name and address of the yoga studio, and did my best not to express frustration at the thoroughness of his inquisition. This was, after all, his job. He had no way of knowing at this stage of the investigation what clues, what individuals, would come to be important. Kat and I, as the discoverers of the body, were, of course, his first and so far only possible suspects.

I was in the middle of recounting, for the third time, what we had been doing in the house, when Al arrived.

My partner walked into the yard, flanked by police officers. One of them, a grizzled man who seemed too old to be a cop at all, let alone a uniformed officer, called out to the detective, "Hey, this is Al Hockey. He used to be on the job. He knows the redhead."

I gave Al a relieved smile, and he winked at me. He extended his hand to the detective, whose brusque manner had already begun to dissipate.

"My partner giving you some trouble?" Al asked.

"Your partner?" the detective said.

"I've been doing some private security work since I retired. Juliet works with me."

"Al left kicking and screaming," the older officer said. "Bullet took him out, but he'd still be here if it weren't for that."

The detective nodded. "I'm about done with my questions," he began. Just then, we were interrupted by a piercing shriek.

"What's going on here? What are you all doing here?" A small woman with pitted olive skin meticulously covered by a smooth sheen of expensive make-up, was standing in the French doors, hands on her hips, her face twisted into an anxious scowl. "What happened?" she yelled.

The detective heaved himself laboriously to his feet and walked over to the woman. At the sound of her voice, Kat had finally roused herself from her stupor. She had not been able to answer the police officers' questions with much more than whispered monosyllables, and I was worried that she was in some kind of shock. Now, she glanced over at the woman and groaned, "Oh, God."

"What? Who is that?"

"My mother-in-law."

Nahid Lahidji's eyes were hidden behind a vast pair of Jackie O sunglasses, but she certainly didn't seem old enough to be Kat's husband's mother. She had the clothes for it, though. She looked exactly like what she was, a fabulously successful Beverly Hills real estate agent. Her trim body was encased in a chartreuse Chanel suit with large gold buttons and matching stiletto pumps. Her black hair was sprayed into a bobbed helmet, and her diamond earrings flashed in the sun. Her thin wrists were heavy with bracelets and bangles, and her lipstick was fire-engine red.

Mrs. Lahidji blew by the detective as if she hadn't even noticed his presence. "Katayoun! What's happened here? Why are the police here? What have you done?"

"What?" I asked, dumbfounded at the absurd accusation. I turned back to Kat, expecting her to blow up at this tiny, designer-clad, green goblin, only to see her close her eyes once again.

"Katayoun! I'm talking to you!" the woman said sharply.

By now the detective had caught up with her. "Excuse me, ma'am," he said, "I'm going to have to ask you a few questions."

She spun on one elegantly appointed heel. "One minute. I'm talking to my daughter-in-law!"

"Mrs. Lahidji," I interrupted. "I'm Juliet Applebaum, and Kat was showing me the house. I'm afraid we found a body in the guesthouse."

"A body!" she shrieked. "The house isn't even on the market yet!"

I was not quite sure what to make of that comment. Was it standard procedure to dump a body only *after* the house had an official MLS listing?

The detective finally managed to refocus Kat's mother-in-law's attention on him.

"Ma'am?" he said. "I'll need to know your name."

"My name?"

"Yes, ma'am."

"Nahid Lahidji. And who might you be?"

The cop identified himself and asked her whether she knew the name of the deceased.

She replied, "A woman? Blond? Fake boobs?"

"Well, I, uh, I couldn't make a definitive call about the breast implants," he said, looking a little embarrassed. "But yes, a blond woman."

"In the guesthouse?" Nahid barked.

He nodded.

"Then it must be the owner's sister. God knows there wouldn't be any reason for another woman to be on the property."

"Do you know her name?"

"Of course I do. This is my listing!"

"Nahidjoon, please." Kat whispered. Nahid paid not the slightest attention to her.

"Ma'am?" the detective asked softly, almost tentatively. Why, I wondered, did the man seem so utterly cowed by this miniature tyrant?

"*Felix,* like her brother. Her first name is Alicia. She's an actress."

Three

I felt terrible leaving Kat in the clutches of her terrifying mother-in-law, but by the time the detectives released us I was desperate to get home. I'd called Peter and asked him to pick Ruby up from school, and had found out that Isaac's stomach flu had returned with a vengeance. I hated the idea of Peter taking him out, even just to do a carpool run, but not even Al could convince the detective that I was needed at home. In fact, he didn't intimidate the supervising detective anywhere near as much as the diminutive Nahid Lahidji did. It was Kat's mother-in-law who got us sprung. After she had engaged in a conversation with the detective in which she'd asked as many questions as she'd answered, she turned to me.

"Business card," she snapped.

"Excuse me?" I said. By then I'd become as silent as Kat.

"Give me your business card. And your driver's license, too."

I proffered the requested documents wordlessly.

"Katayoun!" she said. Kat roused herself, reached into her purse, and handed Nahid her wallet. The older woman rummaged through it, *tsk*ing at the jumble of cards and bills until she found Kat's driver's license. She then reached into her trim gold purse and pulled out a sparking card case. She snapped it open, removed a thick business card printed on creamy ochre paper, tapped all the cards into a neat pile, and handed them to the detective.

"Check the names against the licenses," she said. "And then we're leaving. My daughter-in-law and her friend need to get home. As you can see, they are both in a delicate physical condition."

The detective leafed through the small stack of documents and then handed our driver's licenses back to us. "We'll be needing to talk to you again," he said.

"Of course," I replied.

"We'll see," Nahid said. She poked Kat and said, "Katayoun. Up. We're going home."

Kat struggled to her feet, and I reached out a hand to help her. She shook her head at me, rubbed her eyes once, and then stood up. "I'm okay. Nahidjoon, I'm fine."

Nahid clucked her tongue. Then she turned back to the detective. "I assume when you're done here you'll clean up after yourself. I'm planning an open house for next week, and I can't have you making a disgusting mess here."

His jaw dropped, but by then the woman had spun on her heels and was halfway across the yard to the outside gate, dragging my friend along behind her.

I turned to Al, expecting him to escort me out, but he shook his head slightly. "I'm going to hang out here for a while," he whispered to me. "See if I can't get in to see the body. You go on."

Kat and her mother-in-law had already driven away by the time I got out to the front of the house, and it was a moment before I remembered that I'd left my car in the parking lot at the Coffee Bean & Tea Leaf. Nahid had hustled Kat into her own car, and Kat's Mercedes was still on the street in front of the house. I debated waiting for Al to drive me, but, it wasn't more than a fifteen or twenty minute walk home. In the middle of the trek, I realized that while I'd routinely walked dozens of blocks when I lived in New York City, since Peter and I had transplanted ourselves to the City of Angels—and of SUVs—my walking had been pretty much limited to trips to and from various parking lots, and the odd, desperate perambulation with a stroller, trying to convince a crying baby to nod off. I'd certainly never attempted a mile or so in this late stage of pregnancy. But the walk, or should I say waddle, was good for me. By the time I got home, I had managed to calm myself down sufficiently to fool the kids, if not my husband. We spent what remained of the afternoon playing Chutes and Ladders. Peter seemed to understand that I wasn't in any shape to be alone, so he hung out with me and the kids. He hadn't cleaned up the bathroom after Isaac's latest adventure in emesis, but only because we have always had an unofficial division of labor that makes disposing of the children's various effluvia my purview. There are other household unpleasantnesses my husband assumes responsibility for, including dealing with the cars, plumbing problems, and his mother. Trust me, it's an even trade.

It was only after we got the kids to bed that I could collapse on the couch and recount to my husband the horror that I'd witnessed.

"So the shower didn't have any effect on the progress of

the rigor?" Peter said, when I was done describing the state
of the actress's body.

"Peter!" I said.

"What? It might come in handy some day."

I shook my head. You'd think after eight years of mar-
riage I'd be used to my husband's voracious appetite for the
disgusting detail.

He suddenly seemed to remember that we were talking
about a real person, and not one of his celluloid corpses. He
reached an arm around me and snuggled me closer to him.

"It was pretty awful," I said, leaning my head against his
chest. "Mrs. Lahidji said the woman was an actress. Alicia
Felix. I've never heard of her, have you?"

He shook his head. Then he reached under the couch and
pulled out the laptop he'd stashed there when I'd walked in
the door. I had pretended not to notice that he had been sitting on the couch playing on his computer while the kids
wrestled on the carpet, and I didn't comment now. He tapped
on the computer for a while. Peter had set us up with an
Airport, so we could get a wireless connection to the Internet from anywhere in the house.

"Here she is," he said. "I found her on TV-Phile."

I lifted my head and looked at the screen.

The headshot that decorated Alicia Felix's page on TV-
Phile.com, a website devoted to the minutiae of canceled
television shows and former personalities, was the same one
I had seen in her apartment. It showed a gamine-faced
blond woman with a thick head of tousled hair and a pout
that somehow managed to look both sexy and innocent at
the same time.

Alicia had an impressive list of television credits. She had
appeared in guest roles on almost every major sitcom and
drama in the late 1980s and early 1990s. She had even had a

recurring role in a short-lived drama that I remembered watching when I was in law school. It had featured a cast of stunningly attractive prosecuting attorneys, and a few of us had gathered weekly to watch the show in the student lounge. We weren't fans; rather our purpose was to jeer with our newfound expertise at the glaring errors and misrepresentations in the cases on the television lawyers' make-believe dockets. I couldn't honestly remember this Alicia; there had been too many young blond females in the cast.

Beyond the early 1990s, there were fewer and fewer entries for Alicia. The last listing was in 1997: she had had nothing since.

"What happened after 1997?" I asked Peter.

"Maybe she moved into film." He clicked over to the part of the site devoted to filmographies. Inputing Alicia Felix's name resulted in no hits.

"Does that mean she didn't do any movies? Do they have every single actor listed online? Or could she have had some small roles that don't show up?" I asked.

Peter wrinkled his forehead. "I think the site is pretty thorough. I mean, I know that the casting agents on our movies use it to dredge up information even on the most unknown person who auditions for us. I think this has got to mean she never made a movie."

"Huh." I leaned back on the couch and heaved my legs into his lap, pushing aside the computer. "Will you rub my feet, sweetie? Is helps me think."

Peter lifted my left foot. "It's like a little, tiny sausage bursting out of its casing," he said, poking the swollen skin. His finger left an indentation on my ankle.

"That's nice, honey." I jerked my foot away. "Way to make me feel good."

"Oh stop it." He took my foot back in his warm palms

and began rubbing. "You know I think you're fat little feet are adorable."

"Yeah, right."

He tickled my toes and I giggled. "I do," he said. "You're the cutest pregnant woman around."

I sighed. "You wouldn't say that if you knew Kat. She's gorgeous. She looks like a supermodel who happens to have swallowed a basketball. A very neat, petite little basket-ball."

Peter reached his arms around my waist and heaved me on to his lap, grunting loudly. "I prefer women who look like basketballs, not women who look like they swallow them."

I leaned against his chest, first checking to make sure that I wasn't crushing the life out of him. Why am I one of those pregnant women who blows up to cosmic proportions? Why can't I be like Kat, or like the other Santa Monica ma-trons at my yoga studio?

"How about a root beer float?" Peter asked.

Aha. The answer to my question. "Sure," I said, rolling off his lap.

I followed my husband out to the kitchen, and while he scooped vanilla ice cream into the soda fountain glasses he'd bought me for our anniversary the year before, I mused aloud about Alicia Felix's career.

"Maybe she stopped getting parts because she got too thin," I said. "It was disgusting. She looked like an Auschwitz survivor."

Peter popped the top off four different bottles of root beer. He was involved in a systematic and painstaking analysis of all commercial root beer brands, including ones available only over the Internet at shocking prices. There were literally two hundred single bottles and cans of root beer taking over our pantry. Every night we had to taste-test at least a few. And I wondered why I was so fat. He carefully poured root beer into the ice cream–filled glasses, careful not to the let any liquid foam over the top.

"I doubt that's why she stopped getting cast," he said. "There's no such thing as too thin in Hollywood. You would not believe what some of those starlets look like in their bikinis."

Peter's most recent film, *The Cannibal's Vacation,* was shot on an island in Indonesia. He was currently pretending to be hard at work on the prequel, *Beach Blanket Bloodfest.*

"Oh really? And just how careful an analysis did you make of these gorgeous women in their bathing suits?"

Actually, I was only pretending to be jealous. My husband is adorable, in that kind of thick glasses, mussy hair, skinny, and pale-skin way that seemed lately to have become so fashionable. He pretty much epitomizes nerd-chic. I'm okay-looking, for an average woman. Pretty even, when I'm not bloated with pregnancy. However, in Hollywood, pretty in a normal way just doesn't cut it. Everyone here is beautiful, and if they aren't naturally so, they pay top dollar to get that way. It's enough to make anyone insecure.

"Oh, you know me," Peter said. "Ogling all day and all night. Actually, if you want to know the truth, I did spend a lot of time looking at them. But it was more scientific curiosity. There's something almost extraterrestrial about those skinny girls with the big boobs. They don't look *human.*"

I leaned over and kissed my husband on the lips. "Thanks, honey. You're so loyal."

He buried his head in my chest. "At least I know these are real." He sat up and handed me a root beer float. "Taste this one."

I slurped.

"This one any better?" He handed me the other glass.

"I guess so. But honestly, honey, they all taste more or less the same to me."

He shook his head and sighed. "You have such a primitive palate."

I took another long sip, and said, "Delicious. So, if the concentration camp look isn't a deterrent, then why hasn't Alicia Felix been able to get any work for the past five years?"

Peter lifted his head and got his own drink. "How old was she?"

"I don't know."

He went to the living room and retrieved his computer. He clicked back to the TV-Phile site.

"Says here that she was born in 1973."

I wrinkled my brow. "So she's thirty?"

"Maybe, but I doubt it."

"What do you mean?"

"Her first credit is as 'Bereaved Young Mother' on *St. Elsewhere* in 1983. Something tells me that by 'young' they didn't mean ten years old. She's got to have been at least twenty then. Or been able to play twenty. That makes her birthdate no later than 1963. Or 1964, if she could play old."

I leaned forward and stared at the screen. "No way. She took ten years off her age?"

"It's pretty common," Peter said. "You wouldn't believe who shows up when we put out a casting call for a high school student. Women *your* age walk in and try to fake seventeen!"

"That old and decrepit, huh?" I said.

"You know what I mean. You're young and gorgeous, but, baby, I hate to break it to you, you ain't seen twenty in a long, long time."

"Fifteen years," I said.

"Yeah, well, for an actress like Alicia Felix, thirty-five is old, and forty is the kiss of death. If she was that old, that explains why her career dried up."

I sighed, slurping up the rest of my drink. "That just sucks," I said.

Peter nodded.

"Why is it okay for some of these ancient actors to play virile young men well into their sixties and seventies, but a forty-year-old woman can't get work?"

Peter opened his mouth, but I didn't allow him to get a word in edgewise. I was on a roll. "I mean, do they really expect us to believe that some gorgeous thirty-year-old would ever be married to Sean Connery, or Michael Douglas? Those guys are like sixty years old!"

"Um, babe?"

"What?"

"Catherine Zeta-Jones. Married to Michael Douglas."

"Oh. Right. Still . . ."

"It's unfair," Peter said. "But that's Hollywood. Just be grateful you're not in the business."

"Poor Alicia. It doesn't look like she was in the business anymore, either."

Four

"I want a hard-boiled egg. And a Tab," Ruby said.

"And what?" I was pouring breakfast cereal into bowls, tying Isaac's shoes, and carefully padding Ruby's class project, a diorama of her grandfather on skis (long story), with wadded paper towels so that it wouldn't get crushed in transit to school. All at the same time.

"A Tab."

"A tab of what?" I asked, wondering if it was really possible that LSD had made it to the first grade set.

"A Tab of soda."

"Ruby!" I said, more sharply than I should have. "Speak English."

"I am!" she yowled in righteous indignation. "I do not want cereal! Cereal is yucky! I want a Tab soda and a hard-boiled egg!"

I dropped Isaac's foot, carefully set the shoebox diorama down on the counter, and turned to my daughter, doing my best not to yell. "A *diet soda?*" I said through gritted teeth.

"Yes. Milk is sugary. And sugar makes you fat. And cereal is just stretch, and stretch makes you fat, too. I want an egg, and Tab."

"First of all, it's starch, not stretch, and second of all, how do you even know what Tab is?"

"It's the best diet soda. Better than *Diet Coke*. Madison says so. Madison's mommy lets *her* have it. She buys it at a special store. A store for skinny women." She paused and looked at me critically. "I don't think you've ever been there."

I counted silently to ten, poured milk into the two cereal bowls, and set them in front of my children. Isaac picked up his spoon and began eating. Ruby scowled down at the little yellow balls bobbing in the milk.

"Eat," I said.

She rolled her eyes at me.

"Now."

"Whatever," she said, and lifted her spoon to her lips.

I sat down at the table next to her. "Honey, what's going on with you? Why are you thinking so much about diet stuff? Is it because of Madison? Did she say something to you?"

Ruby didn't answer.

"Honey?"

She picked up her bowl, drank her milk and cereal down in a few huge swallows, and clambered down out of her chair. As she walked to the sink to deposit her bowl and spoon, I looked at her sturdy legs, her bubble butt (something she inherited from her mother), and her waist, still untapered.

"Rubes, come here," I said.

She came over to me, leaned against my legs, and put her

head on my belly. "Hi, baby," she said, sounding a little glum.

"Tell me what's going on, Ruby?"

She sighed and, without lifting her head of my stomach, said, "Madison, Chinasa, and Hannah are on diets. And I want to be on a diet, too."

"Why, sweetie? Why would you want to go on a diet? You're gorgeous. Your body is perfect! You're strong and powerful. You're not fat at all!"

"I know," she said.

I lifted her face in my palms and forced her to look at me. "Well if you know that, why do you want to be on a diet?"

"Because *everybody* is on a diet. All the girls in first grade. Everybody wants to be like Madison's mom. She's really skinny. She can wear Madison's pants!"

"No way!"

"Yeah, she can!"

It's a measure of how sick *I* am that for a brief moment I felt admiration for a thirty-something-year-old woman who could fit into her six-year-old's clothes. Then I came to my senses. "I don't believe that. And if it's true, then it's just sick. Honey, normal women can't wear their little girl's clothes. Normal women just aren't that small."

"Madison's mom isn't *normal*," Ruby said, with disgust at the very idea. "Madison's mom is a *model!*"

"Well, that explains it. Models are insane. All of them. They have a grave mental illness. And I don't want you listening to Madison anymore. Tab! Please. You're a beautiful girl with a beautiful body. And that's the end of it. Okay?"

Ruby shook herself free of my hands. "Okay," she said, and wafted morosely out of the kitchen.

At that moment, as if to punctuate her exit, there was the sound of a huge crash, immediately followed by jack-hammering. Our neighbors were beginning the demolition of their house. We'd received notification a few months before that the young couple who had bought the duplex from the elderly brother and sister who had lived there for the previous sixty years planned to raze the place and build a McMansion on virtually the entire lot. We hadn't paid much attention—after all, we were renters, and had little interest in the effects of the neighbors' activities on property values. For some reason the sheer *volume* of the construction project had not occurred to me. I wrapped my bathrobe around my waist and ran down the steps to our front door, hoping to catch the workers before they woke my husband.

"Excuse me!" I shouted at the hard-hat-clad young man wielding the jackhammer.

No reply.

"Excuse me!" I shouted, again.

This time he raised his eyes, but pointed at his ears and shook his head. That's when I noticed that he was wearing heavy plastic earphones. Lucky him. I waved my hands in the air, and he finally switched off the machine and took off his earphones.

"Yeah?" he said.

"Can you guys wait to do that? My husband works at night, and he sleeps in the morning. You're going to wake him up."

"Huh?" he said.

"My husband isn't going to be able to sleep if you guys keep jackhammering!" I said.

"Lady, we're working here."

"I know that!" I said, exasperated. "But isn't there some more quiet thing you could be doing? Couldn't you leave the jackhammering until after lunch?"

He shook his head. "Lady, city ordinances allow us to begin construction at 8 AM."

"I'm not asking you to stop. I'm just asking if there isn't something more quiet you could do in the mornings."

He shook his head, put his earphones back on his head, and revved up his machine again.

Defeated, I walked back up the stairs to our apartment. I found Peter huddled at the kitchen table, his head in his hands.

"I went to bed at four," he said.

"I know, honey. I'm really sorry. There's nothing I can do. The city lets them start at eight."

"How long is this going to go on?"

"I don't know. Months, I imagine. Maybe even longer. I mean, they're taking the thing down to the ground and re-building from scratch."

"Juliet," my exhausted husband whispered. "Please go find us a house. Any house. As long as it's quiet."

I thought of the bucolic garden in which Kat and I had waited for the police. The jasmine plants. The twittering birds. And the house! The giant tub. The Sub-Zero. The mangled corpse. I pushed that last image firmly from my mind and picked up the telephone.

"You don't want that house!" Kat said, dumbfounded.

"Yeah, I do."

"But someone was killed there! We found her body!"

"I know."

"How could you live there after that?"

I looked over at my husband, drooping in misery over a cup of steaming coffee.

"Easily."

She let out an exasperated groan. "Anyway, you can't afford it."

"I couldn't afford it two days ago, but I'm betting there's some wiggle room in the price now, don't you think?"

"That's sick!"

"Kat, just do me a favor. Find out what the asking price is. And help me make an offer. I want that house."

"Oh, all right. But you know what?"

"What?"

"You are a *sick* person. Really."

I laughed. "I'm not sick. I'm just *cheap*."

Five

WITH Peter awake and able, more or less, to help me get the kids into gear, we were dressed and ready for school almost on time. Before I had kids I never had the problems with tardiness with which I've been plagued ever since. I used to blithely juggle court dates, visits to prisons, interviews of witnesses, and appearances before the appellate court with an aplomb that I thought came naturally to me. My first inkling that parenthood was going to have a drastic effect on my competence was the first time I showed up late for jury selection. I had actually made it to the courthouse in plenty of time. It was the twenty minutes I spent crouched in the ladies room, trying to haul my maternity pantyhose back up over my bloated thighs and mountainous belly, that made me late. My favorite moment wasn't waddling into court, sweat streaming from my forehead, the crotch of my stockings hovering at about knee level. It wasn't even reassuring my client that all was well while I tried surreptitiously to make sure my skirt wasn't tucked up into the waistband of my underwear. No, the crowning moment of my career was when the judge called me up to the sidebar and made me explain my tardiness. And forgot to cover the microphone with her hand.

My attempts to balance work and home kind of went downhill from there. Thus I found myself, six years later, working only a few hours a week, and paying more in late fines to my son's preschool than the monthly tuition—they billed me ten bucks for every ten minutes I was late to pick the little guy up. Extortion, if you ask me.

Peter succumbed to the children's entreaties and agreed to drive them to school. Actually, I think what got him out of the house wasn't really a burst of paternal devotion, but rather the realization that it was Wednesday, and if he ran the morning carpool he could make it to Golden Apple as soon as it opened and be the first uber-geek in line to buy the brand new Promethea and Top Ten.

I took a more languid shower than usual—three minutes rather than thirty seconds—and called Al while I was getting dressed.

"So?" I said my voice slightly muffled by the oversized T-shirt I was pulling over my head.

"So what?" he answered.

"So did you see the body?"

"Yeah."

"And?"

"Typical sex crime. At least that's what it looks like now."

I shivered. "And what's going on with the rats?"

He sighed.

"Are they still there?"

"Yup."

"And?"

"And now it seems some of them are dead. At least it smells that way. We don't know where they are, though. Maybe under the floor, or in the walls."

I gagged, which made putting on lipstick something of a challenge. "No way I'm showing up, Al."

"So what else is new?"

I felt a flash of defensive indignation, but the truth was, he was right. The days I actually made it in to work were dramatically outnumbered by the days I didn't. Still, it wasn't like I took any money out of his pocket. I billed the clients for the hours I worked. The very few hours I worked.

"Anyway, what have we got on today?"

Al sighed. "Barely more than nothing. Just that witness investigation out of Texas. The referral from that friend of yours from law school. I tracked down the address of the witness. He's up by you. In Inglewood."

One of my best friends from law school, Sandra Babcock, had become the terror of the Texas bar. She was an aggressive and talented defense lawyer, operating out of Houston. That made her something of an anomaly in a state where it often seems like most indigent defendants are represented by attorneys whose sole qualification for a career in criminal defense is their ability to catch a nap at counsel table. The appellate court for the Fifth District, perhaps because it understood that it would otherwise force two thirds of local counsel out of business, actually ruled that sleeping through trial does not qualify as ineffective assistance of counsel, a decision which has been a real boon for the hung over and narcoleptic members of the Texas bar, and something of an aggravation for Sandra, whose pro bono clients outnumber her paying ones three or four to one.

She had called a week before, asking for help on a case. One of her clients, a young woman, had been fingered by a

DEA informant who claimed to have passed her three kilos of cocaine for processing into crack. The defendant, a twenty-one-year-old college student, had insisted that she was in Los Angeles visiting family at the time the deal was supposed to have gone down. Sandra had called and asked us to track down the family members with whom she was staying and get witness statements from them. She was hoping that the statements would help in her motion to dismiss the charges. Meanwhile, because it was Texas, the poor kid was rotting in jail, bail not being something the judge felt obligated to provide to an African-American in a drug case, no matter how patently false the charges.

"Why don't I do it?" I said. "There's no reason for you to schlep all the way up here, and, anyway, who knows when or if we'll get paid for this case." Sandra would bill the government for our time, but if she were to receive reimbursement at all, it wouldn't be for a good long while.

"Okay," Al said. "You're better at chatting up regular folk, anyway." That certainly is true. There's no one like Al for getting the lowlifes to spill their guts, but somehow his skills often fail him when confronted with decent, law-abiding citizens. I think the truth is that after twenty-five years on the force, Al just has a hard time believing that there's any such thing as an honest person. My years as a public defender certainly infected me with this cynicism, and it has been more than validated by my experiences sticking my nose into private investigations. I've seen some pretty straight-seeming people do some pretty awful things. Still, unlike my partner, my belief in the fundamental integrity of at least some members of the human race has not gasped its final breath. Who knows how long that will last?

Inglewood is one those strange Los Angeles neighborhoods whose benign, even charming, appearance belies its frightening crime statistics. Little cottages flanked by palm trees and jacaranda bushes nestle on small squares of lawn. There are bicycles leaning against porch steps, and kids playing hopscotch and basketball on the sidewalks. It's only at second glance that you notice the metal bars on the windows and doors, and realize that there are few if any older people sitting out on their porches, even in the warmth of a Los Angeles winter morning. They are bolted and barred in their houses, too afraid of flying bullets and warring children to risk the sun-dappled streets. The young people are out, congregating on the corners, leaning against the broken streetlights and staring at the passing cars with eyes vacant of any expression other than vague menace.

In my years at the public defender's office I'd represented many boys like these. And they *were* boys, still in their teens, although they had lived through enough violence and fear for men twice their ages. It had taken me many hours to get through to these young men, to convince them that I, a white woman from a background so dissimilar to their own that it might have been another country, another era, another world, would represent them not just honestly, but passionately. I'm ashamed to say that many of them never believed me. The ones to whom I got through weren't necessarily those who ended up being acquitted. Like most public defenders, I had relatively few of those—my clients were pretty much always guilty of the bank robberies and drug deals with which they'd been charged. Every so often, however, I made one of them understand that I cared about him, that I knew that underneath the tough hoodlum he presented to the world was a young boy with the same fears and dreams as any other boy, from any other neighborhood, including my own. Those guys stayed in touch with me, writing me long letters from prison, occasionally bragging of their successes in getting their GEDs, or maintaining contact with their girlfriends and children. Many if not most of them ended up back in prison after their releases, but every once in a while there was one who turned his life around. I wasn't arrogant enough to believe I was the cause of the transformation, but I knew it didn't hurt that somewhere in the system he had met someone who took the time to care about him.

I pulled up in front of a small pink house set back from the street. The owners had given up the fight against crab grass and LA drought, and had ripped up their lawn, laid down cement, and painted the whole thing an almost ironic shade of grass green. They'd done their best with window boxes of nasturtiums and geraniums, and there were a few bright blooms poking out from behind the wrought-iron bars covering the windows. An ancient and impeccably maintained Lincoln Continental hunkered down in the driveway, its fins casting sharp shadows across the flat, emerald pseudo-lawn.

I pulled into the driveway behind the Lincoln, careful not to get too close to the highly polished rear bumper. I flipped down my mirror, applied some modest, girly pink lipstick, and buttoned my white cardigan up to the neck. Different witnesses respond to different things, and I'm always careful to look the part—whatever that might be. Given the tidy house, window boxes, and thirty year old car, I was betting that the house contained an elderly couple who would be most likely to confide in a nicely but unassumingly turned out matron. And I was right.

The door was answered by a woman in her late seventies, wearing a flowered dress and a cotton sweater that was the twin of my own. Her sparse white hair was arranged carefully on her head, not quite concealing the mahogany sheen of her scalp, and she had an ironed pink handkerchief tucked into her sleeve. The only affront to the impeccably maintained order of her person was the puffy, veined ankles protruding from a pair of pale blue terrycloth slippers. She had crushed down the backs of the slippers, and her heels hung, cracked and swollen, over the edges. I wriggled my toes as best I could in my too-tight Joan and David navy blue pumps. At this stage of my pregnancy, my feet looked more like those of this old woman than I cared to contemplate.

"Hello," I said, extending my hand. "My name is Juliet Applebaum, and I work for your niece, Lara."

The woman shook my hand firmly and moved aside to let me in. "Yvette Kennedy. Very pleased to make your acquaintance. My sister told me that someone might be coming to talk about her poor child. You come on in."

She led me into the front room, a small neat parlor with carpeting the precise color of the cement lawn. I perched on the edge of a pale pink sofa, marveling at how long it had been since I'd felt the sticky tug of clear vinyl slip-covers beneath my thighs. The only seat in the tidy room not thus protected was a taupe Barcalounger whose cracked pleather seemed not to warrant defense against assault by the human behind. Or, perhaps, it was simply that the recliner had never been empty long enough to allow it to be wrapped in protective sheeting. The old man ensconced in its depths appeared to have been there for the last two or three decades.

"Mr. Kennedy," the old woman said, gently, waking the man from his slumber. He startled, and wiped the corner of his mouth with one large hand. His fingers were smooth and bloated, twisted with age and arthritis. Nothing could hide, however, the massive expanse of palm, and it was clear that this had once, a long, long time ago, been a very powerful man. "We have a visitor."

He looked at me, and then at his wife. "Mrs. Kennedy?" he asked. His voice was deep and hoarse, but time and sleep had rendered it more of a purr than a growl.

"It's about Etta Jean's girl. You know."

He grunted and pushed a bar on the side of his chair. The leg rest swung down, and the back moved upright. He put his hands on his knees and turned his attention to me. He rubbed his gnarled fist across his cinnamon-colored cheek and said, "A gross miscarriage of justice, is what that is."

"I agree, sir," I said.

"I marched with Dr. King in Selma," he said, shaking his head. "You'd have told me then that forty years later we'd be looking at this kind of thing, I would have gone on home. Not bothered missing a day's work."

"Now you just stop, Mr. Kennedy," his wife interrupted. "One has nothing to do with the other."

He sighed loudly, and shook his head.

"Mr. Kennedy. Mrs. Kennedy," I said. "Your niece Lara claims she was here visiting you in August of this year. Is that true?"

"It surely is," the old woman says.

"Are you positive about the date?" I asked.

"Absolutely," her husband replied.

"Really?" I asked. Most people don't remember dates and times with quite this certitude.

The woman nodded, her stiff hair bobbing with the vigorous motion of her head. "There's no mistaking it. Mr. Kennedy is a deacon at our church, First African Methodist, over on Thirty-Seventh Avenue. Lara was with us during the summer baptisms. She came to the Lord, she did. Blessed be his name."

"Amen," her husband said, so loudly it made me jump.

This was about as good as I could ever have hoped. Better even. Nothing like a baptism for an alibi to turn a case around.

"Would you like to see the photographs?" Mrs. Kennedy asked.

I nodded, and to my delight soon found myself leafing through an envelope of pictures clearly stamped with the date and time. There was a series of photos of white-clad young people being dipped backwards into something that looked a lot like the birthing tubs I'd seen advertised for rent in the back of *Mothering Magazine*. Maybe those tubs doubled as baptismal fonts when they weren't being used by natural-minded home-birthers.

"That's Etta Jean's girl, right there," Mrs. Kennedy said, pointing a finger at a rail-thin girl whose robes hung loosely on her gaunt frame.

My complacent glee at the sureness of an acquittal ebbed. Lara had the telltale, hollow-cheeked, brittle-haired look of a crack addict. Her aunt must have noticed my dismay, because she clicked her tongue.

"She looks bad in this picture, I know," she said.

I didn't deny it.

"By the end of her time with us, she was much improved. Much. Isn't that so, Mr. Kennedy?"

Her husband nodded vigorously. "Indeed. That is the truth. She got off that plane, I didn't think she'd be able to walk to the car. Honestly I didn't. But she got back on it a few months later with a spring in her step. Yes she did."

"Was she . . ." I paused, not wanted to insult this sweet older couple. But there was no getting around it, Sandra had hired me to do a job, and do it I must. "Was she using drugs, do you think?"

"No! Of course not," Mrs. Kennedy said sharply.

"Now Mrs. Kennedy, you calm down," her husband said. "You can see why she would ask. Of course you can." He turned to me. "It wasn't the drugs got that girl. She was making her own self sick, no help from any drugs."

"What do you mean?"

"My sister sent her to us because Lara had been making herself ill," her aunt interrupted. "She'd put her finger down her throat, to make herself vomit."

"She was bulimic?" I asked.

"Yes, she was," Mr. Kennedy said. "And that Etta Jean was at the end of her rope. Never could control the girl. You know that's true," he admonished his wife, who had opened her mouth to object. "Never could do a thing with her. Well, we took that girl in, brought her to the Lord, and she kept her food down fine. Yes, she did."

Mrs. Kennedy smiled. "We fattened her right up. Look here." She pulled out another photograph. This girl in the picture was by no means fat, but she was a world away from what she'd looked like in the previous photograph. Her skin looked smoother, her hair was neatly ironed and turned under at the ends, and almost glossy. Her smile was broad. She looked happy. I felt a pang at the thought of what befell her once she'd returned home to Dallas. I was willing to bet all the money in my wallet that her bulimia had returned full force once she'd been thrown into jail.

I spoke to the Kennedys for a while longer, and then told them that I'd send typed witness statements for them to sign and return. I asked them if they'd mind if I took the photographs with me, promising that I'd be sure to have Sandra return them. I left confident that I'd helped Sandra win her case. The word of a deacon and his wife, and the timed, dated photographs, were surely all the alibi Lara would need to provide. Not even a Texas jury could ignore that evidence. There was even a chance that the prosecutor would see his way to dismissing the case before trial. Although, given that this would mean acknowledging what everyone else knew to be true—that his informant was a liar whose interest lay not in convicting actual criminals, but in protecting himself and keeping money flowing into his pockets—perhaps a dismissal was too much to hope for. When I'd worked at the Federal Defender, I'd come across all too many of this particular breed of informant scum. The most galling part of it all is the amount of my tax dollars the government blithely hands over to them as reward for their dishonesty. I'd been involved in cases where the confidential informant had earned millions of dollars setting up drug deals. Now, some of these guys certainly pulled in some actual drug dealers. After all, they were themselves involved in the business, and had been recruited precisely because of whom they knew. A shocking number, however, set up first-time offenders with no history of participation in drug crimes. I'd represented all too many of these folks, people whose sole involvement in the drug trade was at the behest of the informant. They were invariably facing ten-to-twenty-year sentences for their minor roles in drug conspiracies. At first I couldn't figure out why the informants would prey on this kind of person. Then it finally hit me; why turn state's evidence against some gangland thug who is bound to have someone track you down and exact retribution, when the DEA will pay you the same amount of money to set up a first-time loser? It's a simple question of personal safety, and your basic snitch is nothing if not wise in the ways of self-preservation.

On my way home from the Kennedys, I was overcome by an insurmountable urge. Right here, only ten or fifteen miles out of my way, was Beulah's Fried Chicken 'n' Waffles.

It really was too much to expect a pregnant woman to resist. On my way through the overwhelming LA traffic that was quite obviously conspiring with my obstetrician to keep me from my appointment with a platter of wings and thighs, I called Al.

"Where are you?" I asked him.

"Shooting range. Just leaving."

"Good. You're not too far. I'll buy you lunch. Beulah's."

He didn't even reply. He didn't need to. My favorite thing about Al is his encyclopedic knowledge of the lunch counters of the Los Angeles basin. We share a devotion to greasy, budget cuisine. It's what brought us together in the first place. When my first case was assigned to this gruff, sexist gun-toting ex-cop, I never imagined we'd end up friends. In fact, I vowed I'd never work with him again. I'm fairly confident he made the same promise to himself, when he saw me tripping through the office in a black leather miniskirt, acting like god's gift to criminal defense. A week later, after a day spent interviewing a passel of good-natured Hell's Angels, Al took me to Felipe's for a French dip. My first bite of the sandwich served to seal Al in my affections, and I think I earned my place in his when I devoured, in two bites, the purple pickled egg he handed me.

I was dipping my fried chicken in maple syrup when he walked through the door.

"Couldn't even wait?" he grumbled. But he grinned when a platter appeared before him as soon as his butt hit the chair. I'd gotten his order in at exactly the right moment.

While we gobbled our food, I told him about my success with the Texas case. When I was done recounting the tale, he waved a drumstick at me.

"Excellent luck. But will we get *paid?*"

"Sandra will file a request for investigation fees. We'll get something, I'm sure."

He wiped a stream of grease from his chin. "Well, thank God for that. Because we've got nothing on the calendar for the next two weeks."

"Nothing? Nothing at all?"

He shook his head. "Big goose egg. And I've got to pay for the rat problem."

I made a gagging sound. "I'll cover half."

"Nope," he sighed. "My house, my problem. Anyway, I hired a kid to help me out. Cheaper than the exterminator. Remember Julio Rodriguez? I've got him digging around under my house looking for the dead ones."

"He's out?" I asked. Julio was one of Al's protégés. He was a young kid with a talent for computers, who had used his skills in slightly less than legitimate ways. Rumor had it that it had taken upwards of a million dollars to close the holes he exposed in the Social Security Administrations computer system, and I'm pretty sure they never caught up to all the immigrants who benefited from Julio's early-amnesty green card program. The thing about Julio was that he never benefited, financially, from any of it. As far as any of us could tell, he did it all out of a kind of Robin Hood impulse, stealing legitimacy from the government to provide it to his family, friends, and neighbors. Money never changed hands at all.

"Yup. Supervised release, as of two months ago. Poor kid, damn probation won't let him work in the only trade he's got, so he's got to hunt rats for me." In hacker cases like Julio's, one of the conditions of release is always that there be no further contact with computers. It always seems sort of harsh to me. I mean, how's a guy supposed to get a job nowadays if he can't get near a computer? No wonder

Julio's reduced to scraping rat corpses out from under Al's garage.

Al patted his lips with a napkin and hunched forward in his chair. "We're in trouble, Juliet."

I nodded. I knew we were. "I've got five thousand dollars just sitting around in my separate checking account," I told him. "That should hold us for a couple more months. We could pay your salary, and the phone bill at least."

Al shook his head. "I'm not taking it from you."

"That's ridiculous. We're partners, Al. You've sunk money into this. Now it's my turn."

He dipped a finger into his syrup and swirled it around. "No can do."

"Al!" I said sharply. "I'm not willing to give up on us. We're just in a slump. Things were going great. We got paid a ton of money for the Jupiter Jones case. We had those worker's comp investigations. Sandra will get us paid. It's building. Slowly, but it's building."

He shrugged, and then changed the subject. "You doing okay?"

"You mean because of the murder?"

He nodded. Then, in a gruff voice, as if uncomfortable with his own attempt at empathy, he said, "I know it can be hard, first time you see something like that."

"Not as hard as being shot," I said. I spoke from experience. Bullet wounds were one of the few things Al and I had in common.

"I don't know. That's different," he said. At that moment, Al's cell phone rang, and he sent an inquiring glance in my direction. I nodded, and he licked the syrup off his fingers and answered the phone. I could tell by his tone that he was talking to one of his talented and beautiful daughters, the younger of whom was an FBI agent in Phoenix. He was probably in for a long chat, so I decided to do some calling of my own. I dialed Kat's number. She didn't sound entirely glad to hear from me.

"What's wrong?" I asked.

"Wrong? Nothing. I mean, nothing really. It's just that I don't think you're going to get that house."

"What do you mean?"

"My mother-in-law says they're not sure about selling. I mean, they aren't sure it's the right time. Right after Felix's sister's murder and everything."

I asked in frustration. "Why not? That's ridiculous. Don't they *want* to get out of there? Isn't the whole idea of living with such a horrible memory oppressive to them? I have to have it. We're bursting at the seams in our apartment, and that's even without the baby. Peter can't get any work done because of the construction project on our block. We have got to move. And damn it, Kat. That's *my* house."

"You are so morbid, Juliet. Really you are. Why would you *want* to live there?"

I didn't grace that comment with a response. After all, she had seen the living room. What was a dead body compared to hand-blown wall sconces?

"Let me show you some other houses," Kat said. I sighed. "Come on."

"You yourself said that everything out there is crap."

Now it was her turn to sigh. "Well, maybe something will turn up. I mean, this place did, right?"

I was just about to beg off another fruitless house-hunting expedition when I noticed Al trying to get my attention. "One second," I said to Kat.

"Possible insurance investigation," he said, holding his hand over the phone.

"Really? Where?"

"Pasadena."

I looked at my watch. "I've got to pick up the kids soon."

"Don't worry about it. I'll take the meeting myself."

I put my phone back to my ear. "Kat?" I said.

"So? Are you coming?"

"Sure. But is it okay if I bring the kids? I've got to pick them up from school in half an hour."

"That's fine," she said. "I've got Ashkon with me today. He and Isaac can entertain each other." Kat's son was a year younger than Isaac, and nearly three inches taller. He also outweighed my kid by a good twenty pounds. Isaac would never admit it, but Ashkon scared the bejeezus out of him.

"That'll be great," I said.

Al was wiping his mouth with a carefully folded napkin when I got off the phone.

"Good case?" I said.

"Probably not. But it's billable hours. And that's what matters, right?"

I nodded. "Call me and let me know how it goes."

six

KAT and I crammed our three kids into my station wagon, shoving the car seats in on top of each other in a mountain of straps, buckles, and velcro. Despite Kat's entreaties, I wasn't willing to risk the buttery leather of her Mercedes. I'd bought Ruby and Isaac bags of sour gummy bears as a bribe to ensure good behavior on our real estate rounds, and I knew from experience that at least two or three of the sugar-encrusted globs were going to end up adhered to someone's butt. Better that it should be my crud-mobile that suffered the consequences of my lousy parenting.

"Just a couple, Ashkon," Kat said, staring in horror at her son's beatific face as he jammed the candy into his mouth, licking his fingers and giggling maniacally. Given Kat's various food phobias, I suppose it was entirely possible that this was her child's first experience with sugar in his life. He had crammed two-thirds of his bag of candy into his mouth, and he sat in his booster seat with the blissed-out look of someone who has just found the secret to eternal life.

"Sorry," I said. "I probably should have asked you before I gave him those. It's just that since Ruby and Isaac had them . . ." my voice trailed off.

"It's fine, really," she said, looking nauseated. Thank goodness my friend was too polite to yell at me. It probably didn't hurt, I guess, that she was enough of a real estate agent to remember that she wanted to make a sale at some point.

"Okay, so. What do you have to show me?" I asked.

Kat reached into her bag and pulled out a folded piece of paper. "There isn't much new on the market. We saw almost everything the other day. But I found one place we haven't looked at yet."

It took a good forty minutes to wind our way up to Mulholland Drive. The house, when we finally arrived, didn't look too bad, if you happened to be a devotee of bad 1970s architecture. And who isn't, really? I could barely bring myself to get out of the car, and it was only Isaac's urgent need to get to a bathroom that convinced me to go inside.

The listing agent was waiting for us in the kitchen, and I was full of something akin to admiration when I saw the avocado green appliances and orange Formica cabinets. You've got to appreciate that kind of devotion to the palette of the period—and 1973 was such an *interesting* year for colors.

"It's beautiful!" Ruby announced, her voice almost reverent.

"What?" I said, staring at her.

"This house. It's just like *The Brady Bunch!* I want to live here, Mama. Please, can we live here?"

With Peter's purchase of TiVo he and Ruby had lately become devotees of all the television shows we used to watch when we were kids. Ruby was absolutely obsessed with both

The Brady Bunch and *The Partridge Family,* and wandered around singing, "I Think I Love You," and howling 'Oh my nose!' at odd intervals.

"You're right, little lady, this is a beautiful home! Let's see if we can convince your Mommy to buy it for you!"

I shot the listing agent who had made this comment a baleful scowl. He smiled back. Unlike Kat, this realtor looked the part. His blond hair was sprayed and marceled into a high wave that perched on his head like a sparrow on a tree branch. He was impeccably turned out in a black linen jacket and matching pants. I'd never before seen linen so crisp and unwrinkled. A gold ring in the shape of a horse-shoe flashed on one knuckle, and it was all I could do to keep from telling him that he had the thing upside down— all the luck would leak right out of it. Worst of all, I had never met anyone so perky, not even when I had tangled with a religious cult. He had greeted Kat with an effusive hug, and begun to rave about the house as soon as we walked in the door.

My frown at his comment to Ruby seemed to faze him not at all. "This place is a true gem," he shrilled. "Honestly, I can't even believe I'm letting you guys in! I should be sav-ing it for my own clients." He waggled a reproving finger at Kat, as if my friend had forced him to open the doors of this dump to us.

"Now just look at this carpeting," he said, flinging open the double doors to the dining room. "It's in perfect condi-tion, but if you don't like it, you can tear it right up. Who knows what's underneath. Could be parquet!"

Kat winced, and I nearly laughed. The mauve shag car-peting probably concealed something, but it was more likely to be bare cement than anything else.

The real magic of the house, however, was that it seemed to have been designed by someone with homicidal feelings toward small children. I'd never before been somewhere quite so kid-unfriendly. The circular staircases had no railings and led down to cement floor. I kept Isaac's hand tightly in mine, because I didn't trust him to avoid the spiky wrought-iron sconces that were placed just at the level of his eyes.

We drifted aimlessly through one hideous room after another, the children amusing themselves by making faces in the mirrors that lined every wall and some of the ceilings. The master bedroom was nearly the death of Ruby, although it was hardly her fault. How could she have expected that the sliding glass doors would lead to a sheer twenty-foot drop to the asphalt below.

"They must be redoing the balcony!" the agent said, Ruby swinging from his hand. I couldn't bring myself to thank him for grabbing her collar and saving her life.

Finally, once it had become obvious that unlike the listing agent, we were not the types whose cheerfulness could not be dimmed even by peeling bathroom fixtures and water-stained ceilings, he led us out to the garden.

"It's perfect for children. Perfect. There's even room for a play structure!"

I followed his pointed finger with my eyes. "Where?" I asked.

"Right there!"

"In those sticker bushes?"

"It's a xeriscape—a low-water garden. Very fashionable, and environmentally sensitive."

I murmured something noncommittal, then found my attention distracted by the shrieks of a child. Little Ashkon had managed to impale himself on the thorns of one of those succulents.

"Oh no!" Kat screamed, tearing through the garden, tripping over the rusted patio furniture.

"Stay right here!" I ordered my children, sitting them down on the back step—the only area not overrun with child-eating thorn bushes. "Do not move!"

I ran over to help Kat. She was trying to yank Ashkon's arm free of the barbs, but their gyrations served only to entangle him further.

"Wait!" I barked. I waded warily into the garden. Kat held her son still while I carefully disengaged him from his predator, thorn by thorn. Once he was free, Kat lifted him in her arms, and we trudged back to where my kids were sitting, quietly for once.

"Perfect for kids?" Kat snarled at the other agent, who had the grace to blush.

By the time we got back into the car, Ashkon had stopped crying, and had begun showing off his scratches to Isaac, who expressed very satisfactory awe at his friend's bravery. I took off down the hill, as fast as I could.

"Fine," Kat said.

"Fine, what?"

"Fine, we'll get you the Felix house."

"Really?" I smiled at my friend. "Really?"

She had her arms crossed over her chest, and she looked grim. "I just warn you, it's not going to be easy. Nahid is planning a full frontal attack for when the boys decide to put the house on the market. She's lined up a psychic to do this insane 'ghost-clearing' ceremony, and she's already booked a dresser for the open house."

"A dresser?"

"You know, like a decorator."

"But the house is beautifully decorated!"

Kat shook her head. "If there isn't something gilded

in every room, my mother-in-law doesn't consider it done."

"Ah. She must *love* your place."

Kat laughed bitterly. "Not a holiday goes by that she doesn't try to foist some monstrosity off on me. You would not believe what she gave Reza for his birthday this year."

"What?"

"I don't even know what it's supposed to be. It hangs from the ceiling. It's covered in gilt sparrows."

"Ew!!"

"My sentiments exactly. It went right into his study, with every other present she's ever given us. At this point that room looks like Ali Baba's cave!"

"So what do we do? How do we get me my house?"

Kat shook her head. "I don't know. I have to think about it. If we wait until it goes on the market, we'll be screwed. Knowing my mother-in-law, she'll jack the price up and get a bidding war going. I wouldn't be surprised if she manages to convince people that a dead body is good *feng shui*. Our only hope is to get an accepted offer *before* it goes on the market."

"How do we do that? Isn't the owner's boyfriend Nahid's cousin's son or something? They're not going to sell it to us, especially not if they know she can make them more money."

Kat wrinkled her forehead. "I don't know. But that's our only hope."

We rode in silence for a while. Then I said, "What if I went to talk to Felix? What if I offered to help with the investigation of this sister's death? You know, in my capacity as an almost-licensed private investigator, and an experienced criminal defense attorney. I could act as his advocate with the police, that kind of thing."

"You're saying you want to ingratiate yourself with a

murder victim's brother, in order to buy his house on the cheap?" Kat said.

I glanced over at her. "Yeah."

She heaved her feet on the dashboard and tapped her toes. She looked positively disgusted with me. Finally, she said, "That could work."

Seven

WHEN we got home I foisted the kids off on their father with instructions to give me an hour's peace and quiet.

"And you know what would be great?" I said.

"What?" Peter asked, Isaac dangling upside down from his shoulder and Ruby wrapped tightly around his legs.

"An early dinner."

My husband glanced ostentatiously at his watch. My generally constant level of pregnancy starvation had resulted in our evening meals creeping closer and closer to the daylight hours. I couldn't help it. I just couldn't seem to make it past five. I suppose that wouldn't have been so bad if I weren't always hungry again by eight. Yes, all right, I'd been eating two full suppers since the first trimester of my pregnancy. Two breakfasts, too. Also two lunches. So sue me.

"How about if we make homemade pizza?" Peter asked.

"Mmm," I said, wondering how I'd survive until the pies came out of the oven.

"Don't worry," he said, "I'll make you an extra one for tonight. And have an apple if you're hungry now."

Thank God I'm married to an understanding man. So sympathetic was he, in fact, that he had taken, with each pregnancy, to matching me pound for pound. Alas for him he could not breastfeed the pounds away.

I waddled off to Peter's office and logged on to his computer. In a short while I had gathered a very detailed picture of Alicia's brother, Murray Felix. No surprise the man went by his last name only. The name Murray conjured up many things—a *bar mitzvah* boy, a certified public accountant, a podiatrist with bad teeth. But Murray, the fashion designer, on the cutting edge of every trend? I don't think so. So Felix it was. A name that was also a brand.

Felix had launched his label with a collection of old-school preppy clothes, *a la* Ralph Lauren, but with a twist. The men's suits were cut a little tight, with bright colored ties that would not have passed muster at the Harvard Club. The women's gowns looked like fairly conservative classics, but in black and white only, with necks so high and hems so low that they were nearly demure. Except they were each characterized by a plunging back nearly to the buttocks, or a cut-away section that revealed an unexpected peek of the side of a breast. The fashionistas had raved about Felix's quirky creativity, his lush fabrics, his unexpected vision. And the hordes had responded by buying, and buying big.

Within a few years, however, other quirky, unexpected, lush designers had come on the scene, and Felix's star had begun to fade. Then, last year, the man had come up with the marketing coup of all time. He hired as a spokesman an eighteen-year-old rapper from Compton named 9 MM and launched the line that made his career. 9 MM had a brother serving a life-sentence for murder, a mother with three crack cocaine possession convictions on her record, and more street cred than any other gangsta rapper in the business. The clothing line was called Booty Rags and, from the pictures I saw on the Web, seemed to consist primarily of gigantic cargo pants, tight shirts in vaguely Indian patterns, and dresses of torn spandex that revealed significantly more than they covered. Booty Rags were all the rage—everyone from Hollywood starlets, to teenage nymphets, to the well-maintained and impeccably toned matrons of Beverly Hills was prancing through their days draped in the torn and bedraggled finery. For those, like me, whose bodies would not stand up to the rigors of micromini dresses and see-through tank tops, Felix sold T-shirts with 'Booty Rags' scrawled in a facsimile of graffiti tagging. No wonder Alicia's brother was selling his house in Larchmont. He had moved way beyond that pleasant neighborhood, and well into the land of gated estates.

The aroma of baking pizza interrupted my Internet reverie. I followed my nose out to the kitchen and found my husband and son swathed in identical white aprons. Their hair and faces were dusted with flour, and they had rigged up a catapult system out of wooden spoons and elastic bands.

"What's up, guys?" I asked, from what I thought was the relative safety of the doorway.

"Extra dough," Peter said. Isaac leaned back and fired off a grayish clump. The T-shirt I was wearing had ridden up over my round belly, revealing a strip of midriff. The dough caught me right there.

"Ick," I said, peeling off the cold clot. "Gross."

"Yeah!" Isaac squealed. "Really gross. Like brains!"

I winced. "Ick," I said again. "Where's Ruby?"

"She didn't feel like helping. She's down on cooking for some reason. She's in her room, playing computer games."

I left my men to their battlefield, hoping vainly that one or the other of them would become inspired to clean up. I found Ruby hunched over the iMac she had inherited when her father upgraded his system.

"What'cha doing, kiddo?" I asked, sitting down on her bed and picking a bit of pizza dough off my stomach.

"Barbie dress up."

Ruby's favorite computer game was a particularly vacuous one in which she spent her time crafting outfits for Barbie to wear. Her current project looked like a bra and panties in a lime green, with fringes.

"Cool outfit," I said, wondering if I shouldn't hire her out to Felix. She seemed to have his style down pat.

She leaned back in her chair and gazed at her handiwork appraisingly. "It's okay. Mom?"

"What?"

"I need a belly button pierce."

I lifted my eyes from my stomach and stared at my six-year-old, dumbfounded. "You need *what?*"

"I need a belly button pierce. Like Barbie." She pointed at her design. It was only then that I noticed that she'd decorated the doll with a thick gold hoop where her belly button would be. The thing is, though, Barbie is not particularly anatomically correct, and Ruby's ring sat on an empty expanse of virtual belly.

"You don't need your navel pierced, kid."

"Yes I do!" she said. "Barbie has one!" She poked the screen with one indignant finger.

"First of all, Barbie isn't real. She's a doll. And that's just a picture of a doll that *you* made. And anyway, if she *were* real, Barbie would be a lot older than you, Ruby."

"But I'd look really good with a belly button pierce." She lifted up her shirt and showed off her delicious rounded stomach. I scooped her up in my arms and kissed her exactly where she'd hoped to impale a bit of metal.

"Mom!" she objected.

"Sweetie, we're not having this argument. You're not getting your pupik pierced, and that's that."

"Pupik is not an English word, mama."

"I know sweetie. It's Yiddish. It's what your Bubbe and Zayde call a belly button."

She sat up in my lap and gazed at me, her expression carefully devoid of expression. "Okay, well. How about earrings?"

I stared back at her. Had this all been a ploy to get me to agree to pierce her *ears?* Was my little girl capable of that kind of craftily sophisticated manipulation?

"When you're twelve, Ruby. You know that."

She groaned in frustration and heaved herself off my lap. "When I'm *twelve?* I can't wait that long! I might already be ugly when I'm twelve! I might be . . ." she paused for dramatic effect. "I might be *fat!*" She whispered the word, as though it were too horrible even to say out loud. I could have been imagining it, but I swear she shot a horrified glance at the stomach peeping out from underneath my too-small shirt.

I was saved from launching into a defense of my prenatal weight gain by the chirping of the telephone. Peter had reprogrammed all the ringers on our various phones so they did anything but ring. They beeped, they twittered, they squawked.

I left Ruby to her fashion design and went to answer the phone. Kat didn't even bother to say hello.

"She says if I even *talk* to them she'll force me to manage rental units for the next thirty years."

"What?" I asked, perplexed.

"Nahid. My mother-in-law. My *boss*," she snarled. "She

caught me going through the computer looking for Felix's phone number. She freaked. I mean, freaked."

"Why? What did you tell her?"

"I didn't tell her anything." Kat paused. "Okay, I told her that we'd decided to approach Felix to see if he'd be interested in a quiet sale."

"You what?" I'm ashamed to say I shouted. "Why? Why would you tell her?"

"You don't understand the woman," Kat shouted back. "She's a *djinn!* I couldn't help it. I had to tell her."

Now, Peter's mother and I weren't friends. I had never managed to muster sufficient interest in her Hummel figurine and Beanie Baby collections even to feign a relationship. Did I think Peter's mother was crazy? Sure. Did I find her irritating? Definitely. But even I had never thought of the woman who insisted on being called "Mother Wyeth" as being a demon capable of assuming both human and animal form. But then, perhaps I'd change my tune if I had to work for her.

"It's okay," I said to Kat.

"No it's not," she groaned. "You loved that house. We'll never find you anything like it again."

"Spoken like a true real estate agent."

"Oh, shut up."

We both sighed at the same time, and then giggled half-heartedly.

"I'm not giving up," I said.

"I am."

"Look, I'm not afraid of Nahid. She can't hurt *me,* I'm not married to her son."

"But I can't get Felix's number. And even if I could, I can't give you any kind of introduction. She'd kill me."

"There's got to be another way to get to him. Once he hires me, what's she going to do?"

"Sic the forces of evil on you. Curse you and all your progeny for a thousand years." Kat didn't exactly sound like she was kidding, but I laughed anyway.

"You, butt out, okay?" I said. "You're no longer involved. The next thing you're going to do is cash your commission check. Other than that, you're an innocent bystander."

She grunted. "Yeah, she'll believe *that*."

"She'll have to. It's the truth."

I hung up the phone and peeked a head into the kitchen. "How long until dinner?" I asked. Peter and Isaac were lying on their backs on the kitchen floor, their faces covered with flattened pancakes of raw pizza dough.

"Like, ten minutes," my husband said, his voice muffled.

"We're monsters that don't have any faces!" Isaac said, lifting up a corner of his mask. "Get it?"

"I do. You definitely scared me."

"But you didn't scream!"

I obliged with a howl of shock and fear, and went back out to the living room. After a minute, I dialed my friend Stacy, the one person I knew who was sure to have a way in to Felix.

Stacy and I have been friends since college, when our competitive natures and single-minded ambition forced us either to become enemies or intimates. We'd chosen the latter, and had spoken pretty much every day for the last seventeen years. We'd gone to graduate school together at Harvard—me to the law school and Stacy to the business school. She'd moved out to LA as soon as she'd graduated, taking a job at ICA, one of Hollywood's top agencies. She'd soared up through the ranks, swiftly becoming a star at the agency. Through the first years of our careers we were pretty evenly matched, Stacy and I, although she always made much more money than I did. Despite that financial disparity, we excelled at more or less the same pace. I won my first jury trial, Stacy signed her first major star. I appeared on NPR to discuss a Ninth Circuit appeal, she did an interview for *Entertainment Tonight* about hot young women directors. Unlike me, however, Stacy had not let pregnancy and parenting derail her career. She'd limited herself to one child, Zachary, who was brilliant and accomplished enough for a whole pack of siblings. Zach had inherited his mother's looks—he was sharp-faced and attractive, with the same thick head of dark brown hair growing low on his forehead that I vaguely remembered Stacy sporting before she'd begun dying it a succession of glittering tones. She had been a honey blond for years, and had lately taken to wearing her hair swept up in an artfully messy bun at the top of her head, clipped with one or two antique marcasite hair clasps.

It took a moment to convince Stacy's new assistant that she should put me through to her boss. I've been known to keep a pair of pantyhose longer than Stacy keeps one of these poor young things. They never last more than a few months—she chews them up and spits them out, much the worse for wear. To my friend's credit, however, her assistants invariably end up moving up the ranks of the ICA hierarchy, or into a better job at a studio or production company. The assistants might have a miserable few months in Stacy's employ, but she prepares them for a career in Hollywood, and she champions them forever after. Los Angeles is full of her castoffs, and no matter how severe their nervous twitches, or how bad their cases of hives, once they move on to bigger and better things they remember her, if not fondly, then with respect and admiration.

"Jules!" Stacy shouted. "I just got back from the Manolo Blahnik trunk show at Neiman's!"

"Lucky you," I replied, wishing that I, too, could indulge in the purchase of a pair of three hundred and fifty dollar stiletto heels I'd have no opportunity to wear. I have, I'm afraid, something of a shoe problem. For a woman who spends her life in maternity smocks and overalls, I have a rather stunning collection of pumps and strappy sandals. As indulgences go, it's not so bad, is it? And anyway, since I'd discovered eBay, my shoe fetish had come to be satisfied with bargain basement bidding.

Once I'd managed to divert my friend's attentions from the delightful distraction of overpriced footwear, I said, "Felix. The designer. You know him?"

"Booty Rags? Of course. He's a friend." She paused. "Anyway, I've met him once or twice. On the phone. He dressed Fiona." Fiona Rytler was one of Stacy's latest mega stars, a waiflike blond with a classical Shakespearian education and a talent for comedy.

"He dressed her?"

"Yup. For the MTV Movie Awards. He had her in this amazing black dress, like a spider web. Didn't you see it?"

"Uh, Stace?"

"Right, right. What was I thinking? You don't watch award shows."

Peter and I had long ago made a vow that we wouldn't watch the Oscars or any of the other of the multitude of award shows unless and until he was nominated for one. I had a feeling we'd be spending the Oscar nights of our golden years catching reruns of *The Rockford Files* on TV Land.

"Anyway, we were on the phone for weeks working out the dress. He's a sweetheart."

"Can you call him for me?"

"Why?" she asked, suspiciously.

I explained about my investigation.

"Oh, Juliet. When are you going to give this nonsense up? I mean, you can't possibly be making any money at it, can you?"

"We're doing fine," I said, barely managing to keep the annoyance out of my voice. I knew Stacy had my best interest at heart, but she didn't approve of my burgeoning career as an investigator. She, like my mother, felt I should be working at what I was really good at: keeping criminals out of jail. She was convinced that I was wasting my time hanging out with the kids and playing at being a private eye. She was probably right, as I freely admitted to her. Still, I reassured myself that, unlike Zachary, my kids have never had to play a game of soccer with the nanny cheering from the sidelines, and no one else there to notice. In my more content moments I was confident that I didn't want to exchange that for Stacy's glittering career, no matter how bored and frustrated I found myself.

"Really? I mean, I can't imagine there's any money in the investigation business."

"Of course there is!" I said, refraining from mentioning that Al and I weren't earning any of it. "We bill out at more or less what an attorney charges. It's a great part-time job."

"But do you have any clients? I mean, *paying* clients?"

"Well, I might have one if you would just call Felix for me!"

"Is that *it?* You mean you have no other clients at all?"

I gritted my teeth. "We're doing fine, Stacy. I told you. We're in a bit of dry spell now, but it will pass."

She clucked her tongue sympathetically and I gripped the phone receiver to keep from smashing it down in its cradle.

"I'll call Felix for you. But, Juliet?"

"What?"

"I'm worried about you."

"Don't be. We're doing great, Al and I." I was plenty worried about us, myself. I didn't need her help.

Eight

STACY'S intervention inspired in me a sartorial crisis the likes of which I'd never experienced before. I must have tried on every piece of maternity clothing in my closet before flinging the last stretched-out smock to the ground in a fit of pique.

"Damn it!" I snarled.

"Mama!" Ruby said, pretending to be horrified at my language. I rolled my eyes at her. Unless her teacher was lying, she knew worse words than that one, and felt free to use them on the playground.

"What's wrong, honey?" Peter said from under the covers, where he and Isaac were building a fort out of blankets.

The only time Felix could see me was on a Sunday morning. While the rest of my family was playing amidst the pillows and sprinkling bagel crumbs in the sheets, I was forced to confront the terrifying paucity of my wardrobe.

"I have nothing to wear!" I wailed.

"What are you talking about? You've got piles of clothes in there."

I'd been wearing the same maternity and nursing clothes for the past six years, with ever-increasing dissatisfaction; and now that I'd been sucked into a more stylish orbit, it seemed I had an emergency on my hands. I threw a rolled-up sock at my husband's head. "Felix is a fashion designer! I can't wear your old Fantastic Four T-shirt to a meeting with a fashion designer!"

"So go buy something new," he said, entirely unsympathetically. The few times in recent years that I'd had to buy clothes had been exercises more in humiliation than anything else. It was no fun to shop for my rapidly expanding and slowly deflating body, and I had decided just to wait until I was back to something approximating a normal size before I hit the boutiques again. I was obviously going to have to reevaluate that decision.

I was on my way out the door when the telephone rang.

"Please hold one minute for Mr. Brodsky."

A few moments later a deep voice purred into the phone: "Ms. Applebaum. I received your name and number from a mutual friend, Stacy Holland. I'm with the firm of Brodsky, Brodsky & Shapiro. I imagine you've heard of us?"

I had. They were a fairly well-known entertainment law firm in the city, and were not infrequently cited in the trades. "Of course. What can I do for you?" I crossed every finger and toe, praying that he had a case for us.

"My firm has lately been exploring the possibility of engaging in a relationship with an investigative office that specializes in criminal defense. The idea would be to have someone on call when our clients find themselves in unexpected difficulties. Difficulties that require a different kind of expertise to resolve than we possess."

I didn't scream and shout in a combination of joy and relief, but that's only because I clamped my lips shut.

"What kind of difficulties?" I said calmly.

He paused, and my stomach tightened. Had my question caused him to doubt me?

"Perhaps situations where claims are made against your clients, either in the press or simply as rumor?" I asked.

"That's one kind of situation."

"And I imagine there are the occasional brushes with the criminal justice system; situations where hiring a defense attorney might be premature, but where an investigation might prove useful."

"Precisely."

"I think we can certainly help you," I said. "My partner is an ex-police officer, and thus has both connections and experience that is invaluable in all kinds of different situations. And I am a criminal defense attorney, although I no longer practice in the courtroom. I can make sure that any investigation would not endanger future criminal defenses."

"That is what Ms. Holland led us to understand. She believes your firm would suit our needs nicely."

I sent a wordless blessing to Stacy.

"Do you, perhaps, have any references?" Brodsky asked.

I gave him Sandra's name, but I could tell he wanted someone, well, glitzier. I told him I'd need to consult my clients before handing out their names, but I was sure that I'd have something for him. Lilly would talk to him, I just knew she would. And then I made a terrible mistake. It was an understandable error, born as it was of my desperation to close the deal, of my concern for Al, and for my own

professional future, but I regretted the words as soon as
they left my lips: "I've just taken on a rather high-profile
case," I said. "Of course I can't go into detail, but it's a
murder investigation involving a number of well-known
individuals."

"A high-profile murder investigation? Going on right
now?"

"Yes."

"The Felix case? The murder of the fashion designer's sister? You're investigating that? I know Felix quite well. We
represented a company that sought to acquire his a few years
ago."

I gulped and said, "I'm so sorry; confidentiality prevents
me from saying any more."

"Of course, of course. Well, Ms. Applebaum, that certainly is impressive. My partners and I will be watching to
see how that case turns out. Why don't we plan on speaking
once things are resolved? At that point we'll all have a good
idea if working together would be in our mutual best interests."

It was all I could do to keep from strangling myself with
the phone cord. Had I really all but told the man that I represented Felix? I had. And had he really made our hiring
contingent on resolving Alicia's murder? He had. Of course,
Felix hadn't even hired me yet, and even if he did, who
knew if I was ever going to be able to solve the case? What
a fool I was. What a complete and total fool.

In a terrible funk, I made my way to Liz Lange, a maternity clothing store that was so expensive I'd never done
more than casually browse the window displays. A meeting
with the founder of Booty Rags justified a more intensive
scrutiny of their wares, and my misery was more than
enough excuse for some retail therapy. Thirty minutes and

over two hundred dollars later I flounced out of the store wearing a tight, black, long-sleeved T-shirt that showed off my belly, and a grey skirt that did much the same to my rather corpulent behind. The salesgirl had assured me that tight clothes were in for pregnant woman. The idea, I guess, is to celebrate the vastness, not disguise it. Since I was well aware that any attempts at concealment were at best fruitless and at worst pathetic, I was ready to jump on the celebratory bandwagon. Still, I was not quite willing to buy myself a pair of maternity thong underpants—every girl has her limits. A pair of high-heeled black boots that I'd brought with me completed the ensemble, and I felt great, panty lines and all.

The door to my dream house was answered by a small man with a thick shock of black hair and the largest brown eyes I'd ever seen in my life. His sooty lashes were so long they looked tangled, and his lips were full and red. He was beautiful, although certainly not traditionally handsome. He was far too petite for that. He looked like a miniature movie star, a fashion model writ two sizes smaller than normal.

"Hallo," he said, in a vaguely European accent.

"I'm Juliet Applebaum," I said, extending my hand.

"Farzad Bahari," he said, taking it in his own. His grip was surprisingly firm, for such a delicate man.

He led me through the vaulted entry way and into the long living room. A cheery fire was burning in the green-tiled fireplace, and the many sconces were lit, despite the bright midmorning light shining through the leaded glass windows. I surreptitiously buried a covetous toe in the thick Chinese carpet, and determined to convince Felix and his pretty boyfriend not only to sell me their house, but also to toss in the rug.

"One moment. I'll let Felix know you're here. He's in his room. Resting."

"Of course," I said. "This must be very difficult for him. Losing his sister."

Farzad pursed his voluptuous lips for a moment, and then nodded, almost grudgingly. He left me alone in the room and ran quickly up the stairs. I took advantage of his absence to look once again around the room. When Kat and I had been through the house I'd been far too interested in the tiles, wood floors, moldings, and fixtures to look at the pictures on the walls. Now I could examine the black and white photos at my leisure. There was a long row of them, matted and framed behind museum glass. There were one or two that looked decidedly like Robert Mapplethorpes—few other photographers capture the male body with quite that erotic artistry. The others were dramatic, stylized fashion photographs, including two large prints of ethereal models wearing clothing that bore the unmistakable mark of Booty Rag ghetto-chic.

"Those are Avedons," a voice said. I leapt back—I'd had my nose pressed altogether too close to the glass.

"Wow!" I said. "The real deal?" I turned to look at Alicia's brother. He was a tall, thin man with fair hair cropped close to his scalp. His narrow face was dominated by a sharp beak of a nose, made all the more prominent by the diamond stud nestled in the crease above his nostril. He was wearing a black T-shirt in a soft clingy fabric that looked like silk. His narrow hips were having a hard time holding up his voluminous cargo pants, and a pair of black silk underwear peeped above the drooping waist.

"I'm so sorry for your loss," I said.

He nodded, and collapsed into an oversized wing chair, leaning his head back into the nubbly leather. "So you're a friend of Stacy Holland's," he said.

At that moment Farzad came into the room carrying a tray with three small cups and a matching coffeepot. He put the tray down on a side table. Without asking me how I took mine, he spooned generous portions of sugar into each cup and handed them to his boyfriend and me. I took a tentative sip, and then smiled. The coffee was rich and sweet, but plain and strong, too. Much better than the milkshake-like concoctions I'd been drinking lately.

"Mm," I said.

"Farzad makes a fabulous cup of coffee," Felix said, smiling at the smaller man. Farzad sat down on the couch and tucked his legs up under him. He nodded graciously at the comment, clearly understanding that it was no more than his due.

I took another sip, and then warmed my hands around the small cup. "I've known Stacy forever," I said. "Since college."

"Oh?" Felix said, in a voice entirely devoid of interest.

"Did she explain to you why I wanted to meet you?" I asked.

"Sort of. But I'm not sure I really understand. She told me that you were the one who . . . who found Alicia."

"Yes," I said softly. I told him how Kat and I had come to be in the house that morning.

"I told Nahid that lock box was a dreadful idea!" Farzad interrupted. I looked over at him. His face was flushed and he looked angry. "She wouldn't listen. She is just like my mother. Does what she wants."

"You hadn't asked her to put the box on?" I asked.

"Of course not!" he said. "It's a ridiculous idea. Putting your key on the door so anyone can walk in! What's the point of having a five thousand dollar alarm system if you leave the key for anyone to find?"

"Why did she want the lock box, do you know?"

Felix reached across to the couch and laid a calming hand on his boyfriend's arm. "We were just about to put the house on the market," he said to me. "Nahid wanted to be able to get in when she needed to, and to send other agents by to look at the place while we were out of town. She had one of her handymen come and install the box."

"You were out of town?"

He nodded. "At our place in Palm Springs. We'd been there for a couple of months. That's why we wanted to sell the house. To move down there, permanently."

"You'd planned to leave LA?"

He nodded. "Farzad's been dying to get out of the city. And we've fallen in love with Palm Springs. The desert has wonderful energy. So creatively inspiring. We were there working on the preliminary sketches for my autumn collection when we found out about Alicia. So much for the collection," he said, waving his hand as if to bid it goodbye. "I'm not likely to get any of it done now."

"Of course you will. You'll be ready to go back to work in a week or two. It will be a good distraction for you," Farzad said, managing to sound both tender and bossy.

Felix shook his head. "I don't know. I doubt it. Maybe you'll have to do it for me, sweetie." He laughed humorlessly. "It's not like anyone would know the difference."

I gently brought them back to what we'd been talking about before. "So you were out of town when Alicia was killed?"

"Yes," Felix said. He suddenly narrowed his eyes and looked at me. "I'm not sure I understand, Ms. Applebaum. Exactly why did you ask Stacy if you could meet me?"

I explained to Felix that I was an investigator, and that I was eager to help in any way that I could. "I guess you could say that finding her body makes me feel like I have a kind of personal stake in finding out who murdered your poor sister," I finished, lamely.

Felix nodded, not looking entirely convinced. He said, "How can you help? The police are investigating her murder."

"Well, in addition to being an investigator, I was a criminal defense attorney. I can act as your advocate with the police, help you navigate their questions, follow leads they might not be interested in pursuing. I'd be on your side, acting in your interests. You can't necessarily rely on the police for that." I thought of Harvey Brodsky and had a sudden inspiration. "My partner and I provide these kinds of services for people in situations like yours. High-profile individuals for whom relying on the good will of the police is simply not an option, but for whom engaging a criminal defense lawyer might not project the right image."

Farzad nodded, although Felix still looked perplexed, and perhaps a little suspicious.

"Why would I need an advocate with the police?" Felix said.

"Because the police are bound to think you killed Alicia!" Farzad said. "They always blame the family." He turned to me. "Don't they? Don't they always blame the family?"

"Well, statistically, murders are most often committed by someone the victim knows. So yes, they do look to the family."

"But we were in Palm Springs!" Felix said.

I nodded. "And I'm sure the police will rule you out once they verify that."

"No they won't," Farzad said. "They'll just say we paid someone to kill her."

I was surprised by his vehemence. Why was he so sure that he and his partner would become suspects in this grisly murder?

Felix once again patted his boyfriend's arm. Then he smiled at me, uncomfortably. "Farzad was born in Iran. He doesn't have exactly warm feelings toward the police."

I nodded sympathetically. "Of course not."

"He's basically pathologically suspicious of authority," Felix said.

"Have you done this kind of work before?" Farzad asked.

"Yes, I have. Of course my work is confidential, so I can't give you references, but rest assured my partner and I are experienced in this area." Lilly's case qualified as experience, didn't it? "This isn't a service for everyone," I said, hoping my voice wasn't slipping into too oily a register. "Only individuals with a certain public profile can afford this level of protection, or even need it. Most people simply muddle through. Ours is a service appropriate only for the select few." I was definitely going to need a shower when I was done with this interview.

I wasn't wrong in my assessment of Felix's vanity. I've found, in fact, that it's very difficult to overestimate the narcissism of the average wealthy Los Angelino.

"I suppose it wouldn't hurt to have someone on our side," Felix said. "I do have a public profile I need to protect." Then he narrowed his eyes. "But what do you get out of this?"

I was not willing to confess my hope to buy his house on the cheap, and I was getting more and more uncomfortable with my own ulterior motives.

"We pay her," Farzad said. "That's what she gets out of it."

I nodded. "That, and the knowledge that I've done what I can to help find whoever did that to your sister. Finding her is not something I'm ever going to be able to forget." I wasn't lying. The image of Alicia's violated body was there, in my memory, forever.

"How much, exactly, do we pay you?" Farzad asked.

I outlined Al's and my rates. They were reasonable, considering how much money Felix obviously had.

After a moment, Felix nodded. "Okay. We can give it a try. See if it works out."

I hoped my huge sigh of relief was not audible. I leaned forward. "You won't be sorry," I said. "Can I ask you a few questions about your sister? To give me some context for my investigation?"

Felix told me that he and Alicia had grown up in Miami. "My dad owns a Chevrolet dealership. The first thing I did when I got out of there was buy a European car."

After a brief stint at the Fashion Institute of Technology, Felix had followed his sister out to Los Angeles. She'd gone to UCLA and majored in acting. By the time her brother joined her in Hollywood, it was clear to them both that her star was rising.

"She had auditions almost every day, and seemed to get a lot of the parts she tried out for. It was mostly commercials and little one-time roles on TV shows, but she was doing really well. And she was leading this total Hollywood lifestyle. She and her friends would spend every night at parties, or at clubs. She was dating guys you'd recognize from TV, even if you didn't know their names. To a kid like me, it seemed like the coolest scene ever." He shook his head ruefully. "Alicia was terrific. She put me up for almost a year—I slept on this stinky little pull-out futon in her living room. She introduced me to people, even set me up with guys she knew."

"Hey!" Farzad said.

"That was all before you, baby."

"Did the rest of your family know you were gay?" I asked. "Or just Alicia?"

Felix snapped his fingers in the air. "Oh honey, I've been out of the closet my whole life. My mother caught me with our Cuban gardener when I was about fourteen years old."

"Wow!"

He smiled, ruefully. "Let's just say she was *not* surprised. I'd been cutting up her dresses and restyling them for her since I was nine years old. Not many hetero boys can manage a straight seam in velvet."

I thought of my husband and his wardrobe of jeans, khakis, and T-shirts.

"That's certainly true," I said.

"Anyway, I was lucky. My parents were fine with it. They just told me to keep my hands off the help."

Farzad snorted into his coffee cup.

"So Alicia was getting a lot of parts," I said.

"For a while," Felix said. He then told me what I already knew about the downturn in her fortunes.

"That must have been difficult, coinciding as it did with your success."

He shook his head. "It was awful. I mean, not that Alicia was necessarily jealous. She was glad for me."

"She certainly liked having someone to borrow money from," Farzad interjected.

"Farzad! You know full well how much I owe Alicia," Felix said, raising his voice.

The younger man shrugged and made a zipping motion across his lips.

I paused for a minute, and then said, "Alicia borrowed money from you?"

Felix glared at his boyfriend. "Not exactly. I mean, I never expected her to pay me back."

"And you gave her a place to live?"

He nodded. "She worked for that, though. She was our personal assistant." He shot a warning glance at his boyfriend, and I wondered exactly what he was worried the indiscreet young man would tell me.

"What did she do for you?"

"She took care of the house while we were gone, for one. And she did errands and things."

"What kind of errands?"

"You know. Picking up the dry cleaning. Doing the grocery shopping. Making dinner reservations, booking travel. That kind of stuff."

I nodded, imagining what it would feel like to be one's younger brother's maid and errand girl. I don't think I could have tolerated it for a minute, and I felt terribly sorry for Alicia. While my career might not be going anywhere fast, it certainly wasn't sinking into the kind of oblivion that had forced her into this awkward and surely unpleasant situation with her brother.

"What was Alicia planning on doing once you moved to Palm Springs? Was she going to come with you?"

Felix shook his head. "No. She couldn't have. Not if she wanted to keep auditioning and appearing with her comedy troupe. She'd have found some other work, I guess."

"Was she upset at the prospect of your move?"

"She wasn't thrilled. I mean, it meant a lot of changes for her. But Alicia was a flexible person. She would have been fine." He heaved a huge sigh. "I don't know what's going to come of all that now."

"All what?" I asked.

"Palm Springs. The move. Everything."

"Don't be silly, darling," Farzad said. "There's even less of a reason to stay here, now."

Felix rubbed his eyes with his hand. "I can't bear the idea of selling this house, of leaving, with everything so unresolved. I don't know. I just don't know." His voice trailed off.

I felt my tenuous grasp on my dream house slipping away.

We sat in silence for a few moments, and then I changed the subject. I asked for the names of some of Alicia's friends, and after a short pause Felix came up with one.

"Moira Sarsfield. She's known Alicia for ages. They kind of rose and fell together, if you know what I mean."

"Do you have her number?"

He shook his head. "No, but she works at Franklin's, the restaurant in that Best Western, the one right before you get on the 101 in Hollywood. You can probably find her there."

Before I left, I gave Felix and Farzad a printout that Al's wife Jeanelle had made for us of our fee schedule and expense reimbursement policy. My embarrassment at taking the job solely to get my paws on that house kept me from asking for a retainer, and I mentally crossed my fingers, hoping that Al wouldn't kill me when he found out.

Farzad saw me to the door.

"You have a beautiful home," I said.

He raised an eyebrow. "That's right; you were looking at it with a real estate agent. So, had you planned to make an offer? Before all this, of course."

I gazed at him for a moment, and then I said, "You know, Farzad, I'd still like to make an offer. That is if you still plan on selling the house. It would be perfect for me and my family."

He waggled his head in something between a nod and

a shrug. "Well, we'll see how all this pans out. Perhaps you will figure out who murdered poor Alicia, and Felix will be so grateful that he'll sell you the house!"

My plan exactly! "Perhaps," I said. "I'll do my best."

Nine

WHEN I told Al about Harvey Brodsky's call, and about the possibility of us receiving a lucrative contract from him, Al expressed a momentary excitement. I felt terrible when I was forced to explain that it all hinged on how we did with the Felix murder.

"It's most likely a sex crime, Juliet! We aren't qualified to investigate a murder like that."

"I know."

"You solve those crimes forensically!"

"I know."

"With teams of detectives, crime scene experts, medical examiners!"

"I know."

"Not two people operating out of a garage!"

"I know."

He sighed.

I pulled over to the side of Melrose Avenue. This was not

a conversation I could have while driving. "We don't have to solve the crime," I said. "Our job is to help Felix and Farzad navigate through the system. You know, be their representatives to the police. That kind of thing."

He sighed again.

"That's what Brodsky's interested in! Not if we solve the murder or not. He can't possibly expect that."

"Let's hope not," he said.

"Hey, how'd that meeting with the insurance company go?"

"They offered me a job."

"Great! A paying client!"

"No. They don't want the agency. They want me to go work for them. To head up their investigation unit."

"Oh." My stomach sank. Was it all going to end like this? "Oh. Well, then this whole Brodsky thing isn't really important, is it?"

"I turned them down."

"You did what?"

"I turned them down. I don't want to work in some office with some vice president breathing down my neck. I've had enough of that."

"You'd rather work out of your rat-infested garage?"

"Damn right I would. What, do you want me to take the job? Are you trying to weasel out of our partnership?"

"No! No!" I said.

"Good. You're stuck with me, lady."

I smiled and merged back into traffic. After Al and I hung up, I called Peter. The first thing he did was fill me in on the state of the neighbor's construction.

"Jackhammering. All day. I'm losing my mind."

"I'm so sorry, honey. We'll move. Soon. I promise."

"God, I hope so. Anyway, we're on our way to the Santa Monica pier to ride the carousel."

I was free to continue my perambulations around the city. I'd been sure that my husband would not approve of my plan to investigate Alicia's murder, but to my surprise he was remarkably easy going about my efforts. He merely wished me luck, and reminded me that my first priority was to find us a new house. I don't think he thought much of my chances of parlaying an investigation into a house purchase. But he hadn't been out in the real estate trenches like I had. He didn't know just how little there was out there.

I took surface streets over to Franklin's, hoping that I'd find Moira at work. I debated calling the restaurant first, but decided that the benefit of a surprise appearance outweighed any inconvenience of schlepping all the way to Hollywood. I was more likely to catch Alicia's friend in a gregarious mood if I caught her unawares.

Franklin's is one of those dives that for some reason periodically becomes fashionable among Hollywood's almost-elite. The place certainly has a seedy charm to it, with the cracked vinyl booths and Formica counter. But the food isn't much to speak of, and the listless snobbery of the wait staff has always made it and other restaurants of its ilk something of a turnoff to me. It's not that I don't feel sorry for the Juilliard and Royal Shakespeare Company graduates who are forced to earn their livings pouring ranch dressing onto iceberg lettuce salads and swabbing countertops with foul-smelling rags. I was a waitress myself, back in my pre-lawyer days. I have nothing but sympathy for food servers. It's just that I'm never really able to understand why their professional despair need express itself in an ill-concealed disdain for my food choices, my clothes, and me as a person.

Moira was working, if you could call it that, and more than happy to pull herself a cup of coffee from the vast metal urn and sit with me while I ate my BLT.

"It's such a nightmare," she said, dragging the back of her hand roughly across her eyes. It hadn't taken much to start her tears flowing. The mere mention of Alicia's name was enough to jumpstart her grief.

"I'm so sorry," I said again, patting her arm with one hand while the other balanced my leaking sandwich. I swabbed at the dripping mayonnaise with my tongue and put the sandwich down. "Had you seen Alicia recently?"

Moira nodded. "I see her all the time. Like every couple of days. She's my best friend." Her tears were flowing thick and fast, now. "God, Aziz, that's the manager, he's going to kill me. I've been crying pretty much constantly since I found out. The customers aren't real excited about being waited on by some wailing hag."

"You're not a hag," I said. "But maybe you should take a little time off. It's got to be really hard trying to work while you're feeling this way."

"Yeah, that might be nice. But if I don't work, I don't eat and I don't pay the rent, so it's not like I've got a choice."

I nodded sympathetically. "It's not an easy life, acting."

"You could say that. Although I'm not really sure I can consider myself an actor anymore. I mean, I haven't gotten a single part in three years. I'm pretty sure that that makes me just a waitress."

"That's kind of what was going on with Alicia, wasn't it?"

She nodded and tucked her stringy blond hair behind her ear. I noticed a fine, white scar extending along her crown and scalp. Had her hair been clean, and not dragged back on her skull, it would have been entirely covered. I'd seen scars like that once before—on Stacy's mother when she was recuperating at Stacy's house after one of her many facelifts. Mrs. Holland's had been red and fiery, but they'd faded over time. Like Moira, she now looked a bit pressed and pulled, but not too bad. The only difference was that my friend's mother was in her sixties, and Moira was surely not much older than I.

"It's just really hard for women in Hollywood," she said, sighing into her cup of coffee. "A guy is considered young and sexy until he's, like, seventy. But once a girl hits thirty, things start getting really tough. And my God, don't even talk to me about forty." She laughed mirthlessly. "I'll probably just shoot myself before I get there."

It didn't sound like she was kidding, and I patted her on the arm again. There was no comfort I could provide. She smiled wanly. "I'm okay," she said. "You know the saddest part? Things were starting to turn around for Alicia."

I leaned forward in my seat. "What do you mean?"

"Well, she had this new boyfriend, Charlie Hoynes. Have you heard of him?"

I shook my head.

"He's a producer. Film and television. He's pretty huge. He's done lots of things, but what he's most famous for are those vampire movies. The *Blood of Desire* series? They started on cable?"

I'm afraid my familiarity with horror movies borders on the encyclopedic, not a surprise given to whom I'm married. "Those adult ones? Basically soft-core porn?"

"Exactly. He's done other features, but the vampire movies are his biggest. Now he's putting together a one-hour adult drama based on those."

"Based on the porn movies?"

"They aren't really pornography. Just adult entertainment. I mean, there's a difference, isn't there?"

"I guess so." Horror movies I can catalogue, but pornography is a bit out of my field.

She looked defensive. "I don't think Alicia would have done porn. I mean, I know she wouldn't have. It's the fastest way to oblivion. Once you shoot a porno, there's just no way to get back to mainstream film and TV. So the series must be tamer than the original cable movies were."

"She was cast in it?"

Moira nodded. "All but. I mean, she met Charlie at an open call, and she pretty much started dating him right away. I'm sure he was going to give her a part. I mean, he kind of had to, don't you think?"

"I suppose so," I said, no more familiar with the ways of the casting couch than I was with contemporary pornographic cinema.

I wrote down Charlie Hoynes's name in my little notebook. "Was that the only iron Alicia had in the fire, do you know?"

Moira nodded. "Well, I mean, except our improv group. Do you know about that?"

Suddenly, a dark man with a thick bushy mustache and matching eyebrows appeared at our table. "Moira!" he said. "You are only sitting with customer! You are not working, not at all!"

She glared at him. "Can't you see I'm on a break? I'm not some Moroccan slave, Aziz. Here in America we have *coffee breaks.*" She raised her mug at him and shook it slightly. Coffee slopped over the side and onto her hand. "Ow!" she squawked. "Now look what you made me do!"

"Oh no, so sorry," the man said, dabbing at her hand with the damp and dirty dishcloth he held.

She shook him away and he slunk back in the direction of the kitchen.

"Sorry," she said to me.

"No problem. But if you have to get back to work . . ." my voice trailed off.

"Oh, please. Like I care what Aziz wants me to do."

I felt a pang of pity for the poor, beleaguered Aziz. I wanted to follow him into the back and reassure him that all Americans weren't as spoiled and ill-mannered as his employees, but I had work to do, and alienating Moira surely wasn't the best way to elicit information from her.

"You were telling me about your improv group?"

"Right. You've probably heard of us. The Left Coast Players, Spike Steven's comedy troupe?"

I smiled noncommittally, and she chose to interpret it as a yes.

"We've been in the LCP for years, Alicia and I. It's pretty much a feeder program for *New York Live*. Kind of like Second City in Chicago."

"Really?" It had been years since I'd watched the midnight comedy show *New York Live,* but in college I'd been a devoted fan.

"Yeah, like half the casts of the first ten years or more of *NYL* were LCP alumnae. There are a couple of folks on the show right now. Jeff Finkelman. And, well, of course, Julia Brennan. No relation." It was obvious from her tone that *the other Ms. Brennan* wasn't one of Moira's favorite people.

"Do you know them?"

"Who? Jeff and Julia? Sure. We're really good friends. I mean, Julia's a nightmare, and Alicia and I hate her, but we've been friends for years."

Ah, Hollywood, the only place on earth where the definition of 'friend' includes someone you've hated for years.

"Why do you guys hate her?"

Moira opened her mouth to speak, and then snapped it shut. "Look, I can't talk about it."

"Talk about what?"

"Any of it. Julia, the whole thing. Alicia's dead, and it doesn't matter any more. *NYL* has auditions all the time, and the last thing I need is Julia Brennan finding out I've been trashing her."

"Moira, your best friend is dead. If we want to find out who did this to her, we're going to have to ask some really hard questions. Like who might have had a grudge against her. I know you want to protect your chances of getting on the show, but what's more important; that, or finding Alicia's murderer?"

Moira stared into her coffee cup, and I had the sinking suspicion that the answer to that question was not as obvious to her as it was to me.

She sighed. "You know Julia Brennan's *NYL* character, Bingie McPurge?"

"No," I said, vaguely horrified.

"Well, she does this whole bit. Bulimia jokes. Anorexia jokes. Anyway, that's the character that got her the slot on the show. And it's incredibly funny. There's only one problem."

"What? The tackiness factor?"

She smiled politely. "Okay, two problems. The big one, though, is that it's not Julia's character."

"What do you mean?"

"I mean, she didn't make it up. Alicia did. Bingie McPurge was Alicia's character. I mean, that's not what she called her. Alicia just called hers Mia, but she developed her in the improv group. She performed her in our workshops and on our open mike nights. She made it up, she wrote the jokes. Everything."

"Are you serious?"

"Yes. Julia stole the character, and made it on to *NYL* with it. And we just heard she's got a movie deal with Fox. Alicia's Mia is going to be *huge*, and she is never going to get any credit for it at all."

"Was Alicia doing anything about it? Was she going to sue Julia?"

Moira nodded. "She wanted to. But it's really hard to get a lawyer in Hollywood to take on a major studio like that. Everyone she talked to told her it was too hard a case to win. But Alicia wasn't going to give up. She'd never give up. That's just not the kind of person she was."

Moira began crying again, and I gave her a minute. Then I asked, "Moira, was Alicia bulimic?"

"Oh God, no."

"Really?"

"She'd never make herself throw up like that. Too gross. And you have to binge to purge. Alicia would never allow herself to eat that much."

"Was she anorexic?"

Moira considered the question. "I don't *think* so."

"Could she have been?"

She shook her head, but not with any sense of certainty. "Maybe when she was a kid, or something. But not now. Not as an adult. I mean, she was really careful about what she ate—she never ate in front of people, because she thought that was just kind of gross, but she didn't starve herself or anything."

I thought of her emaciated corpse. "Are you sure, Moira? Is there any chance that she was anorexic, and just kept it a secret from you?"

Moira shook her head again, this time firmly. "No. No, I just don't believe it. I mean, we were best friends. We knew everything about one another."

I nodded. Then I said, "Moira, I hate to even ask this question, but you probably understand why I need to. And I'm sure the cops have asked you, or will ask you already." I paused.

"Where was I when Alicia was murdered?"

I nodded.

"Right here," Moira said. "Working with Aziz. Where I always am. Where I'm probably going to be for the rest of my life. In this grease pit with a boss who watches me every goddamn minute of every goddamn day."

"You work nights?" I asked.

"I work all the time. Aziz lets me pull double shifts. It's the only way I can afford to pay for my apartment, my car, and my answering service. Plus the more I work the more he feels like he owes me, so if I ever do get an audition again he won't have any choice but to give me time off to take it."

"The police will probably want a record of it."

"I punch a time clock. They can look at that. And they can talk to old Aziz. He'll tell them I didn't do more than walk outside once or twice for a cigarette, if that."

"Would you mind if I just checked the time clock? I trust you absolutely, but this way I can just cross you off the file, and make it look like I'm doing my job." I used my best beleaguered-working-girl voice and topped it off with a 'you know how it is' shrug.

She called Aziz over, and the obviously good-natured manager supplied me both with Moira's time card and his own firm recollection that she'd been working by his side all evening. He even let me use the office copy machine to make photocopy of the time card. I left the restaurant knowing a little more about Alicia Felix, and with at least one potential suspect firmly in the clear.

Ten

I was still arguing with Stacy when I walked into my house.

"Why *not?* You're being totally unreasonable," I said into my cell phone.

"Why not? Because Charlie Hoynes is a creepy little dope and I'm not going to allow my name to be raised in his presence."

"I won't mention you when I *meet* him. Just on the phone to get him to take my call!"

"Not good enough. You just don't understand how this works, Juliet." She wasn't exactly yelling, but I had to hold the phone a few inches away from my ear nonetheless.

"Sure I do," I said. "If I use your name to get to Hoynes, then he's doing you a favor by talking to me, and if he does you a favor, he'll expect you to do one for him in return."

"Precisely. And what he'll ask for is that one of my clients agree to be in one of his sleaze-fests. And that's just not going to happen."

"So, you just say no! What's so hard about that?"

"He'll *call* me. And I'll have to take his calls! That's what's so hard. Look, girlfriend. We're done here. You can't use my name, and that's that. End of story."

"But I don't know anyone else who knows Charlie Hoynes," I said, but she had hung up the phone.

"I know Charlie Hoynes," Peter said pleasantly.

"What?" I snapped my head up. I was still standing in the entryway to our apartment, my cell phone in my hand. Through the arched doorway into the living room I could see Peter and the kids tumbled together on the couch. Isaac was asleep, his head resting on his father's chest, and a string of drool connecting his pooched-out lower lip to the red plaid of Peter's flannel shirt.

"How do you know Charlie Hoynes?" I whispered.

"You don't need to whisper, he's totally out," Peter said.

"Yeah, Mama, watch this." Ruby reached across Peter's chest and smacked her brother in the head. He didn't stir.

"Ruby!" I said.

She rolled her eyes at me and turned her attention back to the TV. They were watching *Thumbtanic*. Peter and Ruby had rented *Thumb Wars* ("If there were thumbs in space and they got mad at each other, those would be *Thumb Wars*") and watched it pretty much nonstop for two weeks. Now they were on to the all-thumb version of James Cameron's romantic classic. Nothing cracked my daughter up like an ocean full of drowning thumbs.

"How do you know Charlie Hoynes?" I repeated.

"Remember those two producers who pitched me that idea for the abortion movie?"

I groaned. When Peter and I had first arrived in Holly-wood, he had been hungry enough to take meetings with pretty much anyone who would see him, including a producing team that had an idea for a horror movie in which aborted fetuses came to life and attacked a city. It was supposed to be a comedy. Needless to say, Peter didn't take that job.

"Please don't tell me that that's Charlie Hoynes," I said.

"Indeed. Wait a second, it's the 'King of the World' part." He and Ruby poked each other and snickered.

"I'm the king of the world!" Peter said.

"I'm a dentist!" she replied.

Peter turned his attention back to me. "You want me to call him?"

"You don't mind?" I asked.

"Why should I mind?"

"Well, he'll have your number, and you'll owe him a favor."

"Please. Who cares? Go get me the phone."

My generous spouse was somewhat less sanguine when Hoynes not only took his call, but insisted that we join him for dinner the following evening at Spago.

"Ick, Spago," I said, when Peter hung up the phone.

"Don't ick me. This is your fault."

I sighed. "I'll go call a babysitter."

"Nobody old!" Ruby shouted. At her piercing howl, Isaac finally woke up, crying, as usual. Neither of my children has ever managed to arise from an afternoon nap without at least twenty minutes of hysterical tears. I used to wonder if the couple of hours of bliss while they slept was worth the drama of their rising, but then Ruby stopped napping and I quickly realized that an entire, uninterrupted thirteen-hour day with a child is significantly longer than your average human adult can tolerate. The break a nap provides is worth any amount of weeping.

Eleven

THE next day, after the usual Monday-morning horror—
why am I constitutionally incapable of remembering to buy
lunch-making materials when I'm at the grocery store?—I
dropped the kids off at their respective schools and made
my way to Silver Lake. I'd left a message for Spike Stevens,
the director of the Left Coast Players. I hadn't imagined that
I'd reach him early on a Monday morning, but Moira had
given me his home address, and I wanted at least to give
him warning that I was on my way.

Spike lived near the "lake" for which his neighborhood is
named, a reservoir strangely denuded of trees and surrounded by a high fence. His apartment building was a typical LA *dingbat,* an early-sixties multi-unit monstrosity,
mostly carport, with an overhanging second floor and an
outdoor staircase. Generally the only time people outside of
our fair city see those buildings is in the wake of an earth-
quake, when the rubble of crushed cars and piles of cement

is broadcast on the news. Al met me out in front of the building. He hadn't thought much of my idea to interview Spike—he didn't think much of any part of the case, frankly, but Brodsky was too important to us for Al just to ignore what was going on. And it wasn't like he had anything else to do.

I rang Spike's bell, to no avail. While I was writing a note to put in his mailbox, Al pushed open the wrought iron gate that passed for a security system. The lock was rusted open.

"Al!" I said, but he was already halfway up the stairs. Spike lived on the second floor, behind a steel door painted a noxious shade of ultramarine. I tried to avoid looking at it. I'd remained true to my promise that morning and had had no coffee. The combination of caffeine deprivation and the assault on my senses of that garish color was enough to rekindle my morning sickness.

After a few minutes of pounding, a middle-aged man attired solely in pajama bottoms answered the door. His skin was colored an unnatural orange, with streaks along the side of his bulging waist, and I recognized the inexpert application of tanning cream from my own ill-fated exploration of the product. His belly spilled over the waistband of his pants, despite his immediate effort to suck it in. His swift inhalation served only to expand his narrow chest and push his double chin to the fore.

"Can I help you?" he muttered, pushing his lank hair out of his eyes with one hand.

"Spike?" I asked.

"Yeah?" he said suspiciously, rubbing his eyes. He glanced at the flecks of sleep on his fingers and flicked them away. I flinched, trying not to leap out of the way of what Isaac and Ruby so accurately called "eye boogers."

"I'm Juliet Applebaum. I left you a message?"

"Yeah?"

"This is my partner, Al Hockey. We're investigators. We work for Alicia Felix's family."

"Oh, wow. Bummer. You guys want to come in?" He backed away from the door and held it open for me. I walked through the doorway, and for one, brief, nightmare-Sumo moment our bellies rubbed against each other. I blushed, and I think Spike might have too, but it was hard to tell, given the sickly orange hue of his skin.

The room was a small, white-painted box with pale grey indoor-outdoor carpeting and furniture straight out of the Ikea sale aisle. Al and I sat down on a pressed wood and canvas couch that was probably named something like the "Fjärk." Spike settled into a "Snügens" sling-chair and leaned back with a groan.

"Sorry. Up late last night," he said.

"Improv practice?"

"I wish. Catering gig. Premiere at Fox."

"Good movie?"

"Hell if I know. They don't let the help into the screening room. We're supposed to pass the hors d'oeuvres, pour the champagne, and disappear into the woodwork." His tone was matter-of-fact; almost entirely devoid of bitterness.

I nodded sympathetically and said, "You're the director of the Left Coast Players?"

"I am."

"Have you been doing it long?"

He groaned. "Long enough. Twenty-two years."

I stifled my own groan. How could he stand it? How could any of them? Struggling along on the fringes of Hollywood, waiting tables, acting in comedy troupes and television commercials and desperately hoping for a break. It was enough to make a person crazy, or suicidal. Was it enough to drive someone to murder?

Al said, "What can you tell us about Bingie McPurge?"

"Julia Brennan's character? From *New York Live?*" He asked, disingenuously.

"Our understanding is that Alicia Felix created the character," I said.

He sighed.

"Did she?"

"I've gotta have some coffee," he said, leaping to his feet. "You guys want some?"

"Sure."

Twenty minutes later we were sitting at a table in the Starbucks on the corner of his block. Spike had tried to make us coffee, but had been out of filters, milk, and sugar. And coffee.

"Bingie McPurge," I said, once he'd taken his first sip of the coffee he so clearly needed. "Was she Alicia's creation? Did Julia steal her?"

He smacked his lips and moaned ostentatiously, "Ah, the royal bean. Nectar of the gods."

"Spike," Al said sharply.

"Oh, all right. Don't get your panties in a twist. Yes, Alicia had a similar character as one of her Left Coast characters."

"One of them?" I said.

"Okay, her only character. But as I see it, Julia has improved significantly on the idea. Really developed it."

"But it was Alicia's to begin with?"

He nodded. "Alicia inspired the character. Birthed her, if you will. But Julia has made Bingie her own."

I took a gulp of coffee and exhaled with relief as the

caffeine rushed to my head and chased my headache away. "Alicia didn't give Julia permission to 'make Bingie her own,' though, did she?"

He waved his hand. "Permission? Since when does an artist need permission? Art is about taking risks, about gobbling up life. The artist is a selfish being, in thrall to his own creative muse. Who can say from where inspiration will spring?"

I was surprised that Al managed to keep the coffee from spraying out of his nose; his snort of derision was that loud.

Poor Alicia. How frustrating, how miserable it must have been to create something, only to have someone steal it away; and not only that, but to become so successful with it.

"Alicia was planning on suing Julia, wasn't she?"

Spike sighed heavily. "Poor Alicia. She just didn't have a good understanding of the creative muse. She made herself quite unpleasant around this issue."

"What do you mean?"

"Julia told me that Alicia tried to contact her a number of times. Called her. Wrote her letters. I finally had to step in."

"You?"

He nodded. "Julia asked me to. To, you know, see if I could calm Alicia down. Explain how things were. Let her know the steps Julia would have to take should she continue with her harassment."

"Harassment? Alicia was harassing Julia?" Al said.

He winced. "No, that's the wrong word. Forgive me. Julia just asked me to try to calm Alicia down."

"And did you?" I asked.

He nodded. "Yes, I think I did. Look, Alicia was never going to be happy about the whole Bingie McPurge thing. But even she came to recognize that there was nothing she could do about it."

"She gave up her idea of suing Julia?"

He smiled with a certain self-satisfaction. "She seemed, after our conversation, to understand that it would be a bad idea."

"I take it you and Julia are still close. It sounds like she relies on you."

He nodded. "Of course. We're all friends at the Left Coast Players. In fact," he said modestly, "I'll probably be joining Julia in New York soon. I just have to set things up here. You know, find someone who is willing to take over the troupe."

"Oh really? Is Julia helping you get an audition at *New York Live?*"

He shook his head. "She's a doll, and I'm sure she'll put a word in, but this has been in the works for quite some time."

Sure. Sure it had. There was something in Spike's eyes that let me know that he recognized my doubt full well, and, in fact, possessed plenty of his own. Still, I wasn't likely to convince this man to say anything negative about the woman upon whom his future might or might not lie. I was going to have to do the legwork on my own.

"Do you happen to have a video tape of the Left Coast Players? One with Alicia on it?" Al asked.

Spike wrinkled his brow. "I don't, but a few of the players did an appearance on *Talking Pictures* a few years ago. You might try them. They might keep tapes of old shows."

"*Talking Pictures?*" I said.

"It's a public access TV show out of the Valley. Hosted by Candy Gerard. You probably remember her, she used to have a series on CBS back in the mid-seventies, *Mary Jane and Rodolpho in Space?*"

I nodded my head. I vaguely remembered the series from my childhood. It had something to do with a love affair between a girl from the Bronx and an Italian space robot.

"Anyway, Alicia and some of the other players went on the show."

"Was Julia Brennan there?"

"God no. Public Access? Julia was never that desperate. Neither was I, for that matter. Alicia did the show with a couple of the guys. You should call Candy. She might have a tape."

I jotted the name of the show in my notebook, and then asked Spike, "Did Alicia's death come as a surprise to you?"

He wrinkled his brow. "What do you mean?"

"I mean, were you shocked? Or weren't you?"

He closed his eyes for a moment. "Frankly, I wasn't surprised. Don't get me wrong, it never occurred to me that someone would kill her. But Alicia didn't seem like someone who would live to a ripe old age."

"How so?"

He sighed. "Did you ever meet her?"

I flashed on the image of Alicia's brutalized body lying in her bathtub. "No," I said. My voice came out a hollow croak, and I cleared my throat. Al glanced at me, and I smiled reassuringly.

He shook his head. "Well, let's just say that a character with an eating disorder wasn't too great a stretch for Alicia Felix. In all the years I knew the woman, I don't think I ever saw her eat more than a single leaf of lettuce. She was so thin. I mean, they're all thin, all the baby actresses, but she seemed thinner than most. Sometimes she looked positively cadaverous."

I couldn't help but remember, as clearly as if I was holding before me a coroner's photograph, Alicia's sharp ribs, concave belly, and the hollow cup of her pelvis. "She was anorexic," I said.

He nodded. "Of course. I mean, she never said anything, but she had to be."

Here finally was someone who was willing to say what everybody else surely knew. It struck me, without knowing him too well, that Spike was that kind of guy. For all his Hollywood shtick, he seemed like someone who called things like he saw them. Even his self-aggrandizing puffery had just a trace of self-mockery to it. It was as if he was wordlessly letting me know that he was fully aware how ridiculous it was for a man of his age still to be engaged in the miserable rat race that was the quest for stardom. I liked him, orange skin, bloated belly, and all.

"If you told me that Alicia had starved to death, I probably wouldn't have keeled over in shock," Spike said. He took a large gulp of coffee, and looked about to launch into another homily to the speedy brew.

I spoke before he could. "But were you surprised that she was murdered?"

He licked away the pale brown mustache the coffee had left on his upper lip. "That's something else. I mean, who expects anybody to be murdered?"

Al interrupted. "Did she have any enemies?"

He laughed. "Enemies? Honey, this is LA. Everyone has enemies. Hell, your dry cleaner has enemies."

I leaned back in my chair and put a hand to the small of my back where it had suddenly begun to ache. I wondered if other interrogators had to deal with these same indignities—backache, swollen ankles, stretch marks. I shifted in my seat and asked my follow-up question. "Do you know who some of her enemies might be? Would Julia Brennan be one of Alicia's enemies?"

He rolled his eyes at me as if he'd never heard anything

so stupid. "Hardly. Now, if you were investigating *Julia's* murder, that would be a different story. Then it might have made sense to wonder about Alicia's feelings toward her. But I promise you, Julia Brennan didn't consider Alicia an enemy. In fact, I doubt she thought much about her at all."

"And was there anyone else?"

Spike narrowed his eyes, and it was brought home to me, once again, that this was a man far more insightful and intelligent than he allowed himself to seem. "You want to know if I know anyone who would like to see Alicia dead?"

"Yes."

He leaned back in his chair, tented his fingers over his belly, and said, "Alicia was not a particularly nice woman. Don't get me wrong. She could be very charming and friendly, when it suited her purpose. And she did have friends; Moira Sarsfield, for one. But Alicia was ambitious. She was more ambitious than she was talented, I think, but then that's true of most of us. She wanted success, she wanted adoration, she wanted the kind of things stardom brings you. Again, we all want that to a certain degree, but Alicia's desire was more . . . what? Palpable, I guess, than, say, mine. So did she make enemies? Sure. I'm sure she did. But I couldn't tell you who, and it's something of a mystery to me why someone would want to kill her."

"Why? If she was so ambitious, doesn't it stand to reason that she might have trampled on the wrong person?"

He leaned forward again, grabbing his cup of coffee and shaking his head at what he clearly considered my dense lack of understanding. "Alicia never attained any success to speak of. She couldn't have inspired any real envy. That can't be the reason for her murder. You'll have to find the motive somewhere else, my dear."

There was more than a kernel of truth to the man's word. Alicia may have done more than her share of professional trampling, but it surely hadn't resulted in much.

I couldn't resist asking one final question. "Spike's not your real name, is it?"

He pushed his coffee cup away and waggled a finger at me. "Trade secret, my girl."

"No, really."

He winked. "Oh, what the hell. Larry Finkelman, at your service." He extended his hand to me, and I shook it.

"Thanks for your help, Larry."

"Don't mention it," he said. "And call me Spike."

Twelve

CANDY Gerard's talk show was filmed in a long, grey building in a strip mall out in Studio City. There was an Arab grocery store flying a large American flag and advertising Jordanian olives and Israeli newspapers on one side of the studio, and a Vietnamese nail salon on the other. I imagined for a minute soaking my feet in hot paraffin, having my nails painted vermillion, rather than looking for tapes of Alicia Felix. The indulgence of a pedicure was far more attractive, but I doubted that Harvey Brodsky would hire Al and me based on the loveliness of my toes. I had to figure out who killed Alicia Felix, and while I wasn't sure I was going to get any closer to the solution to the crime by watching her appearances on public access TV, it wasn't like I was exactly inundated with better ideas.

I dragged open the heavy metal door of the unmarked studio and walked in. Maybe it was the hypersensitivity of my pregnant nose, but the place stank to high heaven. It smelled like old socks and onions, with a whiff of cheap perfume. It smelled like a tenement just after the hookers and the smack-addicts had been rousted out, and just before the place was demolished. And it didn't look any better. The walls were cement blocks, and exposed pipes trailing filthy streamers of shredded duct-tape sagged from the ceiling. Two young women in short skirts and high heels were lounging on a faded purple couch pushed up against the wall. One of the girls leaned against a broken armrest, her long legs draped across the other's lap. The second girl was holding a tiny mirror and studiously popping the pimples on her forehead.

"Is this where they shoot *Talking Pictures?*" I asked.

The long-legged girl, who had dyed black hair and severely cut bangs, pointed in the direction of a closed door marked "Do Not Enter When Light Is On." There was a large red signal light above the door. She snapped her gum loudly, and the other girl, who had finished ravaging her forehead and was now carefully painting her collagen-enhanced lips a noxious shade of plum that contrasted strangely with her platinum-blond hair, giggled.

"Are you two on the show?"

This reduced both of them to heaps of intense laughter. The black-haired girl actually had to press one long-finger-nailed hand to her inflated chest to quell her hysterics.

"We work over there," she said, finally, pointing to the far end of the hall. A large poster decorated with a silhouette of a naked woman and the words "Man-Eater Productions" marked a set of double doors. Another red signal light glowed over the top of the doors.

"Are you actresses?"

The blond smiled. "Actresses? Sure, that's what we are. Right, Toni?"

"You'd better believe it," her friend said, emphatically. "I'm acting every minute of every working day."

"We're fluffers," the blond said, and winked.

Before I had a chance to inquire just what a fluffer might be, or even to decide if I really wanted to know, the light over the Man-Eater door went out, and a heavyset man wearing a beret and a Sundance Film Festival T-shirt stuck his head out. "Girls, time to get busy," he said.

The two leapt to their feet, dragging their tiny skirts down over their rear ends, and tottered through the door on their impossibly high heels.

"Bye!" the blond called over her shoulder.

"Bye," I replied, and watched them go through the door as I sat down on the couch to wait. I caught a glimpse of a sound stage, decorated with a large, round bed covered in a wrinkled, red velvet spread. There was a naked man kneeling in the middle of the bed, his back to me. Suddenly I had a pretty good idea what a fluffer was. When Toni and her friend had come out to Hollywood from Nebraska, or Alabama, or Anaheim, or whichever small town or city that regularly launched its naïve young women across the country to be chewed up and swallowed by the Hollywood machine, had they imagined that fantasies of stardom would result in jobs keeping male porn stars prepped and ready? Somehow, I doubted it. Like every other wanna-be starlet, like Alicia for that matter, those two girls had probably spent their years in high school playing Emily in *Our Town* or tap dancing through *Bye Bye Birdie,* dewy-skinned and starry-eyed Kim McAfees. They'd honed their Oscar acceptance speeches on the bus to LA, and spent their last two hundred dollars on the perfect set of head shots, designed to make them look like leading ladies, ingénues, comic geniuses. And perhaps it wasn't yet all over for them. Perhaps they weren't permanently doomed to be nothing more than fluffers. Perhaps one or the other of them would become the serious actress she had surely imagined herself to be. But I doubted it. If these girls saw their dreams of stardom realized, it would most likely be in the seedy and depressing part of the industry that already employed them.

When the *Talking Pictures* light blinked and went out, I heaved myself to my feet, using my hands to lift my belly. It was getting harder and harder to get myself out of a chair. Pretty soon I was going to need a hoist and a forklift.

I opened the door and looked inside. The studio was larger than I expected, and painted entirely black. Half was taken up with a darkened set that looked much like the one across the hall at Man-Eater Productions—not much more than a bed. Clearly another porn set. At the far end of the long room, lit with two heavy banks of lights, was a set with two easy chairs. A thin woman with a frozen helmet of orange hair, false eyelashes so long they were obvious even where I was standing a good thirty feet away, and a mouth painted in a shade that almost, but not quite, matched her hair, perched on the edge of her seat. Somewhere under the makeup and taut, surgically altered cheeks and eyes was the ghost of Mary Jane, the girl from the Bronx who'd fallen in love with a robot from Naples.

A young man, no older than twenty, huddled in the other chair. His hair was artfully mussed, and his lime-green polyester shirt was buttoned high on his skinny neck.

"You gotta make sure you put the graphic up, dude," the young man was saying as I walked into the room. "They gotta see the graphic."

"They'll see it," a voice muttered from behind the huge camera hunkered down in front of the set.

"Of course they'll see it," Candy said. Her voice was

roughened and harsh, as if she'd spent a lifetime smoking unfiltered cigarettes.

"All I'm saying is they gotta see that graphic. Plug the movie. That's why I'm here."

Candy rose to her feet. She unsnapped a small microphone from the ruffles of her low-cut blouse, and said to the young man, "Thank you so much for your time. It was a terrific interview. Just terrific, don't you think?"

She stomped off toward me before he could answer her, and I swore I heard her mutter something that sounded suspiciously like, "Goddamn film school brats." Then she noticed me. "Can I help you?" she snapped.

"I'm so sorry if I'm intruding," I said.

She put her hands on her hips. "Can I help you?" she repeated. "This is a closed set."

"I'm Juliet Applebaum. I called a little while ago? I think I talked to your producer. I'm looking for a tape of one of your shows."

She called over her shoulder. "Spencer! Did you speak to someone about a tape?"

The man behind the camera raised his head. I immediately recognized the thick Cockney accent that had answered my call when I'd telephoned after leaving Spike at the café. "Yeah. She's looking for that comedy group. The one we had on a few years ago, remember?"

Candy turned back to me and gave me the once-over with a suspicious eye. "Are you in the industry?"

I shook my head. "I'm not."

She shook her head and began to walk away from me. "My husband's a screenwriter," I said hurriedly. She turned back around, one eyebrow raised. "I'm an investigator," I continued, and then began to explain about Alicia Felix. Candy held up her hand.

"Any credits?"

"Excuse me?"

"Your husband. Do I know his work?"

Maybe. "He wrote the *Flesh Eater* series. The most recent one is called *The Cannibal's Vacation*. He's working on *Beach Blanket Bloodbath* now."

Her whole demeanor suddenly changed. "How fabulous!" she cooed. "I'm a huge fan. Huge. Come on over to my office. We *must* talk!"

Her office was down the hall from Man-Eater Productions and consisted of a room about the size of a storage closet. One wall was entirely taken up with shelves full of plastic videotape boxes marked with dates and names in thick black marker. Candy perched on the edge of a card table and motioned for me to take the single seat, a rickety metal folding chair that I was sure would not be able to carry my weight. I sat down carefully, wincing at the creak of the seat under my behind.

"So, your husband writes those wonderful films," she said. "They're so unusual. So exceptional for the genre. I really consider them to be almost like art films, don't you?"

I blinked. I wasn't quite sure what the technical definition of art cinema was, but I had a feeling it couldn't encompass both Truffaut's *The 400 Blows* and Peter's homage to the undead.

"I'd love to have him on the show!" Candy said. "Give him the exposure he so clearly deserves."

I smiled politely, imaging what my husband would say if I told him he had to drive out to the Valley to appear on public access television with a washed-up 70s sitcom queen. "I'd be happy to pass that along to him."

"Just have his agent give me a call." She reached across the table and riffled through a pile of papers. She pulled a crumpled business card out of the stack and handed it to me. "We're, uh, in between bookers right now, so he should just talk to Spencer, or to me."

"Great," I said, pocketing the card. "So, I'm really hoping to get a copy of the Left Coast Players' appearance on your show."

Candy smiled and waved at the wall of videocassettes. "We've got a complete archive, as you can see. They were on, what, two, three years ago?"

"I think so," I said.

Within no more than two minutes, Candy had pulled out a videocassette in a plastic box marked L.C. Players. "Here it is," she announced. She tried to blow the thick layer of dust off the case, and when that didn't work she rubbed it against her skintight black leather pants. The case left a grey smear of dust along her thigh.

"Thanks so much," I said. "Do you think I can get a copy?"

She smiled. "Do you think your husband will do the show?"

I paused, and she blinked her long eyelashes benignly.

"I'm sure he will," I said.

She smiled again. "Excellent. Come with me."

She led me out the door of her office and to the Man-Eater studio. The light over the door was off, and she pushed the door open, motioning me to follow her.

"Fred!" she called out as we walked into the studio. The man in the beret was sitting in a director's chair, talking to two other burly men. They were the only fully dressed people in the room. A few women wrapped in bathrobes were standing around a long table full of picked-over boxes of donuts and half-empty bottles of diet soda. I looked over at the bed, and froze. Toni was there, hunched over a naked man, probably the same guy I saw from the back. This time it was *her* back I saw, and the realization of what she was doing crept over me slowly. I felt the heat of my blush burning my cheeks, and I was all the more self-conscious because I was the only person who seemed at all shocked by what was going on. I turned my back on the scene, and gulped nervously.

"Can you dub this for me, hon?" Candy said to the beret-wearing man. She handed him the video.

"Sure, Candy," he said.

She turned to me. "Juliet? You don't mind if he does it on a high speed, do you? He can do higher resolution, but it'll take longer."

"That's fine," I said, looking down at my shoes. For some reason I just wasn't capable of looking anyone in the face. Not with Toni and the unidentified man over on the bed.

Candy seemed to notice my embarrassment for the first time, and she laughed. "Never been on an adult film set?"

I shook my head.

Candy nodded in the direction of Toni's busily bobbing head. "The fluffer's got to keep the guys in working order."

"Right," I said, trying unsuccessfully to appear nonchalant. "Of course."

"You know, there's some cutting-edge work going on in the adult-film arena. A lot of studio directors are finding inspiration in adult film directors' creative risk taking. Aren't they Fred?"

"Give me ten, fifteen minutes, and I'll have this dubbed," Fred said, ignoring her question. He tossed the tape to one of the other men.

"Thanks, hon," Candy said. "Juliet, would you prefer to wait in my office?"

"God, yes," I said. They all burst out laughing, and she led me back out the door.

Thirteen

"You know what I love about you the most?" I asked Peter as we were driving to Spago.

"My rock-hard buns and washboard stomach?"

"Those, too. But I was really thinking of how supportive you are. How eager you are to help me succeed in this wild new path my career has taken."

He glanced over at me and narrowed his eyes.

"Juliet?"

"What, darling?" I smiled innocently.

"What did you get me into, now?"

"Nothing. I'm just talking about this dinner."

He turned back to the road, just in time to avoid hitting a bright yellow Humvee that had shot out of a blind driveway directly into our path. He swore under his breath.

"Wow! Great job avoiding that monster truck! You are such a *terrific* driver, sweetie."

"Okay, that's it!" he shouted, and screeched the car

over, right in the middle of Little Santa Monica Boulevard.

"Peter! What are you doing?"

"What? *What?* You tell *me* what. What is going on?"

I leaned over and patted his arm. "Nothing. Really. Let's just get to the restaurant."

He pulled back out into traffic. Within a few moments he was handing the car over to the valet parker with his usual elaborate instructions. The young valet parker just nodded, clearly not understanding a word my husband was saying. Peter has never made peace with that fact that vintage orange BMW 2002s with wood trim, velour seats, delayed wash wipe, and the rarest of Alpina Butterfly throttle injection systems just aren't the valued commodity in the rest of the world that they are around the Applebaum/Wyeth household. The valet took off with a squeal of wheels, and Peter swore again. I wrapped my arm around his waist and leaned my head against his upper arm, the closest to his shoulder that I could reach while we were standing up. He hugged me back, and we walked into the restaurant.

As we were heading over to the table where Hoynes and his guest were already waiting for us, I said, "Oh, Peter. I forgot to tell you. You're booked onto this talk show. *Talking Pictures?* You're shooting next week. Wednesday."

He turned to me, his mouth open, but we'd arrived at the table.

"Hi!" I said brightly. "I'm Juliet Applebaum. And you know my husband, Peter Wyeth, of course."

It was a thing of beauty—by the time the hand shaking was completed, my husband's stunned expression had been replaced by one of resignation.

Alicia Felix's boyfriend, Charlie Hoynes, was a fat man. Not obese, necessarily, but bloated somehow, with an immense abdomen that appeared to begin right under his neck, and continued down, to the tops of his thighs. His thinning hair was cut short, almost buzzed, and a single gold hoop dangled from one bulbous earlobe. His nose was squashed flat, and redder than the rest of his face. It looked like it had been palpated, squeezed, and pressed deep into the flesh between his cheeks. His grip was firm, and somehow sticky, and it was all I could do to resist wiping my palm on my leg when he finally released my hand.

It was impossible to imagine him in any kind of intimate situation with his date, a rail-thin blond with oversized breasts, improbably named Dakota Swain. How could her delicate frame survive contact with his bulk? Dakota had sharp, mouse-like features, and narrow lips outlined heavily in bright red lipstick. She looked incredibly familiar to me, and for the first few minutes of dinner I was distracted by trying to place her. This always happens to me in Los Angeles. During our first few years in the city, I would constantly greet people, sure I'd met them before. I even asked, on more than one occasion, if the possessor of that familiar face was someone who had gone to college with me. I was invariably shut down with a glare, and the comment that the person had just had a guest spot on *Seinfeld*.

But I did know Dakota. I was sure of it. Finally, I just asked her. "Dakota, do we know each other? I swear I know you."

She smiled. "I'm an actress. You've probably seen my work."

I smiled back, doubtfully. "What have you been in?"

"Oh God, what haven't I been in! Sitcoms, commercials. You name it."

Charlie patted her talon-like hand with his broad, damp

one. "And now Dakota is going to be in the latest Hoynes Production, *The Vampire Evenings*. We're shooting the pilot and eight episodes over the next few months."

That's when I figured out why I felt like I knew Dakota Swain. I hadn't caught any one of her various TV or movie appearances, at least not that I could remember. She looked familiar because she looked like Alicia Felix. Like Alicia, Dakota was a skinny blond with fake breasts, approaching forty, and desperately trying to look a dozen years younger. Hoynes clearly had a type.

I smiled noncommittally, and then complimented Dakota on the black spandex midriff-baring top she was wearing. There were two tears in the fabric, carefully placed just barely to avoid exposing her nipples. "Booty Rags?" I asked.

She nodded. "I bought it at Fred Segal. They have the best selection in the city."

I nodded, wondering if she really thought that information would be useful to a woman at the end of her pregnancy.

Through the appetizers, Hoynes grilled Peter on his career, what films he'd written, what projects he'd been up for but hadn't got, what he'd turned down. At one point, his chin glistening with melted butter, and his mouth full of Clams Casino, the producer pointed a finger at my long-suffering husband and bellowed, "So what's your quote, kid? What are you getting now? Two, three hundred K a picture? More? Less?"

Peter smiled sickly and pinched me under the table. I hadn't been paying much attention to what Hoynes was saying; I found myself unable to keep my eyes off Dakota. She was carefully slicing and dicing every item on her plate. She had reduced her smoked salmon to tiny pink shreds, and her blini to a pile of mashed dough. So far I hadn't seen her raise her fork to her lips even once. I dragged my eyes away from her plate and interrupted Hoynes's flow of words.

"So, Charlie, what can you tell me about Alicia Felix?" Awkward, I know, but that's what we were there for, and the guy had been torturing my husband long enough.

He banged his hand down on the table. "Call me Tracker!" he announced in a voice uncomfortably close to a bellow. Diners at neighboring tables looked over at us, and one fastidious-looking man in a black suit jacket and muted grey tie winced.

"Tracker?" Peter said. "Since when are you known as Tracker?"

"Since last year. I had it legally changed."

Peter and I exchanged a look. "Er, Tracker," I said. "What can you tell me about Alicia?"

"What do you want to know?" he asked. At that moment a busboy swooped down on our table and cleared our plates. Dakota pushed her plate away with one hand, and putting the other over her chest, filled her cheeks to indicate how full she was. Of air, I assume, since she hadn't actually consumed a single morsel of her first course.

"Were you two . . . er . . ." I looked over at his date.

He laughed again. "An item? We were; we were indeed. Dakota here knows all about Alicia. I don't keep secrets from my girls, do I, babe? It's all out in the open with the Tracker-Man. You see what you get, and you get what you see!" He reached his fork over to the butter dish, speared a ball of butter, and popped it into his mouth. He smiled at my astonished expression and said, "Atkins diet, babe."

I discreetly refrained from mentioning the breadcrumbs that had been baked onto his appetizer. Dakota looked nauseated at the sight of him eating butter, or maybe by the very idea of butter itself. Or perhaps it was simply old Tracker who made her ill. I was willing to bet that was it. I thought I was detecting a resurgence of my own morning sickness.

"So how long were you seeing Alicia?" I asked.

He wrinkled his brow. "Let's see. Six, nine months maybe? Dakota, you'd know. I met you both at the vampire auditions. When was that?"

"Closer to nine months ago."

I felt decidedly awkward asking him these questions in front of her. How desperate was Alicia, how desperate was Dakota, that the two of them had forced themselves to be intimate with this grotesque man? Because desperation could be the only reason for their choices. Nothing else made sense. As little as I wanted to, I needed to know more. I decided to take Tracker at his word that he was a man who brooked no secrets. "Were you and Alicia serious?"

"Serious? I don't know. I liked her, sure. Just like I like Dakota here." He reached one hefty arm around his girl-friend and squished her close, placing a kiss on her cheek with a loud smack. She furtively wiped the grease left from his lips with a napkin.

"How often did you see each other?"

"Two, maybe three times a week. She was a good kid. She helped me out with my daughter. Dakota's not a big one for kids, are you babe?"

Dakota curled her lip and shook her head.

"Alicia always stayed over on Halley's night with me. I've got the kid every, what is it . . .?" He looked at his girl-friend.

"Tuesday," she murmured.

"Right. Halley's at my house on Tuesdays. So Alicia al-ways came over that night. I'll tell you, I miss her one hell of a lot." He paused, wiping carefully at his dry eyes with his napkin. "Especially on Tuesdays." He sighed at the wearying thought of Tuesdays. "Halley loved Alicia. She really did. And that girl doesn't take to just anyone. For instance," he dropped his napkin and chuckled. "She sure as hell can't stand Dakota, can she?"

"The feeling's mutual," Dakota said, taking a gulp of wine.

Two waiters arrived at our table and lay our laden plates down with a flourish. I was momentarily distracted by the pile of fluffy mashed potatoes sitting next to my lamb chop. I always order according to the side dish. Steak, stew, fish, I like them all. But what really catches my attention is a nice butter-laden gratin, or a mound of pureed squash. I gobbled up a few bites, blissing out at the creamy texture, the buttery flavor. Food always tastes so good to me when I'm pregnant. I looked up just in time to catch Dakota's disgusted expression. I imagined that to a woman who took finicky eating to such an extreme that it nearly qualified as performance art, Hoynes and I were one and the same—overweight, greasy-cheeked gluttons. I felt a spark of sympathy for Tracker. Sure, he'd made his own bed, but how could he stand to share it with such a judgmental twig?

I swallowed the fond in my mouth and continued with my questioning.

"Had you cast Alicia in your vampire series?"

He spread his hands wide. "Hey, nothing's final until the show's on the air, you know? Sure, I was considering using her. I probably would have, you know? But I hadn't made any final decision. I still haven't."

Dakota's head snapped upward. She'd been staring at her plate, busily performing an autopsy on her halibut fillet. "What the hell does that mean, Charlie?" She seemed suddenly to have forgotten his new name.

He patted her hand and chuckled. "It means what it

always means. Nothing's final until it's in the can." He turned back to me. "I got lots of parts for girls in this series. We'll suck 'em dry every week, if you get my meaning." He bellowed with laughter, making the diners at the neighboring table jump in their seats. "Alicia wanted the part of Empress of the Night. Just like Dakota does."

"Did Alicia think she would get that part?"

"She might have. But she knew it was still up in the air. That's just how I work, isn't it Dakota?"

"Tracker, you promised *me* that role. Months ago." Dakota's face was pale, and the hand she had wrapped around her wine glass was trembling, making the liquid slosh in the glass. "You did!"

He sighed and looked at me. "A producer's life—it ain't easy, let me tell you."

"Goddamn you, Charlie Hoynes. Goddamn you!" Dakota shouted. She leapt to her feet and rushed out of the restaurant. Peter and I stared after her. I turned back to Hoynes. It took me a moment to realize that he was not in the least upset. His shoulders were shaking only because he was laughing.

"That is one feisty girl, let me tell you. She'll make a damn fine Empress."

"Don't you want to go after her?" I asked.

He shook his head and placed a huge bite of steak in his mouth. Then, with his mouth still full of food, he said, "She'll find her way back to my house. Or not. Don't worry about it. Dakota's a big girl. She can take care of herself."

I didn't want to spend another minute at the table with that vulgar, greasy-mouthed pig. But I had no choice. Whatever *she* had meant to *him*, Alicia had considered Charlie Hoynes her boyfriend, and as depressing and sad as that was, I needed information from him. I also wondered just how much a role in a soft-core porn TV series meant to Dakota Swain. Enough to run out of Spago and make her own way home, sure. But how about enough to commit murder?

"I take it Dakota and Alicia didn't get along," I said.

He laughed, and I could see a clot of pink meat on his tongue. "I'm honest with my girls. It's all out in the open with me."

"Did they spend much time together?"

"I doubt it. They didn't have much in common, those two. Oil and water."

That certainly rang false. They seemed to have absolutely everything in common, except an affection for Hoynes's daughter.

"Your daughter, Halley, how old is she?"

He took a large swallow of wine and wrinkled his brow. "Let's see . . . sixteen? No, wait a minute. She was born in 1986. That'll make her seventeen. Or was it '87? No, '86, I'm sure of it."

By now my husband had pinched me under the table so many times that I was sure I had a bruise the size of a grapefruit on my thigh.

"And she and Alicia were friends?"

Hoynes nodded, his mouth once again full of food. "Alicia helped her out. Halley's a little bit anorexic. Won't eat. It's just a teenage phase, but Alicia'd been through that when she was a kid, so she knew what was going on with Halley. She got where the kid was coming from, which is more than I can say for Halley's hag of a mother."

Could that really be true? Had Alicia confided in Hoynes that she had been anorexic, when she hadn't even admitted it to her best friend, Moira?

"She told you she used to have anorexia?"

He shook his head. "She didn't tell me anything. She told

Halley. And Halley told her mother. And her goddamn mother called up my lawyer screaming her head off, lunatic that she is."

"I don't understand. Why would that upset your wife?" I said.

"Hell if I know. My lawyer is always getting hysterical phone calls from my ex. Seems the kid went home and told her mother that she hated her—and who can blame her?— and that she wanted to move in with me and Alicia." He laughed, genuinely tickled by the idea. "Like that would have happened. Anyway, Halley said only Alicia understood her, because she knew firsthand what it was like to have this crazy anorexia thing. Barbara freaked out—so what else is new. And when Ms. Barbara Hoynes freaks, she calls her lawyers."

Hoynes scraped his fork against his empty plate, gathering up the last of the juices. "You'd think she would have been glad Halley had found someone to talk to about her problem, wouldn't you? I mean, the goddamn girl didn't talk to *any-body,* not even the shrinks they've got me paying through the nose for. But Barbara's a jealous woman. She just couldn't stand to see Halley close to anyone but her. And especially not one of my girls."

I could sort of understand that. But one might imagine that Halley's well-being would override her mother's vindictiveness or sense of competition. For that matter, one might have imagined that the ex–Mrs. Hoynes would consider herself well rid of her vile ex-husband.

"Did Alicia keep seeing Halley after that?"

"Sure she did. You think I'm going to let Barbara say who I can and can't have in my house? She threatened to take me back to court, but I'd like to have seen her try. Lunatic."

"What would her grounds have been to take you to court?"

"Grounds? You think that woman needs *grounds?* Who knows. She wanted Alicia away from the kid. She thought she was a bad influence, and she told me she'd go to court to keep her out of Halley's life." He belched softly, covering his mouth with a curled fist. "She didn't need to in the end, though, did she?"

"What do you mean?"

"Well, someone took care of that for her, didn't they?"

"Do you think your ex-wife could have had something to do with the murder?"

"Nah, I mean, she's a nut-case, but not a murderer. Anyway, she's got all she can handle with Halley. Girl's back in the hospital."

"She's in the hospital?"

Hoynes sat back, letting out a sigh of contentment and patting himself on the stomach. "Halley's in and out every few months. Whenever her weight drops below eighty pounds, her mother checks her back in. Thank God I've got health insurance through the Guild, that's all I can say. Hey, you know what I just thought of? I should sell my own damn story. Beloved girlfriend brutally murdered. Killers at large. Disease-of-the-week daughter. Make a great TV movie, don't you think?"

I blinked.

Hoynes laughed and said, "Hell, maybe I should option it myself! How about that? Give myself a hundred grand for the rights."

Fourteen

"You owe me big time," Peter said. We were lying in bed, doing our best to recover from our evening with the charming Tracker Hoynes. The man had actually imagined that we'd go out "clubbing" with him after dinner. Was he out of his mind? Had he not noticed that I was the size and shape of a dirigible? Even if I hadn't been pregnant, I would never have gone out dancing with him. First of all, I hadn't been out to a bar since I met Peter and was finally relieved of the obligation to spend my weekends searching for a man. More importantly, however, I knew that if I spent another minute in Hoynes's presence I would end up grabbing a chair and whacking him over the head with it.

"How should I pay you back for tonight?" I asked.

"Find us somewhere to live."

I groaned. "Anything I can do in the interim?" Despite the advanced stage of my pregnancy, I did the best I could to compensate my husband both for our terrible evening and for my lack of real estate progress. Afterward, I put the videotape of Alicia's appearance on *Talking Pictures* on the VCR in our bedroom. The production values were every bit as dreadful as I had expected, given the company with whom the show shared studio space. The tinny music started up, and the camera swooped in on Candy's face. She was harshly lit, the glare coming from above her head and casting the lower half of her face in shadow. She presented a decidedly cadaverous appearance to the camera.

"Hallo, I'm Candy Gerard. Welcome to *Talking Pictures*," she said, staring steamily into the camera. I'm sure it was my imagination, but I could swear she was doing a Marlene Dietrich imitation.

Peter turned to me. *"Talking Pictures?"* he said.

I smiled wanly.

"This is the show *I'm* booked on?"

"Um. Yeah."

"Who booked me on it?"

"Um, I did."

"You do realize you'll have to pay me back for that, too."

"Tonight?"

"No. I'll take a rain check."

"Sure, honey. Now be quiet, here's Alicia."

The Left Coast Players troupe consisted of two men dressed as high school nerds and Alicia wearing a miniskirt, a tube-top, and a ponytail high on her head. One of the men went off screen and returned dressed as a dozen Krispy Kreme donuts, complete with huge, pink cardboard box and sprinkles. Alicia and the donuts engaged in a dance that looked more like simulated sex than Balanchine, and then she started miming eating the donuts. Once she'd faked consuming what appeared to be at least a dozen, she began to stick her fingers down her throat. At that moment, she tripped over the dancing donuts and got her hands stuck in the box. The shtick proceeded for another few minutes, with Alicia trying to get her fingers down her throat to make herself throw up, and something interfering at the last second. The bulimic who couldn't purge. Ha ha ha. Ho ho ho.

"Is it me, or is this really not funny?" I said.

"It's not you."

Finally, the sketch was over, and Candy interviewed the players. Alicia didn't say much, other than to drop the name and contact number of her agent. The discussion was dominated by the donut box, who spoke at great length about the historical and cultural antecedents of urban comedy. Peter was nearly asleep when the half hour was up.

"I can't wait to be on that show," he said when I poked him awake. "Really."

"I'm sorry."

"You should be." He leaned over and kissed me on the lips. "You're lucky you're so damn cute, otherwise I'd be really upset. And honey?"

"Yes?"

"The San Diego Comic Con is next weekend. And I am *so* going."

"Okay."

"Juliet?"

"Yeah, sweetie?"

"Does Felix know you're only representing him to get a hold of his house?"

I sat up. "That's not the only reason I'm investigating this case!"

"But it's the main reason. Don't get me wrong. I want to move as badly as you do. I haven't gotten a minute's work done since that damn construction project started. But it just seems . . . I don't know."

"What?"

"Unethical."

"It isn't. Really. Farzad and I even talked about how much I want the house." I felt a little knot in my stomach. What had been unethical was implying to Harvey Brodsky that Felix was my client even before he'd hired me. But all that was okay now. I'd been hired. And I'd find the killer. And Brodsky would hire us, and Al and I wouldn't have to shut down the agency. I hoped.

I snuggled closer to Peter. "I wish I could see Julia Brennan's Bingie McPurge. I wonder if she's any funnier than Alicia was."

"Wait a sec," Peter said, and took the remote out of my hand. He clicked over to his new toy, TiVo. Within minutes he had an episode of *New York Live* playing on the television set.

"You recorded this?" I said.

He shook his head. "No, but the software thinks I like it, so it keeps recording it for me, I think because I have it catching *Monty Python*. I haven't bothered to correct it yet, so you're in luck."

Julia Brennan didn't dance with a box of donuts, and *New York Live* had a slicker set and better costumes to lend that much-needed air of verisimilitude. Bingie McPurge's attempts at emesis were thwarted by elaborate casts on her arms, by catching her thumbs in a pair of mouse-traps, by a toilet seat that was stuck shut, by a pair of Chinese finger cuffs. But it was the same gimmick exactly. The bulimic binges, and then cannot purge. And it was just as humorless in its more professional incarnation.

"Well, that's pretty clear," Peter said when the skit was over and Julia had gagged her way off screen.

"She stole the character from Alicia."

He nodded. "Definitely. Although it does raise one really important question."

"What's that?"

He pounded on his pillow with his fist and lay back down in the bed, drawing the down comforter up to his chin. "Why in God's name did she bother?"

I laughed. "It's just unbelievably awful, isn't it?"

"Yup."

"Wanna hear something really horrible?" I turned off the light and curled up around him.

"What?" he murmured, already half asleep.

"They're making it into a movie."

"What?" He sat bolt upright.

"You heard me."

"Oh my God!" He collapsed back onto the pillow. "Sometimes I really hate this business."

Fifteen

THE next morning, right as I was walking out the door to drive the kids to school, my phone rang. It was Farzad.

"There is a detective from the LA police department here. He wants to talk to Felix."

"Damn," I muttered, looking at my watch. Peter was sound asleep, and the kids needed to be at school in ten minutes. "Where is he?"

"Waiting in the living room."

"And where's Felix?"

"In the shower."

"Okay, here's what I want you to do. Give the detective a cup of coffee, and tell Felix to take his time getting dressed. I'll be there in half an hour."

"Good," he said.

"Oh, and Farzad?"

"Yes?"

"Don't say anything to the cop, okay?"

He grimaced. "What do you take me for, Juliet? I'm not some stupid American who confesses everything to the secret police."

"Good," I said, and hung up the phone, wondering if I should have pointed out to him that while the LAPD was far from perfect, their powers did not yet include hauling people from their homes in the middle of the night and making them disappear. At least, I didn't think they did. I called Al and told him to meet me there, luckily catching him on his cell phone in the Ikea parking lot. He was only too happy to leave Jeanelle to shop on her own. It wasn't until I was speeding down Beverly Boulevard to dump the kids and get to Felix's house that it occurred to me to wonder what exactly it was that Farzad wasn't dumb enough to confess to the police.

I managed to dump each of my children off in front of their respective schools. I gave Ruby to a mother with whom I'd once shared field trip carpool duties, and Isaac to the nanny of his best friend. I crossed my fingers that both women would sign the kids in correctly and make sure their lunches made it into their cubbies, and tore over to Felix's house. For once, I actually made it in significantly less time than I'd promised.

Farzad answered the door and nodded his head in the direction of the living room.

"Where's Felix?" I asked in a low voice.

He pointed up the stairs.

"Come with me," I said.

We found Felix in his bedroom, sitting on the edge of the bed, his forearms resting on his knees, and his head bent low.

"Hey," I said.

He raised his head at the sound of my voice, and I could see the tracks of tears down his cheeks.

"Thanks for coming over," he said.

"Hey, that's what you pay me for," I replied. "Felix, do you have an attorney?"

He nodded. "Of course. I mean, the business does."

A corporate lawyer adept at contract negotiations and employee disputes was not going to do Felix much good under these particular circumstances.

I sat down next to him and gave him the speech I gave every client about to be questioned by the authorities. Most of the people I'd represented had faced examination by the FBI or DEA, both agencies that tended to employ agents significantly more professional and educated than the average LAPD cop. I hadn't often supervised an interview with a regular police officer, but I was confident in my ability to do so. While federal agents tend at least to simulate a respect for the strictures of the Constitution, they are also generally wilier and more skilled in the art of interrogation. The most important thing he was to remember, I told Felix, was to pause after hearing each question and before replying, both to make sure he understood the question and knew the answer, and to give me time to indicate to him not to reply if I felt that doing so would not be in his best interest.

"Why don't I just tell the cops I won't talk to them?" he said.

"You can do that. It's up to you."

"Will that make them think I had something to do with Alicia's death?"

"It might. But then, they might think that already. It's not what they're suspicious of that matters. It's what they can prove."

He groaned. "I had nothing to do with it, you know that, don't you?"

"Absolutely," I said, although of course I knew nothing of the kind.

"I want to help them find her killer. I really do."

I waited.

"I'll talk to him," he said, finally.

"Are you sure?"

He nodded.

"Okay then, let's go. Don't worry, I'll stop the questioning if I think it's going somewhere it shouldn't."

Before we were halfway down the stairs, the doorbell rang. I introduced Al to our clients, *sotto voce,* and together we went into the living room, where we discovered the detective peering at the photographs on the walls.

"Mapplethorpe," he said, smiling.

Felix nodded.

"He's one of my favorites."

Felix and Farzad looked at each other quickly, and then back at the detective. I joined them in their appraisal, and agreed silently with what I knew was their conclusion. I looked over at Al, who was rocking back and forth on his heels, his eyes nearly bugging out of his head at the photographs. My partner is, like many aggressively masculine men, not particularly comfortable with gay people. To his credit, though, his political commitment to the libertarian cause makes him a live-and-let-live kind of guy.

"Detective Antoine Goodenough," the cop said, extending a large hand with tapered fingers.

Felix's hand disappeared into Detective Goodenough's proffered mitt, and he very nearly smiled a greeting.

I stepped forward and introduced myself. "I'm Juliet Applebaum, and this is Al Hockey."

The detective raised one, arched eyebrow.

"I'm an attorney, and a friend of Felix and Farzad's. I hope you don't mind if we sit in on the conversation."

He paused, and looked for a moment like he was going

to object. Then he smiled pleasantly. "Where were you on the job?" he asked Al.

"Hollywood," Al said. "Been retired nearly ten years now."

The detective nodded. Then he turned to me and said, "You're the woman who found the body, correct?"

He'd recognized my name from the report. "Yes," I said.

Detective Goodenough was a tall man, with broad shoulders and a slim waist. His skin was the color of cinnamon, and a glint of russet was just visible in his shorn brown hair. His lips were thin, and he wore a narrow line of moustache as if to enhance, or deflect, attention from them. His eyes were almond-shaped, lending his face a faintly Asian cast. He looked like a Tartar, I decided. A very handsome, African-American Genghis Khan.

He reached a hand into his pocket and removed a silver card case. Unlike the one floating around in the bottom of my purse, his was untarnished, and had no lint-furred sucking candies stuck to its surface. He flipped it open with an elegant finger, removed four business cards, and handed one to each of us.

"I'm new to your sister's case," he said to Felix. "I wanted to come by to tell you how very sorry I am for your loss."

Felix bent his head. "Thank you," he murmured.

"I've read the reports prepared by the detectives who first arrived on the scene, as well as the crime scene and forensic files."

"Detective Goodenough," I interjected. "Is the case now yours?" Had the LAPD reassigned the case because they were either biased enough or savvy enough to assume that Detective Goodenough would be more adept at eliciting information from Alicia's brother than a heterosexual officer?

"Please, sit down," he said, welcoming Felix and Farzad

to their own living room. We followed his bidding. "This crime is a very high priority for my department. I want you to know that we're devoting as much of our resources to it as possible. I'm now the lead detective on the case, but the entire department is working hard to find Alicia's murderer."

For what felt like hours, Detective Goodenough asked question after question about Alicia's life, her childhood, her career. Al took his usual careful notes, and I listened closely.

"Did Alicia have any problems growing up? Was she, say, involved with drugs?" Goodenough asked.

Felix shook his head. "No, not at all."

"Not at all," Goodenough said, with a smile.

Felix smiled back. "Well, no more than was normal. You know, she smoked pot a little. Maybe even did some cocaine. Hell . . . we . . ."

I interrupted him quickly. "Felix," I said.

He turned to me. "What?"

"I think the detective just wants to know if Alicia had any kind of a drug problem." I stressed his sister's name.

He nodded, and turned back to the detective. "She didn't have a drug problem. At all."

"Did she have any other problems?"

Felix nodded. "She had an eating disorder when she was a teenager."

Goodenough made a note, and asked, "Any other issues?"

Felix shook his head.

I wanted to know more, however. "She was anorexic as a child, wasn't she?" I asked.

Felix nodded.

"Severely?"

He nodded again. "Enough to be hospitalized a couple of times. She made it through, though. She went to this inpatient facility back home in Florida for the whole summer before her senior year of high school. That cured her."

But had it? I thought of her emaciated corpse with the pang of horror complicated by pity that struck me every time that image entered my mind. "Are you sure the problem hadn't recurred?" I asked.

Felix shook his head. "Look, I'm a fashion designer. I can tell you—all women have an eating disorder. Alicia was no worse in the end than any one of the women who model my clothes."

I thought this wasn't saying very much.

"Was she ever *dangerously* thin? I mean, after that time she had to go to inpatient treatment?" I asked.

Felix shook his head, but Farzad said, "She was always too thin. Always."

"Farzad!" Felix snapped.

"You spend too much of your time with models," Farzad said. "Alicia *never* ate enough, and she was *always* too skinny."

Felix shook his head and turned to the detective. "You'll have to excuse my partner. He's Iranian, and he's gay. He has no idea what a normal-sized woman looks like."

Al shifted uncomfortably in his seat. Thank goodness none of the other three men seemed to notice.

"That is ridiculous!" Farzad said. "Iranian women are *beautiful,* and stylish. And for your information they are not fat! They are very thin. Too thin, in fact, like your models. A woman should look like a woman! Not like a little boy. A woman should look like her!" He pointed to me, and all of them turned and fixed appraising gazes on my body. I could tell that Felix thought I was anything but normal-sized, and I blushed furiously.

"Except not so pregnant," Farzad said.

"My sister was thin, but not abnormally so," Felix said.

Detective Goodenough seemed to decide that we'd covered this topic in far more detail than necessary, and he reassumed control of the interview. He was, in the end, more thorough than I would have expected, and I was both impressed and made a bit anxious by his attention to detail. He jotted down a long list of every one of Alicia's friends, family, members of her comedy troupe, people she came in contact with through her work as Felix's assistant. He asked about boyfriends, and Farzad told him about Charlie Hoynes. I was glad not to have had to provide that information myself. It was surely something he needed to know, but I have a very hard time, both because of my training and because of my temperament, cooperating with the police, even when I know I should. A useless, even counterproductive holdover from my public defender days.

When the detective asked about people with whom Alicia had had conflicts, Farzad brought up Julia Brennan.

"Oh, don't be so melodramatic," Felix said at his boyfriend's characterization of Alicia's feelings toward the successful actress. "Alicia didn't hate Julia. She was just a little jealous. Who wouldn't be?"

Farzad pursed his lips. "She was planning on suing the woman. And what about the letter?" he said.

"Farzad!" Felix nearly shouted.

"What letter?" the detective asked.

"Julia Brennan had her lawyers send Alicia a letter."

"A threatening letter?" Al asked.

Farzad glanced over at Felix. "I would say so," the Iranian man said. "The lawyers told Alicia that if she continued to claim the character was hers, they would sue *her*."

"But the character *was* hers!" I said.

"Since when does that make any difference?" Farzad replied.

"What was Alicia's response?" I said.

Felix spoke. "She didn't have time to respond. At least, I don't think she did. She got the letter just a little while before . . . before . . ." his voice trailed away.

Detective Goodenough turned to Farzad, "Do you think this woman, Julia, felt the same way toward Alicia as Alicia felt toward her?"

Farzad waggled his head in his half-nod, half-shake. "I have no idea. All I know is that Alicia hated Julia Brennan. It's hard enough to make a name for yourself in this business without someone stealing your ideas. Frankly, I wouldn't have been surprised if *Alicia* had killed *Julia!*"

"Farzad!" Felix said sharply. "Alicia would never have hurt anybody. She was not that kind of person, and you know that."

Farzad waved a hand in the air. "Whatever."

It was time for me to step in. Nothing they were saying was exactly against their interests, but at the same time I wasn't eager to expose my clients bickering to the curious eye of this very intelligent police officer.

"Detective, are there any other questions you have for Felix and Farzad?"

He nodded, fully aware of what I was doing, and then spent a few minutes going over the two men's alibis for the night of Alicia's murder. He took down the names of the maid and cook who kept the Palm Springs house in running order.

Felix sighed, and his eyes welled up with tears. "I just thought to myself, 'I'll have to get Alicia to call him with the phone numbers.'"

"She took care of that kind of thing for you?" the detective asked.

Felix nodded. "I've never had much of a head for details. And I'm so busy with my business. I have an assistant at work, of course, but he never had to deal with any personal stuff. I guess he'll have to, now."

"What kind of personal stuff?" Goodenough said.

"Oh, you know. She would take the clothes to the laundry. Make sure the cars got serviced. Deal with the house-cleaner and the gardener. Plan our dinner parties."

"Buy our toiletries," Farzad said. "You wouldn't believe the different unguents Felix uses. Every part of his body has its own lotion, and God only knows where Alicia would get them all. If you think *I'm* going to be able to do that for you, sweetheart, you've got another thing coming."

Felix seemed about to rebuke the younger man, but I shot him a warning glance. Instead, he said, "Alicia did all those errands that it's hard for a busy person to get to. You know."

I did know. I'd run out of deodorant over a week before, and I had no idea when I'd make it to the drug store. I was counting on it becoming apparent if things got out of control. For now I resisted the urge to sniff under my arm.

Goodenough tapped his pen on his notebook. "Alicia was your older sister, yes?"

Felix nodded.

"She didn't mind running these kinds of errands for you?"

"No. Alicia had always taken care of me. Even when we were kids. This wasn't any different. Anyway, she needed the money, and I needed the help."

I could see that the detective didn't buy that any more than I had. He was probably a younger sibling. Perhaps the

relationship between Alicia and Felix was every bit as un-
complicated as Felix claimed. Perhaps not. It was hard to
imagine an older sister who wouldn't resent buying her little brother's toilet paper and toothpaste, or even his two-
hundred dollar bottles of algae and placenta wrinkle cream.
And a history of having been forced to babysit a younger
sibling was, I thought, more likely to instill antipathy,
rather than a willingness to continue a lifetime of selfless
devotion. Still, Felix seemed entirely unaware there might
be anything unusual or unbelievable about the way he characterized his relationship with his sister. Theirs had either
been a very special bond indeed, or he was a singularly insensitive man.

Detective Goodenough finally wrapped up his questions
and left.

After the door closed behind the handsome detective,
Farzad whistled through his teeth. "Mmm," he said.

"Oh, please!" Felix replied.

I looked over at Al, who was blushing. It was, I thought,
the first time I'd seen him turn that shade of crimson.

I interrupted Felix and Farzad's banter to reassure myself
that neither man was worried about the interview. They
were more interested in discussing the relative attractive-
ness of their interrogator than going over his questions, so
there wasn't anything more for Al and me to do.

We found Goodenough leaning against the hood of my
car. He stood up when he saw me, shot his cuffs, and
stepped forward.

"Ms. Applebaum, Mr. Hockey," he said mildly. "I wonder if I might have a word."

"Of course."

"Ms. Applebaum, you said that you're an attorney?"

"I am."

"How long have you known Mr. Felix?"

"Not very long."

"How long?"

"I met him after the death of his sister, if that's what you're asking."

He looked surprised.

"Felix has retained us to assist him during the course of the investigation of his sister's murder," I said.

"How do you mean? Are you acting as his defense counsel?"

"No, of course not. He doesn't need a defense attorney. My partner and I are merely assisting Felix and Farzad to navigate these very unfamiliar waters."

He narrowed his eyes at me. "Do you have a ticket?"

"Excuse me?"

Al interrupted. "I do. Juliet works with me."

Goodenough turned to Al. "You're a licensed private investigator?"

Al nodded.

"But she's not," the detective said.

I was, in fact, in the process of getting licensed. The exams weren't a problem; after all, I'd successfully taken and passed both the New York and California Bar Exams. The private investigator's exam was nothing compared to those horrors. However, while Al was certainly qualified to supervise me, my hours weren't exactly regular, what with taking care of Ruby and Isaac, and spending much of my first trimester vomiting instead of working. I was still nearly one hundred hours short of what was required for me to get licensed.

"Our goal isn't to get in your way, Detective Goodenough," I said.

The tall man smoothed the fabric of his expensive suit and picked an invisible piece of lint off the sleeve. Where did an LAPD cop get the money for those clothes? "Of course not," he said.

"Is your working theory of the case that it was a home invasion by a stranger? Using the lock box on the door?" I asked.

He waggled his head in something between a nod and a shake. "That's one possibility."

"Have there been other, similar, cases in the city?"

"If you're asking whether we've had a rash of Charles Manson–like murders, then the answer is no. But of course there have been other home invasions."

Now it was my turn to raise my eyebrows.

"Two young men in Watts were killed when rival gang members broke into their homes last week," he said. "And a mother of three was strangled in her bed while her children slept in the next room."

"Domestic violence?" I asked.

He nodded. "We've arrested the children's father."

"But nothing like this?"

He shook his head. "No. No other rich, single women have been stabbed to death in their bathtubs."

I had a feeling there was another adjective he might have substituted in that description. It took a very generous definition of the word to describe Alicia as rich, but she was most certainly white.

"Was there evidence of sexual assault?" I asked.

He pursed his lips and gazed at me, appraisingly. Finally he said, "I suppose it doesn't hurt to tell you. She had had sexual intercourse within the previous twenty-four hours, but there was no evidence of assault."

"How did you rule out rape?"

"No sign of bruising or tearing, and the presence of Nonoxynol 9."

Well that seemed pretty clear. It's a rare rapist who is both gentle and solicitous enough to use a condom. Alicia had most likely had consensual sex a day or so before she was killed.

"Did her body turn up any other evidence?" I asked. "Fingernail scrapings? Hairs?"

The detective shook his head. "As I'm sure your partner will explain to you, Ms. Applebaum, our information sharing cannot be the two-way street you would like it to be. I'm trusting you to turn over to me anything you discover. I will not be able to do the same. I'm sure you understand why not."

I sighed. Of course I did. And I was used to being on the short end of the informational stick. As a public defender, what I knew was always limited to what my client was willing to tell me, and what I was able to pry out of the prosecutor, sometimes with the help of a judicial order. I didn't expect Detective Goodenough to come entirely clean. Nonetheless, he'd already told me enough to convince me of one thing. I just didn't believe Alicia was the victim of a random act of violence. Sure there were killers who didn't rape their victims, but more often than not, this kind of stranger-attack was a sex crime. Perhaps the very fact that Alicia had been naked and in the shower was in and of itself sufficient to satisfy her killer's sexual perversion. But I doubted it. The lack of any kind of physical violation seemed to preclude a stranger attack. Furthermore, Alicia had been murdered by someone who knew how to get the key out of the lock box, or someone who had keys to the house. Now, again, it was possible that there was a serial-killer/real estate agent on the loose in the greater Los Angeles area, but I didn't believe that, and I was certain Detective Goodenough shared my doubts. No. Alicia Felix had been

murdered by someone who knew her well enough to gain
access to her home. I hoped to God it wasn't her brother, because I had every intention of figuring out who had killed
her. And I seriously doubted Felix would sell me his house if
I ended up putting him in jail.

ON my way home I stopped at the supermarket. We were
entirely out of breakfast cereal, and I didn't relish trying to
force something else down my finicky children's throats in
the morning. It was hard enough getting them to eat a
small bowl of organic chocolate crispies. Anything else was
beyond them, and me.

Once inside the store I surprised myself by remembering
deodorant, and a new tube of bubblegum-flavored toothpaste for the kids. I was so pleased with this feat of deep-
pregnancy recall that I decided to reward myself with a
donut. I still hadn't gotten that life-size box of Krispie
Kremes out of my mind. The pastry counter offered my
honey glazed favorites in boxes of four, just enough, I told
myself, for my perfectly sized little family. I ate my donut as
I waited in line behind an elderly woman with a hand
tremor who was insisting on paying by check. The confec-
tion went down altogether too fast. While the ancient
woman consulted her calendar for the date, and laboriously
filled in and then crossed out the number "19" in the spot
for the year, I decided that not only wouldn't Peter really expect me to bring him a donut, but that since I was eating for
two, I really deserved another one myself. As long as I still
had two left for Ruby and Isaac, I was fine.

Once I was in the car, I recollected what the kids' dentist
had said about sugary snacks late in the day, and the need
for better toothbrushing. Well, I'd been trying, but I couldn't

get the kids to brush with anything resembling the commitment the dentist demanded. I was going to have to limit the amount of sweets they were allowed. Therefore, it was my duty as their mother to eat the other two donuts.

I'd like to say I felt sick, or regretted my gluttony. I didn't. In fact, I felt like I could easily put away another four-pack. But turning the car around and heading back to the pastry counter was beyond even me, wasn't it? I checked my watch. Alas, I didn't have time. I had to pick up the kids from school.

I started feeling bad while I was waiting out in front of Ruby's school in the pick-up line. I don't mean physically bad. Physically, I was just fine. No, what got to me wasn't abdominal discomfort, but rather a bit of good old fashioned self-hatred. A group of moms had gotten out of their cars and were chatting amiably as they waited for the doors to open and the children to pour out. I joined them, and was confronted with the ugly truth. I was, by far, the fattest woman there. Now granted, I was pregnant, and moreover I wasn't really *fat* by any stretch of the imagination. At least not fat like any normal person would consider fat. After all, when not under the influence of a developing fetus I fit more or less comfortably into a size 10, and could even manage an 8 if I was willing to forgo respiration. The problem was that these were all *Los Angeles* mothers. Not all were actresses, or even in the industry at all. In fact, these particular women were mostly stay-at-home mothers. But nonetheless they looked, to a one, like they had just walked off a movie set. They weren't dressed particularly glamorously—a pair of tight yoga pants and a stretchy T-shirt was the style of the moment. But they were all thin. They were aerobicized and stepped and Zone-dieted down to a svelteness that only a town that idolized the broomstick likes of Calista Flockheart and Lara Flynn Boyle could have considered normal. Alongside them, I felt hugely, lumberingly, hideously fat. I'm fully aware that it is simply unreasonable for a woman who has given birth even to just one child to have an abdomen that looks good in hip-hugger pants and a belly button ring. Still, it bothered me that my belly button, after three pregnancies, was going to look more like a deflated party balloon than a body part that deserved its own jewelry, and that even if I had a pupik-plasty or whatever that surgery was called, I still would never have the courage to bare my midriff.

I made as much small talk as I could stomach and then made my way back to my car, pulling my shirt over the behind that suddenly seemed bigger than anything that could easily fit into my station wagon. I thought of the donuts, each of them in turn, oily and coated with its grey scum of sugar. For the first time in my life I felt, or at least understood, the compulsion of women like Alicia. I wanted to run to the nearest ladies room, stick my finger down my throat, and get rid of the pounds of carbohydrate and fat that would soon be taking up permanent residence on my thighs.

Then the image of Alicia's emaciated, vandalized body sprang before my eyes. Was that really what I wanted to be? I looked out the window at the woman gathered together in front of the school. How many of them maintained their slimness by denying themselves basic sustenance? How many of them vomited up any item not on the paltry list of foods they considered acceptable? I was willing to bet that it was more than a few. Not many of us ended up like Alicia, institutionalized and force-fed, but we were all completely crazy when it came to food. Felix was right. We all had eating disorders. It was only a question of degree.

Just then, the door to the school burst open, and the children began to pour out. I caught sight of Ruby's gleaming red curls immediately. When she saw my car she smiled widely, revealing the gap where her front tooth had just begun to grow in. I smiled back and waved. I was damned if I was going to let my little girl grow up feeling the way I did about my body. Ruby was going to be proud of how she looked, and take pleasure in every morsel that passed her lips, if I had to tie down every Tab-drinking mother in the city of Los Angeles and force-feed them Ding-Dongs from now until doomsday.

sixteen

I didn't notice the Mercedes parked in front of my house. If I had, I might have hustled the kids off to the park, or to the movies, or anywhere at all to avoid the scene that greeted me when I walked into my apartment. Kat was huddled in an armchair, her face mottled with a humiliated blush, and her hands knotted in her lap. She was staring out the window, doing her best not to look at her mother-in-law and my husband, who were sitting side by side on the couch, their heads bent together in an altogether disturbing tête-à-tête. While I stood in the doorway, Nahid's tinkling laugh filled the room, and she reached out one manicured hand, pushing at my husband's sweatshirt-clad chest, as if he had said something so witty, so daring, that she needed to swat him for it. He laughed in reply, and leaned ever so slightly into her.

I coughed, loudly, and released my hold on Ruby's and Isaac's hands. They flung themselves into the room and onto their father's lap, reminding him, I hope, that he was married, and that flirting with middle-aged, artfully sculpted real estate agents was a singularly inappropriate activity.

Nahid looked at me, and her smile turned acid. Kat shot me a worried glance and turned back to the window. For a moment, I felt a tightening in my stomach. I shook it off, firmly reminding myself that Nahid Lahidji was not *my* mother-in-law. She couldn't scare me. Could she?

"Hello Kat, Mrs. Lahidji. What's up?" I said in a sprightly voice.

Peter set the children on the floor and said, "Guys, go play in Ruby's room for a minute, we've got grown-up things to talk about."

"But we just got home!" Ruby whined.

"And you said we'd play *Bionicles* today!" Isaac said, matching her tone.

"Give us a few minutes, kids," I said, shooing them out of the room. "Daddy will be in to play with you soon."

As soon as they were gone, I said, "Can I get you something to drink? Coffee? Tea?"

Kat raised a grateful face, and nodded, but Nahid said, "No, no. We're fine. Your *darling* husband has already made us very comfortable." I could swear she batted her eyelashes at him.

"Well, what can I do for you?" I asked, settling myself on the ottoman that passed for a second chair in our living room.

"Juliet," Peter said, "Mrs. Lahidji is worried about the whole house thing." There was just the tiniest hint of 'I told you so' in his voice, and I scowled at him.

"Juliet, dear," Nahid said. "I'm sure you had only the best intentions. After all, I know just how desperate you must be to move from here before the baby is born." She waved a condescending hand around my living room, as if to say that of course no one could imagine bringing a child into such desperate and meager surroundings. "But I'm afraid I must ask you to refrain from disturbing poor Felix and Farzad. They've gone through so much."

"Disturbing them?" I sputtered.

"Katayoun has told me of your *plan*."

"Kat!" I said to my friend. She winced, and shrugged as though to ask me what I had expected from her. Clearly I should not have imagined that she would withstand the force of nature that was her husband's mother.

Nahid said, "She has told me everything. That you have befriended the poor grieving man. That you have worked your way into his confidences. All to convince him to sell you the house. Sell it *below market value!*" The outrage, the horror in her voice filled the room.

"Listen, Mrs. Lahidji, you're being ridiculous. Yes, of course I'm interested in the house, and maybe my motives weren't entirely altruistic at first. But I'm not trying to cheat Felix out of anything. Anyway, Felix has hired me to investigate his sister's murder. He's my client."

She shook her head furiously. "How long do you think you'll be working for him if I tell him you're just after his home?"

"First of all, he knows I'm interested in his house. That's the reason Kat and I were there in the first place. Second of all, how long do you think you'll be his real estate agent if I tell him you care more about the price of his house then you do about finding out who killed Alicia?"

She sputtered for a moment, and then seemed to deflate just the tiniest bit. "Look my dear," she said. "We are both on the same side here. We both want this situation with Alicia resolved as quickly as possible so that the house will be free to be sold. Let's not argue."

I turned to my husband. "Sweetie, give me your seat," I said.

"Huh?"

"Your seat. My back is killing me."

He leapt to his feet and gave me a hand up off the ottoman. "Maybe I should see how the kids are doing," he said.

"Good idea."

I sat down on the couch next to Nahid. "Mrs. Lahidji, I promise I won't go behind your back, okay? If Felix ever decides to sell me the house, I promise you'll not only be the first to know, but I'll make sure you're involved in the sale, okay? You'll be able to advise him on a fair price."

She pursed her lips together, and then stretched her mouth into a smile. "Very good, my dear. That is all I was asking."

"On one condition."

Her smile died. "What is that?"

I reached over for my purse and pulled out my little notebook. "Let's talk a little bit about Alicia. Did you know her?"

"We should not discuss this unpleasantness."

"How else will we achieve our mutual goal of resolving the issue quickly?"

Nahid narrowed her eyes. "I'd met her. But only once, when Farzad first had me over to look at the house. She was there, cleaning up after a dinner party. Or, rather, she was ordering the maid to clean up." Her tone of voice made it clear that she had not liked Alicia.

"Did you talk to her?"

"No, my business was not with her. I was there to appraise the value of the house. Whether she liked it or not."

"What do you mean?"

"Well, the girl obviously didn't want her brother to sell

the house and move permanently to Palm Springs. She would have had to get a *job.* Find someplace to live. God knows how she would manage that. She was supposed to have been an actress, but Farzad said she hadn't gotten a part in years. She was nothing but her little brother's nanny!"

I looked up from my notebook, surprised. "Farzad told you that? He told you that she didn't want Felix to move?"

Nahid waved a dismissive hand at me. Her diamond ring caught the light, and we were both momentarily distracted by its brilliance. "Lovely, isn't it?" she purred. "I will tell your husband where my husband bought it. His cousin, Momo, is in the diamond business. He'll give you a special deal."

It looked like the glass shade on the Czechoslovakian floor lamp in my Bubbe's old apartment. Only larger.

"That's okay," I said. "You were telling me about what Farzad told you?"

"Farzad didn't need to tell me anything. The girl threw a tantrum as soon as she realized what I was doing. She began screaming at Farzad, telling him she would tell her brother he was trying to throw her in the street. She was like a wild person. Tears, howls. Awful. So tacky. So low class."

"What did Farzad do?"

Nahid smiled. "He yelled right back at her! Farzad is like his mother, Lida. No one has ever won a fight with my cousin Lida Bahari. She is the most formidable woman I know."

Kat and I sat in stunned silence for a few moments, contemplating just what a woman scarier than Nahid would be like.

"What did Farzad say to Alicia?" I asked, finally.

Nahid laughed. "He told her he'd throw her out right then if she didn't close her mouth, and then he chased her out to the guest house where she lived. Such a scene. The two of them, screaming like a couple of fishwives. Farzad is just like his mother. Only prettier." She laughed again.

Suddenly, Kat leaned forward. "Nahidjoon, maybe we should go. Juliet probably has things to do."

I scowled at her. She had been too afraid to speak a word the entire time, and now she mustered up the courage to cut our conversation off just when things where getting interesting?

Nahid nodded. "I must get back to the office. And you," she said to Kat. "You need to get to work on those rental units. I need a full inventory of tenants and rents by the end of the day."

Kat sighed, following in her mother-in-law's wake out the door.

Once the two women had gone, I sat for a moment in my quiet living room, pondering what Nahid had told me. There was no love lost between Alicia and Farzad. If he had had his way, and it appeared like he had been about to, she would have been out on the street. I was supposed to be finding out who might have had a motive to kill Alicia, and instead I kept coming up with people whom *she* would have liked to see dead.

Seventeen

THE next morning I dropped by Felix's house. I found Farzad in the dining room conferring with two very young women over a pile of fabrics printed with black and white photographs.

"Hello, Juliet," he said, when the housekeeper had shown me in. "Come, tell us what you think of these. Gorgeous, aren't they?"

I fingered a corner of the soft gossamer fabric, and then held it up. "Are these crime scene photographs?" I asked, trying not to sound as horrified as I felt.

"Yes, aren't they fabulous?" one of the young women said. "*So* edgy."

"And so bloody," I said. The length of silk I was holding had the image of a woman sprawled on a bed. Her head hung over the side, dripping a pool of black blood onto the floor. "What are these for?"

"Felix's new line," Farzad said. "Mostly formal-wear. He's having problems with the final designs."

"Gee, I wonder why?" I said.

Farzad smiled thinly. "I know what you're saying, but Aimee and Bethany have been working on these for months. Long before Alicia died. It was Felix's idea to use the Weegee photographs, and it cost a fortune to get the rights. We can't exactly just toss the entire line because he's having a personal crisis."

I didn't reply. What good would it have done to point out to my client's partner that he was an insensitive ghoul?

"Felix is resting," Farzad said. "Is there something important? Should I wake him?"

"No, don't. Actually, I've come to talk to you." I shot the girls a glance.

He gathered the fabric swathes into a pile and dumped them into the arms of one of the girls. "These are fine. Call the factory and tell them we'll have final designs by the end of next week."

"Are you sure?" the girl said. "I mean, if they get set to go, and we don't have the drawings for them, they're going to freak."

"That's Felix's problem, darling, not yours."

"Okay," she said, doubtfully, and headed out of the room. The other girl scooped up their two identical Burberry totes and followed.

Farzad sighed and collapsed onto a leather Morris chair. He kicked off his embroidered slippers and tucked his feet up under him.

"I spoke to Nahid Lahidji yesterday," I said, sitting down on the couch.

"Ah, Auntie Nahid, the dragon lady. I must call her."

"She's pretty anxious to get your house on the market."

"No more anxious than I am. But we're both going to have to wait. Felix won't even talk about it."

"He just needs some time to deal with everything that's happened. I'm sure once Alicia's murder has been resolved, and—he's further along in his grieving process, he'll be ready to contemplate leaving Los Angeles."

"You may be right." He glanced at me. "Or it could be wishful thinking, couldn't it?"

I didn't answer. I felt a twist of guilt. Farzad and I both knew that I was hoping that his poor lover would grieve quickly enough to sell me his house before I was forced to buy something else.

I eyed the leather ottoman tucked in next to the couch I was sitting on, wondering if it would be indelicate to heave my aching feet up on it.

"Please, relax," Farzad said. "You must be exhausted."

I nodded gratefully, and put my feet up. "I understand from Nahid that Alicia was very upset at your plans to sell the house."

He wrapped his arms around his knees. There was something feline about Farzad—graceful, elegant and utterly consumed with his own comfort. "Of course she was. She was furious. She was going to have to pay for her own apartment."

"Did she try to convince you and Felix to stay in LA?"

"Look, we all knew that this was really for the best. Alicia had always been much too dependent on Felix. It was time to cut the cord. Even she knew that."

"But did she try to convince you to stay?"

He ran a careful hand through his thick hair. "Alicia was an actress."

"Meaning?"

"She threw a fabulous tantrum. But Felix and I had our minds made up."

"And did she realize that? Did she come to terms with it?"

He laughed. "Alicia never came to terms with anything in her life. She managed to convince Felix to keep her on salary, to do whatever he needed done in the city, God knows what that would have been. She was working on him to keep the house as a sort of *pied á terre*. And who knows, she might have succeeded."

I sat forward a bit and fixed my eyes on him. "It's ironic, don't you think?"

"What is?"

"Well, here Alicia was trying so hard to convince Felix not to sell the house, and now she's dead, and he can't bring himself to sell."

"I don't know if it's ironic, but it's definitely typical of Alicia."

"How so?"

He laughed again, without the slightest hint of humor. "She was the most stubborn woman in the world, and you've met my auntie Nahid, so you know I know what I'm talking about. Alicia would never rest until she had her way. I'm not at all surprised that she's manipulating her brother, even from the grave."

I wasn't sure how to respond to this, and decided that it was best to let the bitterness of his words go unacknowledged. "Farzad," I said. "Why are you so eager to leave Los Angeles?"

"This place is toxic, darling. Truly toxic."

"How do you mean?"

"I've been here since I was a teenager, ever since I left Iran. For ten years I've been trying to become an actor. You know how many parts I've gotten?"

I shook my head.

"Eleven. Eleven roles in movies and television. What do you think of that?"

"That actually sounds pretty good to me."

He stretched a leg out, and then tucked it back under him. "You know how many times I played a terrorist, of those eleven?"

I was afraid to guess.

"Seven! Seven terrorists, two taxi drivers, one shooting victim, and a Mexican gardener. And I'm not a man without connections. Felix knows many people—famous people, directors, producers, actors. Still, with all his help, I am never more than a terrorist or a cabbie."

"That must be incredibly frustrating."

"Worse. Worse than frustrating. It eats you up inside. Makes you feel small and useless. Ugly. I can't stand it anymore. But acting is like a disease. It infects you. I can't be in the city and not be an actor. So I must get away."

"And what do you plan to do in Palm Springs?"

"I will take care of Felix, take care of the business. We'll be a family. Who knows, maybe we'll even adopt a baby."

I blinked, and then reminded myself that a lot of people who seem far too self-absorbed to be parents end up rising to the occasion.

"And Felix? Is he as eager to leave Los Angeles as you are?"

"LA is bad for Felix, too. It's full of people who want something from him. The pretty boys want to model in his shows, the actresses want free dresses. Everybody pretends to be his friend, and everybody wants something. Felix knows this. Sure, he's seduced by the honey of their words, but he sees right through them. As I do."

That all too familiar feeling of guilt stabbed me in the stomach. What was I but yet another person who wanted something from them? Here I was, manipulating myself into their lives, pretending to be interested in helping, but really only wanting a chance to tape my children's drawings up on that Sub-Zero. Farzad obviously could tell what I was feeling, because, after gazing at me for a moment, he winked.

I said, "But will moving to Palm Springs really get Felix away from it? He's still going to have to deal with the models and actresses, and the demands of his job."

Farzad plucked a loose thread from the sleeve of his creamy white shirt. He wore his French cuffs unbuttoned and hanging over his narrow wrists and hands.

"Perhaps," he said. "But the farther we are away from it all, the less it will influence him. The less it will damage us."

"Damage you? As a couple?"

He looked away, as if regretting his words.

"What do you mean by damage?" I said, insistently.

He shook his head. "Oh, nothing. We're fine. Rock solid. It's just that LA is a toxic city. We are much happier in Palm Springs."

Perhaps it was as simple as he claimed—perhaps he wanted to leave Los Angeles because of the extent of the demands on Felix's time. I couldn't help but wonder, however, if there were some more particular reason. Was their relationship in jeopardy? Had something else precipitated Farzad's insistence on a move?

Try as I did, I couldn't get any more out of him on that topic. Instead, I turned to another line of questioning. "Was the fact that you were both actors something that made you and Alicia closer, do you think?"

He waggled his head in something that might have been either a nod or a shake. "It gave us something in common, certainly. We could complain to one another about our agents, about auditions, that kind of thing."

"Something to bond over?"

"Yes, well, until it got to be too much for me."

"What do you mean?"

"You know how Alicia's career had been going. After a while I didn't like to talk to her about things too much. She was . . ." He paused and looked up at the ceiling. "She was kind of a black hole. You know. An abyss. Too much failure in one place."

I blinked.

"It wasn't like she was depressed or anything. She wasn't that kind of person. She was always moving, always hustling. It's just that . . . well, that kind of bad luck can be contagious," he said.

I nodded slightly, not enough to indicate that I agreed, but enough, I hoped, to keep him talking.

"But things had gotten better recently," he said, as if to reassure me.

"Between the two of you?"

"Better for Alicia. There was that series with the man she was sleeping with, Hoynes. It really seemed like that was going to work out for her."

I thought for a moment about Dakota Swain. How sure a thing had the vampire series been, really?

"Alicia and I used to go to the gym together sometimes," Farzad said suddenly. "We both work out at Corps Sain on Sunset. I mean, she used to. I'd better make sure they've canceled her membership. They're probably still charging her credit card.

"Did Alicia work out a lot?"

He laughed. "Alicia? What do you think? The woman was obsessed with her weight. She was a compulsive exerciser. She was there every day for at least two hours."

"Do you think she was really cured of her anorexia? When I . . . er . . . saw her, she didn't look . . ." I searched for the word. "Normal, I guess. She was so terribly thin."

"Normal? What's normal? Like Felix told that detective, Alicia was no thinner than plenty of other Hollywood actresses. But yes, she was much too thin. She obsessed about what she looked like. Her weight wasn't the only thing. She worried about her clothes, about her face, everything. Worry is too weak a word."

"But do you think she still had an eating disorder?"

He waved the question away. "Of course she did. Who doesn't? Half the people I know are getting their meals delivered by that high-protein diet guru. Alicia was crazy, sure, but she was no crazier than a lot of other girls."

I thought about my adventures in the land of Krispy Kreme. "Did she do any bingeing?"

"Bingeing?"

"You know, eating huge quantities and then forcing herself to vomit."

"Oh, you mean like Mia, her comedy character. That was fiction, only. Alicia would never have done that. She had tremendous control. She never ate anything she didn't want to eat. It was amazing." A note of admiration crept into his voice.

"What about plastic surgery?" I asked. If Alicia's best friend Moira had had a facelift, then Alicia probably had one as well.

Farzad laughed. "My dear, you think we all look this good by accident?"

I gazed into his face. He winked at me. "A little nip here, a tuck there. Bigger breasts, a cleaner jawline. Everyone does it."

I surreptitiously patted the loose flesh that made up my double and triple chins. Maybe my squeamishness about carving up my face and body was silly. After all, everyone was doing it. A little nip. A little tuck. Was it really so bad?

I thought of Moira's scars, and the tight, shiny faces of the women Peter and I met at industry parties. In a world like this, did *normal* have any meaning?

"Did you two use the same doctor?"

"We two?"

"I'm sorry. I thought you meant that you'd had something . . . er . . . done," I mumbled hastily.

He laughed at me. "Alicia's doctor was Bruce Calma. In Westwood, at UCLA. He's the best. Everyone uses him."

I noted the name, even though I could see no way that Alicia's plastic surgeon had anything to do with her death. Still, the picture of her was becoming clearer and clearer to me. She was an ambitious woman, verging on the desperate, engaged in a battle with time that, despite diets, exercise, and surgery, she was doomed to lose. Could it possibly have been this ambition, this battle, that got her killed?

Eighteen

"HOW about this one?" Peter said, holding up a brown checked shirt.

I shook my head. After I had left Farzad, I had swung by my house and picked up my husband for a quick trip to Fred Segal. My ostensible excuse was that I wanted to check out the Booty Rags line in the stores—see what it looked like, how it was displayed, even ask the salespeople how well it was selling. The truth was, however, that hanging around a fashion designer had inspired in me a need to shop. Worse, it made me realize just how woefully lacking my husband's wardrobe was. For all the contrived tatters of Felix's clothing line, he and Farzad were always dressed to the nines. Now, I wasn't fool enough to want my husband draped in a pair of butt-baring cargo pants, but there wasn't any reason he couldn't buy some new clothes. I had to satisfy my shopping jones somehow, and I certainly I wasn't willing to spend any more money on my own ballooning self.

Fred Segal was the perfect spot. It was achingly trendy, and chock full of celebrities and the random LA wealthy. Despite that, I knew they'd have enough classic men's clothes—read jeans and T-shirts—to satisfy my fashion-phobic husband.

Peter presented me with another flannel shirt, this one in a blue check.

"Honey, the whole point of this exercise is to buy you something *other* than flannel shirts and khakis."

"Should we really be spending the money? I mean, aren't we supposed to be saving for a down-payment on that house you were going to find for us?"

Since when had my husband become so adept at passive-aggression?

Peter poked listlessly at the artfully displayed clothing, and I dug through a pile of shirts until I found one I liked. I brought it over and held it up under Peter's chin. "This one's cool," I said.

He grimaced, fingering the pink rayon. "It's got little teapots all over it."

"They're cute!"

"Juliet, I can't wear *teapots*. I just can't. Toasters, maybe. But not teapots."

"Fabulous shirt," a smooth voice said. I turned to find a young man with spiky black hair, wearing hip hugger jeans and a mint green T-shirt. He nodded approvingly. "Leo bought one of those the other day. And I think Justin's got it in blue."

I didn't bother asking who Leo and Justin were. I just put the shirt back on the rack.

"Can I pull some things for you?" the young man asked.

"Sure," I said, at the same time as Peter said, "No thanks."

"Can you find some more . . . *traditional* stuff?" I asked.

The young man heaved a sigh and nodded. He pulled a blue wool jersey off the rack and handed it to me. "Like this?"

It felt like it was woven from spider webs, soft and delicate, yet resilient.

"Perfect," I said, handing it to my husband.

"Wow, this feels great," Peter said, sounding surprised.

"Why don't you take it to the fitting room," the sales-clerk said. "I'll bring you some other things. Pants, too?"

"Definitely," I said.

I left the two of them, purposefully ignoring my husband's desperate glare, and wandered off to the shoe depart-ment. I was modeling a pair of bright red, doeskin ankle boots for the mirror when I saw Charlie Hoynes's girlfriend, Dakota, across the floor, holding up a stiletto-heeled alliga-tor pump. "Can I see this in an eight and half?" she called to the clerk who had helped me cram my swollen feet into the boots.

"I'll be with you in a moment, Madam," he said.

"Go on, it's okay," I said to him, then I smiled at Dakota. "Hi, it's me. Juliet Applebaum? From the other night?"

She looked me up and down, as if trying to decide whether to recognize me or not. "Of course. Spago."

"Right."

She put the shoe back on the display and fingered the leather thong of a pair of sandals. Finally, she said, "I sup-pose I owe you an apology."

"No, of course not." I limped over in my too-tight, too-high boots.

"I love those boots."

"Aren't they great?" I held one foot out, lost my balance, and then, just like that, fell onto my behind.

"Oh my god!" Dakota said, running over to me. She grabbed my arm and tried to heave me up. My bulk was just too much for her, and she toppled over, almost in slow motion. By the time she was next to me on the floor we were both laughing so hard the tears were streaming down our faces. I rolled over on one side and, using a chair for support, yanked myself to my feet. I held out my hand to her and hoisted her up. She was so light I nearly pulled her all the way over on to me. That set us off even more, and soon I had to sit down in a chair. "Stop!" I cried, holding my belly. "I can't laugh anymore or I'll pee in my pants."

"Are you okay?" she asked. She was almost hyperventilating.

"I'm fine." I wiped the tears from my eyes. "God, that was insane."

"No kidding."

"I'm really not this big. I mean, normally."

"You're pregnant."

"Right. And huge. Especially my butt."

"Well . . ."

"My son once said to me, 'You know, Mama, other ladies get pregnant only from the front!' "

We giggled again for a moment, but when the salesclerk showed up with Dakota's shoes, we calmed down.

"Gorgeous," I said.

She slipped them on and strutted around the room. "Yeah, but can I afford them?"

I pulled the box over to me, looked at the price, and whistled. "Wow. Twelve hundred bucks."

"I know," she said, sighing. She sat back down and took them off her feet. "I should just buy them. The series is going to go, I'm sure of it."

"Buy them!" I sure couldn't shell out the four hundred bucks the red boots cost, and I wanted *someone* to make an inadvisable, even insane, purchase, otherwise what was the point of the whole shopping trip?

"I shouldn't," she said. "I'm still paying off these." She grabbed a breast in each hand and squeezed.

"Really?" I said. "They look so real!"

"They'd better look real. I paid Bruce Calma four thousand bucks for them."

"Huh," I said. "Same doc who did Alicia."

"I'm not surprised. Everyone knows he's the best. Not many doctors are as good as he is on both boobs *and* faces. I wouldn't use anyone else."

"Did you know she'd gone to him as well?"

Dakota shook her head. "Alicia and I didn't talk much. For obvious reasons."

"That can't have been easy," I said sympathetically.

Dakota frowned—or at least I think she frowned. Her brow remained entirely unwrinkled, her eyebrows stayed in the same position, but her mouth turned down at the edges. "Tracker Hoynes is a pig."

I caught myself in time to keep from nodding in agreement.

"Anyway, as soon as the pilot shoots, I plan never to see the cretin again." She held the shoes up. "I'm going to buy them."

"You should."

Suddenly, she scowled at me. "I suppose you think I had a good reason to kill Alicia Felix."

I had been, in fact, thinking exactly that. Two desperate women competing for the same last-chance role. What better motive for murder was there in Hollywood?

"I can't say I was particularly upset when she got killed," Dakota continued. "You probably think that makes me a terrible person."

I didn't reply.

"I didn't kill her."

Again I remained silent.

"I didn't."

"You should buy the shoes," I said. With a last, longing look at the buttery crimson boots that were slowly cutting off the circulation to my feet, I tugged them off and put them back in the box.

"I'm going to," she said.

"I haven't laughed like that in a long time."

She smiled. "Me either."

By the time I returned to my men's department, Peter was out of the dressing room and waiting for his purchases to be wrapped by the now-sycophantic salesclerk.

"When you see this bill you are going to be so sorry," my husband said.

"Don't worry about it. I just saved us four hundred dollars."

Nineteen

I decided to visit Charlie Hoynes's ex-wife not because I thought that anyone in her right mind would feel sufficiently rivalrous over ol' Tracker's affections to kill his current girlfriend—especially not when there seemed to be a virtual harem of skinny blond women at the man's disposal—but because Hoynes had been so adamant about his ex-wife's loathing of Alicia. I didn't imagine that jealousy over your daughter's affections provided quite the same motive as that over your lover's or husband's, but interviewing her seemed the only sensible thing to do.

A few minutes on the web was enough to give me Barbara Hoynes's home telephone number and address. She lived in Brentwood, plenty close enough to my house to warrant a quick trip while Peter was getting the kids to bed after dinner. It was too dark to see what ersatz architectural style Hoyne's ex-wife had chosen for her house. Unlike most of her neighbors, Barbara hadn't lit the front of her home with floodlights and tracking beams—or perhaps she simply hadn't turned hers on. I could see enough to know that the place was large. She'd clearly come out well in the divorce, or had money of her own.

The woman who answered the door looked nothing at all like the two other women with whom Hoynes had chosen to spend his time; neither did it seem like she'd ever looked like them, even when she was young. She was shorter, first of all, and a brunette. She hadn't had the assistance of a plastic surgeon—on the contrary, Barbara Hoynes looked her age, and then some. She looked like a middle-aged woman who had spent many sleepless nights worrying about her daughter in the hospital.

"Can I help you?" she asked, in the wary tone of a woman not looking forward to dealing with the demands of a late-night solicitor.

Since I knew this was a woman who despised her ex-husband, I figured the easiest way to get her to talk to me was to align myself with her. "Ms. Hoynes, I'm so sorry to bother you in the evening. My name is Juliet Applebaum, and I'm investigating the circumstances of Alicia Felix's death, particularly her relationship with Charlie Hoynes. I was hoping you would be willing to answer a few questions. Just as background really."

She gave a dry bark of laughter. "Is Charlie a suspect?"

"It's too early to rule anyone out, of course," I said, letting rest the implication that I had any legitimate business drawing up lists of suspects.

She leaned against the doorjamb, crossing her arms over her chest. "What do you want to know?"

I put my hands to my back, which wasn't aching more than usual, and winced. "Do you mind if I sit down?" I asked, looking vaguely around me. I was standing on the long flat porch, but there were no benches or chairs in evidence. I winced at the imaginary pain.

Barbara was obviously fighting an internal battle. She didn't want to ask me in, but neither did she want to force a pregnant woman to stand, sway-backed and uncomfortable, outside her door. Finally, she said, "Why don't we just sit on the steps." She checked the latch with one finger and then let the door slam shut behind her. Frustrated, I followed her down a step or two and settled myself next to her. Without the light from inside the house, I could only just barely see her face.

"Did you know Alicia Felix?" I asked.

"I never met her, no."

"Had your daughter?"

"Yes."

I did my best to make out her expression in the dim light from the streetlamps. The moon was far too thin and too high in the sky to be of much use. "Were they friendly?" I asked, pretending I'd heard nothing from Hoynes himself.

Barbara didn't answer, and I could swear I could see the knot of her jaw working, as if she were gritting her teeth. Finally, she said, "My ex-husband takes a sick pride in parading his girlfriends in front of his teenage daughter. Alicia Felix was just one of them. I doubt Halley thought much about her at all."

I considered this, and decided to confront her with at least part of what Hoynes had told me. "I was under the impression that Halley was a bit closer to Alicia. That they had some things in common."

This time, Barbara's voice came suddenly, and harshly. "In common? No. No, they had nothing in common. That woman did her best to worm herself into my daughter's affections, but they had nothing in common."

"Your ex-husband made a statement that Alicia was helping Halley in her battle with anorexia." Well, it was a statement. Not sworn, true, but a statement nonetheless.

Barbara leapt to her feet. "Helping her? Helping her? Is that what that miserable son of a bitch said? Exactly how was that wretched woman helping my child? By traipsing around in front of her like some kind of human skeleton? By giving her lessons in how to starve herself to death? What kind of help is that? What does he think, that Alicia was some kind of role model for Halley? Is he out of his mind?"

I opened my mouth, but before I could say anything, she wrenched the front door open.

"I don't need to talk to you anymore. None of this has anything to do with me, or my daughter. Charlie Hoynes is a sick cretin, and I'd bet every dime I have that he's the one who murdered that horrible woman." She slammed the door, leaving me sitting on the steps in the dark.

Twenty

THE next morning, for lack of anything better to do, I called Dr. Calma's office. It would have been only marginally more difficult for this particular chubby, pregnant Jewish girl from New Jersey to get an audience with the pope than with the plastic surgeon to the stars. It took an entire morning to get beyond the receptionist's assistant or perhaps it was the receptionist's assistant's receptionist—anyway, when I did finally reach the woman, I was told that Dr. Calma had no time to speak to *anyone*, especially not someone investigating a murder, and that he had, in fact, just turned away an interviewer from *Redbook* magazine. Dr. Calma was being profiled in *Vanity Fair*, and even other periodicals were simply too prosaic and pedestrian for the great man to waste his time with, so who exactly did I think *I* was?

Out of desperation, I called back, and, hiding my voice by reinvigorating the New Jersey accent I'd long ago lost, tried make an appointment. That inspired a bout of pitying mirth. Wasn't I aware, the receptionist asked, that without a personal referral the wait to see His Gloriousness was nearly six months? And that even *with* a letter from a previous patient I'd be lucky to get in before the *summer?* My obvious frustration inspired a brief but inspiring lecture on the desirability of Dr. Calma's talents.

Finally, just as I was about to fling the phone to the floor in frustration, the woman said, "Please hold."

I nearly hung up. I'm not sure what kept me on the line, but within a few moments the woman came back. "My goodness, this is your lucky day."

"What do you mean?"

"That was Dr. Calma's nine thirty-five. She has a callback this morning for a Spielberg film. She canceled, even though I told her that Dr. Calma wouldn't see her again if she did. So if you can be here in twenty-two minutes, the appointment is yours."

I managed to get dressed, drop the kids off at school, and make it to Beverly Hills in just under half an hour. Thank God the good doctor had valet parking, because if I'd had to troll the streets looking for a space I would have been even later. As it was, the scowl on the receptionist's face when I walked in at nine forty-three made me feel like a misbehaving schoolgirl.

She pursed her lips and gazed ostentatiously at the clock.

"I'm sorry I'm late."

"Lucky for you the doctor is a bit behind schedule, otherwise you would have forfeited your appointment."

She handed me a clipboard, and I took it to a long, white couch. There were at least fifteen women waiting to see the doctor, and there was only one seat left in the crowded room. They were mostly of a certain age, although a few were quite young. I figured the younger women for breast enhancement or liposuction. Most of the older women looked as though they had already had those procedures. They were surely in for facelifts, although it was difficult to imagine why they thought they needed them. Surprisingly, I wasn't the only pregnant woman in the room, although I was certainly the largest. The other two were the olive-on-a-toothpicks one sees in Los Angeles gyms, stairmastering away any semblance of a pregnant body.

I glanced down at the clipboard in my hand. It was the usual patient information sheet. I debated handing it back to the receptionist and letting her know that I was just interested in talking to the doctor, but frankly the woman scared me. I laboriously recorded my history of caesarian sections, my father's heart disease, my mother's high blood pressure. By the time I was done I had acquired a whole host of psychosomatic ailments. Headaches, backaches, nausea. I was trying to decide whether I saw spots—I sort of thought I did—when the receptionist cleared her throat.

"Have you finished with that?" she said.

I leapt to my feet, assuming that she wanted the form back because I was about to be seen by the doctor. Wishful thinking, that. An hour later, I was still cooling my heels in the waiting room, entertaining myself by looking through photo albums full of before and after pictures. It didn't seem quite fair; the before photos of the facial surgery were all harshly lit and featured women with hair hauled back from their foreheads, their faces stripped of makeup. The after shots, on the other hand, had clearly benefited from the ministrations of makeup artists and soft-focus camera lenses. Still, the difference post-surgery was pretty dramatic. Dr. Calma appeared to be carving away years.

The liposuction pictures were even more remarkable.

It was all I could do to keep from pinching my expanding thighs as I leafed through the pages. However, my favorites were the breast enlargement photographs. Neither Dr. Calma nor his patients seemed interested in moderation. I suppose it's like buying a pair of shoes. The small ones aren't any cheaper.

After I'd been waiting for nearly an hour an a half, the nurse in the lavender scrubs who had periodically been peeping her head into the room and announcing everyone else's name, called mine. I followed her down a long hallway, past half a dozen closed doors, to a small exam room furnished in tasteful purples and pinks. The nurse and the wallpaper matched perfectly.

"Please take everything off and put on this gown," the nurse said, handing me the most beautiful hospital gown I'd ever seen. It too was lavender, like the nurse's scrubs, and had pale pink lace on the collar and hems.

"Um, I'm really just here to talk to the doctor," I said, backing away from the proffered gown.

The nurse shook her head. "Everything off, dear. It opens in the front."

She left me alone, and I stood fingering the gown. Finally, I stripped off my clothes, leaving the white socks with red jalapeños that I'd grabbed from my sock drawer. They clashed terribly with the elegant hospital gown. The gown was made for a woman who was rather less vast than I. It might have been *designed* to close in the front, but it gaped around my protruding belly. I did my best to hold it closed and sat on the edge of the pink exam chair. The seat was tilted upward like a birthing chair, and it was upholstered in a slippery vinyl. I kept sliding off the edge, and I wished for a set of stirrups on which to prop my legs to keep me from falling right off.

I sat there for much longer than any woman should have to in a too-small hospital gown. By the time Dr. Calma burst into the room, followed by his lavender nurse, I was feeling about as dejected as I ever had in my life. What exactly was I doing there, half naked, waiting for an examination for which I had absolutely no need?

The doctor was much younger than I expected, or perhaps he was just a satisfied consumer of his own products and procedures. He was handsome, in a kind of Ken-doll way. His face was tanned an unnaturally even brown, and his hair was impeccably waved. One lock hung over his eye in a facsimile of rakishness that probably enchanted his patients. I was too irritated by my long wait to feel even remotely captivated.

"Okay, so what have we here?" he said, standing a few feet back from me and staring at me critically.

How far was I planning on going with this charade. "Dr. Calma," I began.

"A little mother!" he interrupted. "When are you due?"

"In a couple of months, but—"

"Hmm, I hope I'll be able to fit you in. Most of my little mamas come here a bit earlier to arrange for their tummy tucks. Let the nurse know when the c-section is scheduled for, and she'll check on my availability. If I'm booked we'll have to do it after the birth. Two months of recovery is usually enough. You don't want to look like this longer than you have to." He shocked me by reaching out a hand and gripping the hammock of fat that was slung below my pregnant belly. I jumped.

"Yup, we'll get rid of all this jelly for you! You'll be sleek and trim in no time. Stand up."

"Dr. Calma, I have a few—"

"Up you go!" he said, hoisting me to my feet. "We should do some lipo here," he said, pushing aside the gown and tracing a warm hand down my hips and outer thighs. "And in here as well." I was gratified that he refrained from actually touching my inner thigh; he just pointed at it. "*Upper arms*—that goes without saying."

Upper arms? What was wrong with my upper arms?

"Turn around, please."

Despite myself, I turned my back to him.

He raised the hem of my gown and clucked his tongue. "We can certainly solve this problem," he said.

Problem? Was my rear end really a *problem?* I mean, I knew it was, well, sizeable, but wasn't that a good thing? And anyway, I was *pregnant!* I glanced back over my shoulder and nearly groaned aloud. He was right. I was looking at one huge, gelatinous problem.

"Now, let's get to your face. You can have a seat."

I collapsed onto the chair, too horrified by the state of my belly, hips, thighs, upper arms, and above all my butt, to continue arguing.

He leaned in and peered at me closely, so close, in fact, that I could smell the warm cinnamon of his breath.

"Not too bad, considering how old you are," he said. "We'll just need to botox the forehead and lip, maybe tug back the jowls." He traced a finger along the edge of my jaw. "We'll erase these fine lines by the sides of your eyes, and get rid of this mole, and that'll be all. Practically nothing!"

"What mole?" I said, and then I blushed. I hadn't intended to shout.

"This one," he said, pointing at a freckle on the side of my lip.

"That's a beauty mark!"

"Hmm. Well, it's up to you. I'd take it off, but it's certainly your decision. Some people are rather inordinately attached to their moles."

"It's not a mole!" The doctor's attack on the freckle of which I was, in fact, very fond, finally roused me from the stupor of self-loathing his criticism had inspired. Unfortunately, it also prevented me from continuing with my plan of delicately and carefully bringing up Alicia Felix. "I'm not actually here to schedule *any* surgery. I just wanted to ask you a few questions about one of your patients, Alicia Felix. She was murdered last week, and I'm representing her family in the investigation of the crime."

Dr. Calma stepped back, looking horrified. "You're not here for a pre-surgical consultation?"

"No."

He snapped the medical chart closed. "I'm sure you understand how very busy I am."

"Yes, and I'm sorry. I know it was ridiculous for me to come here like this, but there was simply no other way for me to get in to speak to you."

He shook his head, clearly furious. "Haven't you ever heard of the doctor/patient privilege? I'm not going to tell you anything about one of my patients!"

"But Alicia is dead, Dr. Calma. And, anyway, I'm just trying to find out anything about her that might shed light on who *murdered* her, and why."

He spun on his heel. When he reached the door, he turned back to his nurse. "You can submit your questions in writing to my attorneys. Florence, have the front desk give her the information." He turned back to me. "You know, you really could use some work. I'd be happy to talk to you about that. Anything else is quite simply out of the question." And with that blistering comment about my appearance, he left the room, closing the door behind him with a firm click.

"Tsk tsk tsk," the nurse clucked.

"Sorry," I said.

"Don't worry, hon." She patted my hand. "Someday you'll probably be grateful for Dr. Calma's discretion. He's a wonderful plastic surgeon. The best."

"I'm sure he is." I gathered the robe around me and clambering down from the exam chair."

"Here, hon, let me help you." She took my arm and hoisted me down.

"Thanks. I'm not getting around real well lately."

She laughed. "Of course you're not. My goodness, you should have seen me with my twins. I was as big as a house. I had to get my poor husband to help me roll over in bed!"

I smiled. "I know the feeling."

"Now, hon, what did you say that poor girl's name was?"

"The murder victim? Alicia Felix."

She nodded. "Wait right here. I'll be right back."

I dressed quickly and sat down on the doctor's stool to wait for her. I wasn't about to risk the exam chair again.

Within a couple of minutes she returned with two of the large photo albums that I'd looked through out in the waiting room.

"There's no harm in showing you these," the nurse said. "After all, Alicia posed for the photographs." She began turning pages until she found what she was looking for. "Here's your friend."

The page she handed me was one that I recognized from my earlier perusal. It showed two photographs of a woman's torso. Her face was turned away from the camera, leaving visible only a sheaf of long, blond hair. In the first photograph, her breasts looked almost prepubescent; they were nothing more than small, flat discs on which perched pale nipples. Her ribs stuck out farther than they did. The bones of her clavicle were sharp, and the hollow of her sternum looked deep enough to sink a finger in up to the second knuckle. The "after" picture could not have looked more different. Alicia had been as uninterested in the concept of less-is-more as the rest of Dr. Calma's patients. Or perhaps it was the doctor himself who preferred melons to oranges. Alicia's new boobs were certainly lovely. They were round, and gravity defying, with nearly invisible scars. However, they looked somewhat bizarre, I thought, set on top of that bony torso.

"Pretty, aren't they?" the nurse asked.

"Oh yeah," I said, trying to sound enthusiastic. "Really nice ones."

"Now, she had a double procedure. Lots of girls do. You'd probably want to consider the same thing. Here, let me show you." She picked up the other album and flipped through it until she found the page she was looking for. I hadn't spent enough time with the face book while waiting for my appointment—I'd been too eager to move on to boobs and hips. Alicia's photographs were toward the back.

I took the book from the nurse and stared intently at the pictures. Alicia had had her face pulled and tugged to remove all wrinkles. She'd also had her nose narrowed slightly, and, if I wasn't mistaken, she'd had some kind of implant put into her chin.

"Isn't she lovely?" the nurse breathed.

"Oh yes," I said. And she was, in a kind of ethereal, hollow-cheeked way.

"Dr. Calma works wonders. He really does. You should make another appointment. He could turn you into a princess!"

"I'm sure he could."

Here again was more evidence of Alicia's desperate attempts to make herself ever more beautiful, ever young.

There was something so achingly sad about the lengths she went to in what was doomed, finally, to be a failed endeavor. Alicia, and all the women in that waiting room, were engaged in a hopeless battle against an enemy that there is, ultimately, no way to fight. We all grow old, no matter how much we carve away at our bodies, no matter how much silicone and botox we inject. We can suck out the extra pounds middle age deposits on our hips, but the years will pass with an inexorable certainty. I glanced at myself in the full-length mirror on the wall of the exam room. There was no getting around it; everything the doctor said about my body was probably true. I was only in my mid-thirties, but I was heavy, and getting older every day. But was the answer really to hack and chop and diet and starve? Or was there some other approach to this inevitable collapse?

Twenty-one

"HAVE you lost your mind?"

I sighed deeply into the cell phone. "Probably, yes."

"Exactly how are we going to bill the client for that? I'm pretty sure our automatic billing program has no entry for 'plastic surgery consult,'" Al said.

"Very funny."

By the time Stacy blew into the restaurant with her hands extended before her like a blind woman, I'd had to endure a good ten minutes of that kind of abuse.

"Read me the specials," she said as she sat down.

"Why? What's wrong with your eyes?"

"What are you talking about? Nothing's wrong with my eyes. I just had my nails done, and I don't want to touch the menu."

I looked at her gleaming burgundy fingernails. "And you give me grief about *my* work ethic? Getting your nails done before lunch!"

She tossed her hair over her shoulder. "My girl comes to the office. I did an entire morning's worth of telephone calls while she was doing my hands and feet."

I leaned back in my chair and gaped at her. "You have manicures and pedicures in the office?"

"Of course. Like I've got time to go to a salon every week? I don't *think* so."

What would I do without Stacy and her excesses to remind me what's wrong with Hollywood?

"What's next? Getting a bikini wax at your desk?"

She laughed. "Could you imagine? Crouching naked on my hands and knees on top of my credenza?"

"On your hands and knees?"

"You know. For when they do the—"

"Too much information, Stace!"

"Oh, please. Don't tell me you've suddenly become a prude. Like you've never had a Brazilian bikini wax."

"Uh, no." I couldn't even remember the last time I got near a *bathing suit,* let alone required the services of a sadist armed with pink wax and a bunch of cloth strips.

"Well, that's just disgusting," she said. "What's the salad of the day?"

I looked down at my menu. "No-carb Cobb."

"Perfect." When the waitress came, however, it was clear that the choice was far from perfect. By the time Stacy had finished substituting goat cheese for the blue, sliced turkey for the bacon, and adding two extra hard-boiled eggs, she'd made it into something different all together. But that's my friend in a nutshell. She's a woman who knows what she wants. Exactly, precisely, completely what she wants.

"I'll just have the regular Cobb salad," I said to the waitress, smiling to let her know that I knew just what a relief it was to have a pleasant, easy-going person like myself to wait on.

The girl shook her head. "That blue isn't pasteurized."

I wrinkled my brow. "Excuse me?"

"Blue cheese? Listeria?"

I sighed. The pregnancy police were everywhere. "Okay, I'll have the goat cheese, instead."

"Ma'am!" she said, outraged. "That's even worse! How about some Kraft slices?"

I closed my menu and stretched my irritated frown into a smile. "Why don't you just hold the cheese altogether."

"Of course. And I'll give you a plain vinaigrette." She raised her eyes from her pad and appraised me critically. "Unless you'd like the nonfat?"

"Vinaigrette is fine," I said sharply.

She turned away, looking miffed.

Stacy spread her hands on the table and blew on them. "Harvey Brodsky called me this morning."

I winced. "I'm such an ingrate. I haven't even thanked you yet for that referral." I'd gotten a message to Lilly that Brodsky might be calling her, but I'd never called Stacy to express my gratitude, and I felt bad. It should have been the first thing I'd done.

"You haven't gotten the job yet," she said.

"I know."

She waggled her fingers in the air. "He seems pretty excited about this murder you're investigating. My sense was that if this came out well, he'd be interested in putting you and your crazy partner on contract."

"That's basically what he said. And that's why I called and asked you to lunch."

Stacy interrupted me, suddenly calling out to the waitress.

"We'll need two black napkins here!" She turned to me. "I don't want white fluff all over my suit. And that black top of yours doesn't need any more lint than it already has."

I glanced down at my maternity smock and sighed. It wasn't particularly linty, but there was a swath of pale green toothpaste where Isaac had wiped his mouth across my belly. When the waitress returned, I dipped a corner of my newly acquired black napkin in my water glass and dabbed at the stain. Something about the general sloppiness of my appearance reminded me of my adventures in personal improvement. "I went to see a plastic surgeon yesterday," I said, and recounted the horror of my visit. "Can you believe he actually wanted to do all that stuff to me?"

"Ridiculous." Then she paused. "What did he want to do to your face?"

I tugged back on the skin at my jaw.

"Hmm," she said.

"Hmm what?"

"Nothing. I mean, it's absurd, of course. Only . . ." her voice trailed off.

"Only what?" I scowled at her.

"No, no. I don't mean for you. I'm just thinking about myself. I mean, about my own jaw line." She patted at her jaw with the pads of her impeccably painted fingers. "Don't you think I'd look better like this?" She pulled the skin back toward her ears.

"No," I said, without looking.

"No, really. I mean, lately it's just getting kind of, I don't know, heavy. Droopy."

"Stacy, what's up with you?"

She dropped her hands to the table. "Nothing. You know. Just the usual. Andy."

"Oh no, not again!" I said. Stacy's husband has a notoriously roving eye. The two of them have been separated and reconciled more times than I can count.

"No, no. He's not seeing anyone. I mean, I don't *think* he is." Stacy shook her head. I looked closely at her. Was that the glint of a tear in her eye?

"What's going on, sweetie?" I said, softly, reaching out and patting her hand, well above her still-drying nails.

"Nothing. Nothing. It's just, you know. It's just so much easier for men. Andy's still so young. I mean, we're the same age, but for him that's young. Thirty-five for a man is nothing. But for us . . ."

"For us, what?"

She looked down at her hands, shaking her bright blond hair down over her cheek. "It's older. A thirty-five-year-old woman is just older than a man of the same age. If he wanted to, Andy could be dating women ten, even fifteen years younger than he is. How many twenty-year-old guys would be interested in me?"

I leaned back in my chair. "First of all, hundreds. Thousands even. You're gorgeous. You're successful. You're rich. If you weren't married you'd be beating them away with a stick. But second of all, why would you ever *want* to go out with a twenty-year-old? Remember what the guys at college were like?" I shivered. "Is that really what you want? Some self-obsessed, overgrown child with no staying power?"

She laughed bitterly. "Isn't that exactly what I've got?"

"Oh honey." I tried to lean over the table to give her a hug, but my belly got in the way. At that moment the waitress arrived with our salads, and we disentangled ourselves and dug in.

"Well?" Stacy said, taking a delicate sip of her iced tea.

"What gives? Why the urgent lunch? How can I help you seal the deal with Harvey Brodsky?"

"Julia Brennan."

"The comedienne? What about her?"

"Can I?" I reached a fork toward Stacy's plate.

She pushed it toward me, wordlessly, and I scooped up some of her cheese. With a glance over my shoulder to make sure the waitress wasn't watching, I sprinkled a bit over my salad. Stacy laughed.

"What?"

"You know what I love about you?"

"What?"

"You're perfectly willing to stare down a murderer with a loaded gun, but you're afraid of some self-righteous dingbat of a waitress."

I sighed. "You should see me with my hairdresser."

She laughed again.

"Anyway, Julia Brennan," I said. "Is she a client of ICA?"

"She is."

"Would you be willing to get me an introduction?"

Stacy lifted a heavily laden lettuce leaf to her lips and chewed contemplatively. "Why?"

Briefly, I told her about the Alicia Felix connection.

Stacy stabbed her lettuce leaves angrily and took a huge mouthful of food. "I can't believe you," she muttered.

"What?"

"Juliet, you really expect me to introduce you to one of my agency's clients so you can accuse her of stealing her character from someone? You take the cake. You really do."

Of course she was right. Had I really asked my friend to go out on that kind of limb? "I promise I'll be delicate."

She set her fork down, clattering it in her plate.

I said, "I just want to talk to her a little about the conflict she had with Alicia. I want to make sure Alicia really had dropped her claim against Julia, like the director of Left Coast said she had."

"Are you planning on accusing Julia of murder?"

"No!" I did my best to manufacture a tone of outrage, but that was, of course, exactly what I was doing. Not necessarily accusing the woman, but investigating her. I wanted to find out exactly what was going on between those two women. What was the extent of the conflict? How far had it gone? Had Spike really succeeded in getting Alicia to drop her plans for a lawsuit?

Stacy was glaring at me, balefully, and I finally said, "You're right. Of course you're right. You can't introduce me to her. I'll figure out something else."

Stacy looked thoughtful. "Did she really steal that character?"

"Absolutely. I mean, I have a videotape of Alicia doing it on some incredibly lame public access TV show out of the Valley years ago."

"Maybe she stole it from Julia!"

"That's not what the director of Left Coast says."

"Left Coast?"

"Left Coast Players. The comedy troupe."

"I think I've heard of it. Hmm."

"Hmm, what?"

"Just, hmm. Do you mind if I tell this to my partners?"

Oy. Of course I should have anticipated this. The last thing I wanted was to precipitate the ruin of someone's career. Particularly not someone who I was hoping would talk to me. "Maybe you shouldn't."

"Why not?"

"I don't know. Let me figure out what's going on, first. Okay? Give me some time to get a handle on what happened to Alicia. When I do, then we'll talk about it again."

"*When* you do?"

"*If* I do."

Stacy smiled. "I was just teasing. I'm sure you'll figure out what happened to her. You always do. You can do anything you set your mind to."

I shook my head. "I wish that were true."

"It is," Stacy said firmly. And that, in a nutshell, is why our friendship has survived so many years, and our two such divergent lives. Stacy and I, for all the entirely different things we value, are each absolutely convinced that the other is not only the smartest woman out there, but is capable of absolutely anything. We're one another's greatest fans. Everyone needs a friend like that.

Twenty-two

I left the restaurant with plenty of time to pick Ruby up at school. I'd arranged for Isaac to go to a friend's house for a playdate, but I hadn't been able to unload Ruby on anyone—perhaps due to her recently acquired habit of gagging and holding her nose whenever offered a snack that didn't fit precisely into her guidelines of acceptable foodstuffs—so I was going to have to take her with me. Hers was not an entirely inconvenient presence, however. I was fixating too much on Alicia and her various body-image problems and career anxieties. I wasn't blind to the possibility that my concentration on those issues was more a reflection of my own neuroses than a realistic assessment of what might have caused Alicia's murder. I had to explore other avenues, and the one I decided to devote the afternoon to was Kat's mother-in-law, the formidable Nahid Lahidji. I was betting that Nahid would be less likely to rip my head off if I showed up at her office with a delightfully cute child in tow.

Ruby greeted me with a hug and her usual prattle about the day's events. Her brother invariably answers the question, "How was school?" with a scowl, and the comment "a *little* good." Ruby, on the other hand, always has a long list of items that require discussion. Our trip in the direction of the Lahidji real estate office was taken up with a monologue on her new social studies unit, the American Indian tribes of Southern California. Ruby's teacher, a young woman fresh out of the education program at Harvard, was a devoted and energetic soul, but if she had a failing it was her desperation to single-handedly right the wrongs of centuries of American racism and xenophobia. The six-year-olds studied slavery, the trail of tears, the Japanese internment in World War II, the expulsion of the Mormons, current English-only initiatives, and the problems faced by illegal immigrants. Whatever one thought the general depressing nature of the material, Ruby was reading well, could add a mean column of numbers, and was more adept at navigating a computer than I. So who was I to complain?

"You guys still talking about that epidemic of obesity?" I asked.

Ruby shook her head and in a voice dripping with disgust said, "We're on another *unit,* Mama. That was the *last* unit."

"Oh. Okay. And what about Madison? Is she still on a diet?"

No response from the back seat.

"Rubes? What's going on with Madison and the other girls? Are they still on diets?"

"Madison doesn't play with me anymore."

I looked in the rearview mirror. Ruby had her knee propped up under her chin. She was dabbing her tongue on the fabric of her jeans, making a large, round wet spot. "Why not, sweetie?"

She shrugged.

"Ruby? Honey? What happened?"

Her eyes were dry, but her lip trembled. "I said I wasn't going to be a diet girl anymore. And Madison said only diet girls can play with her."

I felt a sinking in my chest, and an overwhelming urge to tear off Madison's perfect little head. "She's a stinky girl, Ruby. She really is."

"I know."

"Are the other girls still diet girls?"

"Some of them."

"Well, don't play with them. Play with the ones who aren't. Those are the smarter girls."

"I know."

"I'll tell you what, honey. I'll call Madison's mom. And your teacher. I'll tell them—" Ruby's wails interrupted me. "What? What, honey?"

"Don't call! Don't call! They'll call me a tattletale. Pinky swear you won't call!"

"Okay, okay, honey. I won't. I won't call." I pulled over into a strip mall. "Want some ice cream?" I said.

"Okay. And can we go to the library, afterwards?"

"Sure! What a great idea!" I'm ashamed to say that I pretended to my daughter that my sole reason for agreeing to the library stop was for her edification and pleasure. She was fooled, but only as long as it took for me to settle down in front of one of the computer terminals. Then she scowled at me and stomped off in the direction of the children's department, warning me over her shoulder that she intended to read "lots of *inappropriate* books!"

I put Nahid's name into Google and got over five hundred hits. Most looked to be property listings, but there were a number of write-ups in local real estate magazines,

and even the real estate section of the *Los Angeles Times*. The
reporter for the *Times* had clearly found Nahid to be a more
interesting subject than the run-of-the-mill realtor profiled
by his section. Nahid was the daughter of an Iranian general
and close confederate of the Shah's who had been executed
during the Iranian revolution. Her husband, a military man
who served under her father, had also been killed. She had
escaped to the United States with her mother and son, and
had, with only the portion of the family fortune that had been
invested abroad and was thus safe from the greedy fingers of
the new regime, begun a lucrative real estate business. She
received her real estate license in 1983, a mere two years after arriving in the United States. Nahid's hardness, her ag-
gressiveness, suddenly made sense to me. Here was a woman
who had been torn from her luxurious lifestyle, seen her father and husband murdered, and who had single-handedly
supported her mother and son and, I would bet, countless
cousins and friends, ensuring that their transition to life in
America would be easier than her own. Reading about Nahid
didn't make me like her any more, but now I admired and
respected her.

Over the course of the past twenty-five years, Nahid
had become one of the wealthiest and most powerful realtors in Los Angeles. She still sold primarily residential
properties ranging from Brentwood mansions to smaller
homes in better neighborhoods, but she also owned both
commercial buildings and residential multi-unit dwellings
all over the city. Nahid Lahidji was a very wealthy woman.
I shifted over to the LexisNexis real property listing and
looked up her various holdings. While most of them were
mortgaged, there were no liens, second mortgages, or tax
violations on any of them. Her finances seemed entirely
secure. So much for my notion that Alicia's objections to

the sale of her brother's house would cause Nahid some kind of financial hardship. On the contrary. The house in Larchmont was a bargain by Nahid's standards, and the commission on it was small change to her. So why was she bothering at all? Probably as a favor to Farzad and his mother. As for why she had gotten so angry with me for my interference, I imagined that Nahid was simply a woman who did not like her plans to be disrupted in any way.

I jotted down a few URLs for the more helpful sites and then went to find Ruby. She had, in fact, found herself something entirely inappropriate to read. I discovered her stretched out on a bench in the children's section, chewing on the sleeve of her shirt, and reading *Seventeen* magazine.

"Hey!" I said. "You are way too young to be reading that junk."

She continued leafing through the pages, teeth busily gnawing holes in the sequined turtleneck she'd made me order off a website called "Gurlsdreemz" after swearing to me that she couldn't live without it.

"Ruby! Stop chewing on your clothes. You're ruining that shirt."

She spat the fabric out and rolled over on her back. "Can I have a prescription to this magazine for my birthday?"

"Sure," I said.

"Really?" she asked, obviously shocked.

"Your seventeenth birthday."

"Mom," she said.

"C'mon kiddo. We need to get going."

"Wait a sec. I want to show you something." She paged through the magazine until she came to a photograph of a skinny model wearing a pair of jeans that hung on her narrow hip-bones like clothes on a hook. She wore no shirt, and had her arms wrapped around her virtually nonexistent breasts.

"See?" Ruby said.

"See what?"

"See her belly-button ring? Isn't it pretty?"

I grabbed my daughter around her waist and hoisted her to her feet, groaning at her unaccustomed weight. It had been a while since I'd tried to pick this big girl up. "You're not getting your pupik pierced, my love. Let's go."

"No."

"Come on, honey. We have to pick Isaac up in an hour, and I have something I need to do before then."

I wish I could say I sounded as patient the fifth and sixth times I told Ruby we had to leave. It would be truly wonderful if I could report that we walked out of the library hand-in-hand, an accommodating child and a devoted parent. Alas, it's more likely that we resembled a screaming banshee and the banshee's ill-tempered herder. Thankfully, Ruby's sobs had abated by the time we reached Nahid's office.

The boss herself wasn't there, but Kat was. I was shown back to her tiny office by a lovely young receptionist with dark, waist-length hair, and gold fingernails with tiny jewels imbedded in the polish. I found my friend hunched over her computer, a stricken look on her face.

"Hey, Kat," I said. "What's up? What are you doing?"

"Evicting someone," she replied morosely. She tugged out the pencil that had been holding her hair up on the top of her head and combed it through the locks that tumbled down over her shoulder. "What's going on? Has something happened with Farzad and Felix?"

I shook my head. "Not that I know of. I was hoping to have a little chat with your mother-in-law. You know, just background stuff."

"She's not going to talk to you. I mean, she might talk *at* you, but she's not going to let you interview her." Suddenly

Kat seemed to notice Ruby's presence. "Hi honey," she said. "How are you? How's school?"

Ruby plopped herself down in the corner of the office where Kat had a small pile of toys. Ruby picked up a toy by the edge, her face wrinkled in a pout of utter disgust, as though she were handling a dead rodent, rather than a Matchbox car.

"These are *boys'* toys," she said.

"That's because they belong to Ashkon," I told her.

She sighed heavily and began to drive the car over the carpet with an ostentatious listlessness. No matter how hard I try, no matter how many gender-neutral toys I buy, my children still persist in acting out the roles assigned to them by contemporary culture. Why is it that that continues to surprise me?

I turned back to Kat. "Have you heard anything new?"

She glanced down at Ruby and then at her open office door. I pushed the door closed with my toe.

"What's going on?"

"I was going to call you today. You know the lock box?" she said.

"On the door of the house? What about it?"

"Well, the boxes have a little chip inside them."

"A memory chip?"

"Exactly. And someone was messing with the lock box on Felix's house."

I leaned forward excitedly. "What do you mean?"

Kat reached into her desk drawer and pulled out a lock box. It was grey, with a black hasp that fit through the door handle, and a little metal trap door in the bottom. Then she reached into her purse and pulled out a little keypad.

"This looks just like the one on Felix's door. You see this keypad?"

I nodded.

"It's called a programmer. Every agent has his or her own programmer, with a four-digit code. You snap your programmer into the box, input your code, and the box opens and you pull out the key." She punched in four numbers, and the metal trapdoor opened. She yanked out a little drawer. I nodded again; I knew all this. I'd seen her use the lock box on Felix's door.

"The chip in the lock box remembers the previous ten numbers."

"It does!"

"Yeah. You know that detective on the case? The really nice-looking black guy with the weird name?"

"Detective Goodenough?"

She nodded. "He came by and asked Nahid to show him how the box worked. She accessed the codes for him. I know all this because she called me into her office to make sure that the most recent number on Felix's lock box was mine; which it was, of course. There shouldn't have been anybody else's number in there, except maybe Nahid's or her assistant's, if one of them had tried the lock box after it was put on. Because, remember, the house wasn't really on the market."

"But there were more numbers in the box's memory?"

"In a way. There was mine, like I said, and before that someone had input the same number nine times."

"What was the code? Do you know who it belonged to?" I asked, holding my breath.

She nodded. "Detective Goodenough traced the number. He called to ask Nahid if the woman worked with us or if she had another reason to have gone to the house."

"And?"

"The code belonged to an agent at Crowden Century 21,

in Bel Air, named Marilyn Farley. Nahid asked me if I knew her, or had told her about the house, but I hadn't. Anyway, it couldn't have been her."

"Why not?"

"Because Marilyn's on bed rest—she's pregnant with twins. She hasn't been allowed up except to pee for nearly two weeks. Nahid had me call her. The detective had already been to see her, but she was so desperate for distraction that she talked to me for almost an hour."

"Has she been home on her own, or is there anybody who can testify that she's really been home like she's supposed to be?"

Kat smiled. "I asked her that. She said her husband is afraid to leave her alone, so whenever he's not with her, he has his mother or her mother stay there."

I nodded. "Good job," I said. "Tell me if you get sick of this real estate business. You might have a future as an investigator."

"I wish," she said wistfully. "Wouldn't that be cool? But Nahid would never let me go. She likes having me right here, where she can watch me."

"Did you ask Marilyn if she has ever lent anyone her number, or if anyone else knew it?' Could someone have taken it and used it?"

"You can't just lend the number. You have to have the programmer."

"Could someone have reprogrammed *their* programmer with *her* code number?"

Kat shook her head. "No. Only the Board of Realtors can change the code on a programmer."

"So whoever it was has to have used her programmer, right?"

"Yup."

"Or had some access to the Board of Realtors."

"Right."

"Where's her programmer now?"

"Here's the really interesting part," Kat said. "It's lost."

"What do you mean?"

"She told me that the detective asked to see her programmer, and she went to give it to him. Except it wasn't in her purse. The day she went on bed rest, she did an open house. She told me that she knows she had her programmer that morning, because she used it at the house, but she hasn't seen it since. She didn't notice it was gone, because she hasn't had to use it since she's been in bed."

"So maybe someone at the open house got hold of her programmer."

"That's what I was thinking."

"Does she know who was there?"

"She said it was a zoo. I mean, you know what the market's like. If it's a halfway decent house you can get a couple of hundred people at an open house."

"What about the sign-in sheet? Isn't there always a sign-in sheet?"

Kat nodded. "Marilyn told me that Detective Goodenough got the sheet from her office. But sometimes people don't bother signing in."

Then I thought of something. "But even if someone stole the programmer, he still couldn't *use* it, right? Unless he knew her code number."

Kat winced. "Marilyn swore me to secrecy."

"Kat!"

"You promise you won't tell? She'll definitely get fired if you tell."

"Of course I promise. I mean, I won't tell unless I absolutely have to."

She sighed and leaned closer to me. "She said she'd been having a horrible time remembering anything since she got pregnant. She kept forgetting her code number, and even had to go back to the Board once to have them input a new number."

"Please don't tell me she wrote the number on her programmer."

Kat nodded. "On a sticker."

"So whoever it was who took her programmer also got the code number."

"Right."

"Does Detective Goodenough know that?"

"I don't know. She must have told him, don't you think? I mean, it's a murder investigation."

For far too many people, self-interest trumps civic responsibility. "When was that open house?"

"Right before she went on bed rest. Just about two weeks ago."

"Before Alicia was killed."

Kat nodded.

I wrinkled my brow. "So someone went to the open house, stole the programmer, and then used it to break into the house and kill Alicia."

"Yup," Kat said.

"But Alicia was in the guest house. Would they really have needed the programmer to get in there?"

"The courtyard is entirely fenced in. There's no access either to the garage or to the side yard from the guesthouse. The only way out is through the main house."

"Still, it seems like pretty convoluted coincidence, don't you think? You just happen to find the programmer, it just happens to have the code written on it, and there just happens to be a lock box on the door of the person you want to kill."

"Maybe the person stole the programmer first, and that's what gave him the idea of using it to get into the house and kill her."

"Maybe. Or maybe he went to an open house hoping to steal a programmer, and just lucked into the number. However it happened, why did he bother inputting the number so many times? Why didn't he just use the stolen programmer once, to get in?"

Kat paused, thinking.

"What do you get out of inputting the number?" I murmured more to myself than her.

"What do you mean?"

"What happens when you input the number again and again? You erase the previously recorded code numbers, right?"

Kat nodded. "Right!"

I leaned back in my chair and winced. My sciatica was killing me. "Someone was trying to hide the codes that had been previously used. They were making sure no one would know who had been there before them."

At that moment, Ruby jumped to her feet. "Mama!"

I looked over at her.

"Mama! It's almost five o'clock!"

I looked up at the clock hanging on Kat's wall. "That's right honey. Good job reading the time."

She scowled at me. "*Mama!* We're late picking Isaac up from his playdate!"

We most certainly were.

Twenty-three

WHEN we arrived back home, I dumped the children with their father and called Detective Goodenough. Unlike every other cop I'd ever tried to reach on the telephone, he actually answered his own extension. His voice was deep and resonant, and he projected a stern authority, even over the fiber-optic lines.

The detective reassured me that he was following up on the open house attendees, and greeted my tentative request for a copy of the open house register with a bark of laughter. He was steps ahead of me on the Board of Realtors, as well, and was already in possession of the names and addresses of everyone on the Board, as well as of the various employees. It wasn't surprising that he refused to share that information, either, but that at least I could acquire for myself quite easily over the Internet.

Goodenough was polite, but he neither needed nor wanted my input on his investigation. And who could blame him, really? As far as he was concerned, I was at best an overly aggressive defense attorney, and at worst a busybody pregnant lady.

I hung up the phone feeling frustrated, and called Al, who volunteered to find out who was on the Board of Realtors. We'd sit down together and figure out if any of the members had a connection to Alicia. I took on the rather hopeless task of tracking down the list of people who had attended the open house. I knew Goodenough wouldn't share the sign-up sheet with us, and I doubted that Kat's friend, the pregnant, bedridden real estate agent with the bad memory, would be able to recreate it for me.

Feeling a bit better about my lack of progress, I wandered into Peter's office where the rest of my family was crouched on the floor, building the Bottle City of Kandor out of Legos.

"So, I've got some bad news," Peter said.

I groaned. "What?"

"I've got to fly to New York for a meeting."

I lowered myself to the carpet and leaned against him. I nestled my head against the smooth warmth of his ancient flannel shirt and felt the soft give of the layer of flesh that had lately overtaken his once-thin chest and belly. I toyed with the broken button on his shirt cuff. "Bummer," I said. "When?"

"Tomorrow."

I groaned again, and Peter kissed the top of my head.

Ruby, always on the lookout for any physical contact between her parents that didn't specifically include her, picked her head up from the pile of bricks she was snapping into the shape of Krypto the Superdog. "We should go with you, Daddy."

He ruffled her curls with his hand. "I wish you could, sweetie pie."

"It's been a very long time since I've seen my Bubbe and Zayde," she said.

"Not that long," I reminded her. "Bubbe was just here when Mama and Daddy went to Mexico."

"That was months and months ago," she said.

Suddenly, I thought of Julia Brennan, and *New York Live.* I might not be able to investigate the people who'd shown up at Marilyn Farley's open house, but Goodenough couldn't keep me away from Julia Brennan. I pushed against Peter's chest, leveraging myself into a sitting position. "Honey, you know, that might not be such a bad idea," I said.

"What?" Peter said.

"We should go with you to New York! We'll see my folks, and I can do a little follow-up on this case."

"Tomorrow? You want to go to New York with me tomorrow?"

"Sure! It's a great idea. Ruby and Isaac will stay with my parents, and the two of us will have a romantic couple of days in the city."

"Are you allowed to fly? I mean, aren't you too pregnant?"

"The airlines let you on up to thirty-six weeks, and I know Dr. Kline won't care."

"But I'm going to be *working*. And, anyway, do you know how much a ticket will cost at the last minute?"

"Nothing, if we use frequent flyer miles. I'm going to get on the phone and see what I can do." Suddenly I narrowed my eyes at him. "Unless you don't *want* us to go with you."

He smiled a sickly smile. "No, no. I can't think of anything more fun than flying cross-country with the kids for a two-day visit with your parents."

Lucky for us, the flight the studio had booked Peter on

still had two seats available for frequent flyers. I gulped, and paid full fare for the third seat, reassuring myself that at least it was tax deductible. I was, after all, working on a case. Maybe I'd even be able to bill some part of the fare to Felix's account—if it didn't turn out to be a total waste of time, that is.

What I didn't remember until we actually arrived at the airport the next morning is that the Screenwriters Guild requires that all its members be flown *first class*. Not Business Class, and most certainly not, God forbid, coach. Peter boarded the plane at his leisure and began snacking on warm nuts and champagne, while I did my best to browbeat two people into swapping seats so that Ruby and Isaac would be sitting next to me. My entreaties fell on deaf ears. No one was willing to swap their aisle and window for any one of our three middle seats. Finally, I walked up to the florid man in the New York Jets sweatshirt sitting in the aisle seat next to Isaac and handed him an airsickness bag.

"His name is Isaac, and he usually stops vomiting twenty minutes or so after take-off. I find it helpful to have a second bag at the ready, just in case he fills the first."

The man's face turned even redder, and he leapt to his feet and stumbled over himself on his way to the seat that had been assigned to me.

The flight attendant came over at this point, her perfectly made-up face twisted into a grim smile. "You're going to have to take your seat, Ma'am."

"Okay, I just need another minute," I said.

"We can't push back until you sit down, Ma'am," she said firmly.

"I know, and I'm so sorry. I'll be just a second." I craned my neck to find where Ruby's seat was, and knelt down to point it out to her.

"*Now,* Ma'am."

I stifled my irritation—you can never win an argument with a flight attendant. I once represented a woman who had an altercation with a stewardess over whether her stroller could fit in the overhead compartment. My client ended up getting charged with assault, all because she had tapped the stewardess's name badge and told her she was going to report her to the airline. My poor client, a harried mother of three, was taken off the airplane in handcuffs.

Now, the flight attendant seemed to notice my belly for the first time. Her face tightened into an expression that looked suspiciously victorious. "Ma'am, we don't allow women in advanced stages pregnancy to fly." She smiled at me maliciously. "You'll have to come with me."

I looked her dead in the eye and said, in a voice so shocked and horrified that I nearly frightened *myself,* "What are you talking about? I'm not *pregnant!*" I lifted a trembling hand to my chest. "I've never been so offended in my life."

Ruby opened her mouth as if to protest, but I squeezed her shoulder.

The flight attendant blushed a deep red, and stammered, "Oh. Oh no. I'm so sorry. I didn't mean . . . I'm so. . . . Oh, *no.*" She stumbled away from me back up the aisle. I turned my attention to the young woman in the window seat. She stared back at me over her copy of *The Joy Luck Club,* and then smiled.

"All right," she said. "You win." She got up, and I pushed Ruby into the seat she vacated.

"It's 23B," I said. "And thank you."

"No problem. When are you due?"

I winked at her, snapping my seat belt closed.

Here's the irony of that particular flight. The truth was, Isaac never vomits on airplanes. He's a *terrific* flyer. In fact, unlike his sister, who heaves her food at the drop of a hat, he almost never gets sick. However, I'd forgotten about his recent bout of stomach flu. Worse yet, the red-faced man hadn't given me back the airsickness bag I'd handed him. Isaac did indeed fill more than one bag, but the second didn't have the airline's logo printed on it. With remarkable quick thinking for a six-year-old, Ruby grabbed my purse, dumped the contents into her lap, and handed it to me while I held Isaac's head in my hands. Peter and I were going to need to make a stop at the Kate Spade boutique.

At the end of the five-hour flight, my ankles had swollen to the size of basketballs, and Ruby, Isaac, and I were covered in a combination of orange juice, chicken gravy, and other things too disgusting to contemplate. Ruby's hair resembled a pile of brightly colored autumn leaves, so that gave me some idea about what was probably going on with my own. We tumbled out of our seats and found Peter waiting for us at the door to the plane. His smile slowly faded as we approached.

"Have a nice nap?" I asked him.

He shook his head. "I didn't sleep for more than an hour or two. I watched that new Sylvester Stallone movie."

If there were any justice in the world, the heat of my scowl would have burned a hole right through his chest. I handed him our flight bags and waddled after the children who had scampered out ahead of us.

"I forgot my Lactaid!" he called after me. "So I got a really bad stomachache from the ice cream sundae. And you know how much I hate caviar. The gravlax was covered in it."

It was all I could do to keep from flinging myself at his throat.

Twenty-four

IT was over lunch the next day at the Union Square Café that I finally forgave my husband. His meeting was in the morning, and he'd begged off a business lunch in order to meet me. The kids were at my parents' house in New Jersey, being stuffed with New York bagels, Stella D'oro cookies, and other delicacies unavailable in the wilds of California. Peter and I had had a lovely night on our own at the St. Regis hotel, one of those indulgences you are permitted only when traveling on the tab of someone far richer and more spoiled than yourself. The movie studio for which Peter had agreed to rewrite a Victorian Frankenstein romp qualified nicely.

While Peter had been stuck in meetings, I'd spent the morning replacing the purse I'd sacrificed on the altar of Isaac's roiling stomach, and was feeling pretty darn content. I'd even managed to find a maternity store in Soho that had, hidden on a crooked rack at the rear of the store, a few items in my size. At five feet tall, I'd never before considered my-self an XXL, but the tunic with Chinese writing all over it was too cute to pass up purely because of size-related shame. I was a little worried that the letters might actually spell out something like "Ugly, fat, white woman," or "Many years of bad luck to wearer," but I suppressed that concern as soon as I realized how good the top looked with my new faded, flare jeans.

"Hey! You look adorable," Peter said as soon as I walked in the door of the restaurant.

I smiled brightly and showed off my purse. "What do you think?"

He blinked. "Is that new, too?"

"No, I spent the morning hosing the vomit out of the old one. Of course it's new!"

"Isn't it the same bag?"

"Not at all. This one has a thin red stripe in the fabric. See?" I held the bag out to him and he nodded suspiciously. "And the other one had blue piping, not black."

"Nice," he said.

We sat down at a table by the window, and I spent a de-lightful few minutes perusing the menu, specifically avoiding anything that could be considered even remotely kid-friendly. I was seriously considering an entire meal of shell-fish and carpaccio when I remembered that Ruby and Isaac's absence didn't liberate me in any real way, after all. I was carrying around my very own diet regulator. I would have to make due with grilled flank steak sandwich and fries, but I satisfied my urge to misbehave by ordering a glass of red wine. The New York waitress didn't bat an eye, merely brought me my drink with a practiced flourish, and I tossed off half the glass with equal aplomb.

As we waited for our food and made short work of the breadbasket, Peter said, "We've got an appointment to go to the set of *New York Live* after lunch." I'd sent Peter to his meeting with instructions to ask if anyone there had a connection to *New York Live* that might result in an introduction to Julia Brennan. "One of the producers of my film used to write for the show. She made a call for me."

"That's fabulous!" I exclaimed, nearly toppling my chair as I leaned to kiss my husband on his rough, stubbly cheek. Peter is the kind of guy who shaves only when not to would result in his being taken for an Orthodox Jew, or an Amish farmer.

The *New York Live* set was an old theater, the Stanley, on 43rd street at Broadway. Rehearsals took place on the stage, and the red velvet and gilt of the hanging curtains and proscenium, combined with the hilarious antics of the actors, lent the proceeding something of the hysterical air of late 19th century vaudeville. We walked in on a lesson in pratfalling. A man with a bulbous forehead and a red, fleshy proboscis was flinging himself from a ladder onto the stage while a hovering crowd laughed and leapt out of the way. I recognized some of the actors from the show, including Julia Brennan.

After a particularly dramatic tumble from the top of the ladder, the man limped off the stage and a young woman with a clipboard and an officious air called a break. We told her that we'd come to see Julia, and she called up to the stage, catching the comedienne right before she went off with the others. Julia came up to the row in front of ours and, leaning back over a chair, extended her hand in a friendly greeting. She was about twenty-five or -six years old and tall, taller than she seemed on television, with large hands and sharp, bony features. She looked somehow androgynous, manly even, like a transsexual who has given up the struggle for persuasive femininity and must content himself with a casual ambiguity.

"Randy, the assistant stage-manager, tells me you write those cannibal movies," she said to Peter.

"Yup."

"Love them. They're fun." Then she looked at me. "What can I do for you?"

"Ms. Brennan," I began.

"Julia."

The ancient seat springs groaned as I shifted my weight. Even had she not been so tall, Julia, standing there, would have loomed above me; but as it was, I felt like one of the Munchkins talking to the Great and Powerful Oz. She seemed to notice my discomfort and sat down, still in the row ahead, her long legs crossed and her arms resting on the seat back.

"I'm an investigator. I work for Felix. Do you know who he is?"

"The fashion designer? Sure! Tariq Jones, one of our younger comedians, does a bit spoofing his line."

I smiled, wondering what name Tariq could come up with that would seem more farcical than "Booty Rags." "I think you knew his sister, Alicia Felix."

Julia narrowed her eyes at me for a moment and then assumed an expression of heartfelt sympathy. "Yeah, it's really awful. I heard all about it from Spike Stevens."

"Felix has hired me to look into the circumstances of the murder."

"And that's why you want to talk to me?"

"I'm trying to get a sense of what kind of person Alicia was. What might have been going on in her life."

"Uh huh."

"I understand that in recent years you two had some . . . difficulties."

Julia raised an eyebrow. "Difficulties? What do you mean?"

"The character you do on the show, Bingie McPurge. It's based on Alicia's Mia bit, isn't it?"

"Based on? Hardly."

"Well, Alicia was doing Mia long before you were doing Bingie McPurge, wasn't she?"

Julia stood up suddenly. "I don't think I should be talking to you. My lawyers are dealing with this."

I lifted a mollifying hand. "I'm just doing the best I can to find out about Alicia. Her disappointment over her career seems to have been one of the defining things about her, and your success with a very similar comedy schtick was clearly a source of frustration for her."

Julia folded her arms in front of her, but she didn't walk away. "And? So what? I certainly hope you're not trying to say that I had anything to do with her death."

Now it was my turn to pause. I hadn't made any such implication, had I? "No. But you can't deny the similarity of the characters."

"Let's just say that Mia inspired me."

"Did Alicia ever speak to you personally about Bingie McPurge? Or were all your contacts through your lawyers?"

Julia unfolded her arms and seemed to relax. "She certainly tried to."

"What do you mean?"

"Look, I won't lie to you. You know Alicia was upset. She called my agent a few times, pretty hysterical. We even had to ask Spike to try to mellow her out. Anyway, there wasn't much she could do, was there?

"Wasn't there? Weren't you afraid she would, say, sue you?"

Julia shook her head. "She might have threatened that, but she didn't have any grounds, and she knew it. Sure, she had a character that was a bulimic. But I didn't steal any of her jokes—honestly, why would I have? Alicia was no writer. Her routine basically consisted of gagging noises. Even if she had tried to sue, my agents, lawyers, the studio people, everyone said that she didn't have a leg to stand on. Anyway, Alicia was, like, forty years old." Julia looked at me, as if assessing whether or not I was close to that witching age. "She couldn't play the part anymore. It was ridiculous."

Then Julia leaned over and lowered her voice. "I'll tell you something; you should be looking at a whole different part of Alicia Felix's life if you want to really get to know what she was like."

"What do you mean?"

Julia smiled. "She was a freak. I mean, really. My lawyers found out all sorts of stuff about her."

I deliberately forced my face to remain blandly neutral.

"What kind of stuff?"

"That woman was insane. I mean, really nuts. You want to know why she died, you should look at her website."

"Her website?"

At that moment, a voice called out. "Actors, places. Let's go!"

Julia turned her back on me and loped in the direction of the stage, her long legs carrying her like an elegant stick insect. Right before she reached the end of the row she turned back. "Hey," she called. "Don't you want to know where I was the night Alicia was killed?"

Her jocular tone struck me as so inappropriate I didn't even reply.

"I was here, in the city. I have been for weeks. We've got rehearsal every day but Sunday, and the show is live on Saturdays."

"Okay," I said. It wouldn't take too much to follow up on her alibi. And even if it stuck, there was always the possibility that she had arranged for someone else to do the murder. Although the truth is, it's a lot more difficult to find a hit man than you might think.

Julia said, "I hope you find out who killed her. I really do. Whatever Alicia and I thought of each other, nobody deserves to die like that."

The woman sounded absolutely sincere, and genuinely unconcerned. Her callousness might have been a product of her success, or simply of her youth. Whatever its source, she didn't sound like someone who would have felt compelled to murder in order to protect her career. I wasn't ready to dismiss the possibility of her guilt absolutely—after all, she might have been a better actress than the few minutes of the show Peter and I watched indicated—but something told me that my short list was down another suspect.

Back at the hotel, I logged on to the Web and found Alicia's website. I spent a good hour going through every page, but I could find nothing on the site that made Alicia seem any more bizarre than any other wanna-be in Hollywood. For that matter, I could find nothing that would have inspired the letters from the young girls that I'd seen tacked up on the bulletin board in the guest house. The site consisted of no more and no less than a series of photographs of Alicia in various theatrical incarnations, and her at once lengthy and spotty filmography. The closest I got to "freaky" was a series of photographs of Alicia in which she was naked, although her arms were wrapped tightly around her body, hiding everything from the lens. She looked lovely, almost ethereally beautiful, but also frightening. Alicia was just so thin. Like a half-starved Ophelia. Was this what Julia was referring to? Was it Alicia's anorexia that made her, in the eyes of Bingie McPurge, a freak?

Twenty-five

ON the way home to Los Angeles, Peter gave me the first class seat. All the way onto the plane, I was the happiest woman on earth. So happy, in fact, that I was wishing for thick fog over LAX so we would have to circle the airport for a couple of extra hours. I was the first one on the plane, and I settled myself excitedly in my overstuffed seat, two fashion magazines and a mystery novel tucked into the back pocket of the seat in front of me, my shoes kicked off, my hand ready to receive my orange juice and cup of warmed nuts. Then my seatmate joined me. My very, very large seatmate. My very, very large seatmate, with a sinus condition. The man snorted and snuffed his way through an entire box of tissues before we had even taken off. I refused to allow myself to be troubled. I put my headphones on, turned the volume up loud, and pushed back against the massive elbow that had worked its way across the armrest and into my seat.

The headphones were no match, however, for the twins

sitting in the seat in front of me. When their frazzled young mother made it onto the plane, seconds before the door closed, dragging two car seats with her, I nearly burst into tears. *My* babies were in coach! Far away from me. I was liberated from them, free to enjoy an adult-only universe. And here, in first class, was a mother traveling with a set of infant twins. A set of twins who, apparently, had outgrown their naps. They could not have been more than eighteen months old, and neither of them shut up for the entire flight. They screamed, they cried, they wailed, and no matter how loud I turned up the volume on my headset, I heard them. Worst of all, I had to pretend I didn't care. I had to pretend that, unlike the other sour-faced denizens of first class, I, as a mother, had sympathy for the young woman. I knew her pain. And I did. I really did. Yet I still wanted to throttle her and her wretchedly behaved children.

By the time the flight attendant dumped my hot fudge sundae in my lap, I had grown somewhat fatalistic about the possibility of enjoying my flight. Her cheerily apologetic "Oopsie!" didn't even bother me. Neither did the snicker of the fat man with the runny nose. Or the resounding wails of the twins as their mother put them down for a moment to pass me a handful of baby wipes so I could swab ineffectually at the sticky, wet stain on my slacks.

Peter, on the other hand, reported that the children had been so tired from their two days with my parents that they'd both fallen asleep as soon as the plane took off. He'd spent the flight happily rereading a copy of *Dune* he'd found in the seatback pocket. Once again I had to restrain myself from beating him about the head and shoulders.

The studio had arranged for a car to pick Peter up and take him home, and the look on the driver's face when he realized that three sticky urchins, one of them pregnant, were going to be joining his client in the impeccably maintained Lincoln Continental was a cross between horror and despair. He was even less pleased when it became obvious that our luggage could barely fit on a single cart. The poor man had to lug both booster seats himself. I did dump out the cookie crumbs, sand, and gobs of melted gummy bears before handing him the seats. There was nothing I could do about the crusted-on yogurt, short of throwing the seats away and starting fresh.

My cell phone rang almost as soon as we got settled in the car. It was Al.

"Where are you?" he shouted into the phone.

I held the receiver a few inches from my ear. "On the ten heading for home.

"So?" Al asked. "What did you find out?"

"One dead end after another." I told him about my conversation with Julia. "How did you do on the Board of Realtors list?"

"Got it," he said. When I first met Al, he had been something of a Luddite, suspicious of the Internet, certain it was a tool of the government for spying on innocent and unwary citizens. While he's still convinced that the FBI and NSA are amassing piles of information on individual taxpayers, a suspicion that has lately begun to sound less and less crazy to me, he has grown adept at using the Internet for his own purposes, both professional and otherwise. While once he had to rely on buddies on the force to whisper in his ear, he can now find almost anything out with a few clicks of the mouse. He also uses the Internet to keep in close touch with his militia and anti-tax cronies.

"Read me the list of names," I said.

He did, but unfortunately I didn't recognize any of them.

"I'll email it to you," he promised.

One of the joys of flying from east to west is that that
time difference allows you much of your day once you're
home. Peter took pity on me after my hellish flight and volunteered to stay home with the kids. I called Kat and browbeat her into arranging a visit with Marilyn Farley, who was
still stuck in bed, trying to stave off the delivery of her
twins. I told Peter, albeit half-heartedly, that I would take
Ruby and Isaac with me, but they were busy getting back in
touch with their stuffed animals and action figures and were
unwilling to leave the house.

Kat met me in front of Marilyn's bungalow in the neighborhood known to real estate agents, and to real estate
agents alone, as Beverly Hills Adjacent. The rest of us call it
Los Angeles. Kat was leaning against the door of her car,
and she looked just terrible.

"Hey," I said, walking up to her.

She smiled wanly.

"What's wrong?"

"Wrong? Nothing's wrong."

But she was clearly lying. Her face was drawn and thin,
and her pregnant belly looked like it was hanging from her
shoulder blades like a basketball on a hanger. Her skin was
pallid, and almost green.

I opened the door of her car and got in, motioning for her
to do the same. She followed me and leaned her head against
the steering wheel.

"What is it, sweetie?" I said, patting her shoulder. "Is it
this investigation? Is Nahid giving you a hard time?"

She shook her head. "No, no. Nothing like that. I'm just
under pressure. You know, with the baby coming. Nothing's ready. I haven't moved Ashkon out of the nursery. I
haven't set up his big boy bed. There's just so much to do."

I sighed sympathetically. I hadn't made any preparations

for my baby, either. But by the third, you just sort of assume everything will fall into place.

"It'll work out, Kat. It's just a matter of one intense weekend's worth of work. If you want, I can give you a hand. We'll go shopping for all the stuff you need, including Ashkon's new furniture."

She sat up and shook her head. "That's sweet of you, but it's not just that."

I waited.

She seemed to muster up her courage. "Sometimes, when I'm feeling stressed out . . . I . . . well . . ."

"What?" I asked softly.

She sighed. "God, this is so embarrassing. It's just that I thought I was over all this. I mean, I *was* over it all. And then last week I just started doing it again."

"Doing what?"

She rubbed her hand across her mouth, swallowed, and then said, "I used to be bulimic. I mean, I guess I still am."

For a moment, I was surprised. And then I wasn't at all. Kat's confession made all too much sense. Her thinness always seemed somehow unnatural to her. Here she was, this beautiful, voluptuous, middle-eastern woman, who somehow managed to be rail-thin even while pregnant. While virtually every Persian woman I've ever met has been fashionably thin, Kat always looked like someone on a drastic diet. It was as though her flesh seemed empty—missing its accustomed fullness and heft. Her sharp cheekbones cried out for a layer of padding, her neck sank oddly into a bosom too round and soft for her bony chest and torso.

"You've been making yourself throw up?" I asked, doing my best not to sound judgmental.

She nodded. "I know it's awful. For the baby, especially."

"The baby will probably take the nutrients it needs from your body. I'm more worried about you."

"I should go back to my meetings."

"Like AA?"

"Yeah, but for bulimics. I stopped going a few years ago. I didn't need it. But now I guess I do."

"Do you have a therapist?" I asked.

"I did."

"Maybe you should see her again, too."

"I don't have time! I mean, I told you, I've got like nine million things to do, and Nahid is running me ragged at work."

"And here I am, making things even harder for you. Please, Kat. Make time. Call the therapist. You can't keep doing this to yourself. You'll make yourself sick. And at some point the baby will start to suffer, too."

She closed her eyes, as if to keep her tears from falling, and then said, "We'd better go in. Marilyn is expecting us." She opened her door and walked out, leaving me to follow behind.

This eating disorder thing was so tenacious, so impossibly ubiquitous. Was there a woman in the city of Los Angeles who was not somehow stuck in its claws? What was most remarkable to me was how it could rear its ugly head years after Kat had assumed she was cured, after she had moved beyond that kind of mindset and behavior. Just like, for that matter, Alicia Felix.

MARILYN Farley was lying in bed, on her left side, looking about as bored as any woman has ever looked. We were shown to her room by an older woman who could only have been her mother-in-law, given the combination of politeness and impatience with which Marilyn treated her.

"It's great to meet you!" Marilyn said, a bit hysterically. "God, I'm so pathetic. You just can't have any idea how horrible this is. I've been stuck in this bed forever. I'm not even allowed to roll over! I'm just supposed to lie here on my left side and hope I don't have to pee more than a few times a day. I can't even read, because the medication they have me on gives me blurry vision. So all I do all day is watch crappy movies on cable. There was the one really horrible one about a cannibal wedding that gave me nightmares for days."

I blushed. "Yeah, That's not the greatest movie. I'm so sorry about the bedrest." I could never have managed it. Who would drive carpool? Who would go the grocery store? Who would run out to the shoe store to buy the pair of pink ballet slippers without which the recital could not proceed? Then I gave it a moment's reflection. Would it really be so bad? Trapped in bed watching movies? Even Peter's movies? With no other responsibilities? I wondered if there was something I could do to induce a little preterm labor of my own.

Marilyn, despite her understandable embarrassment at having lost her programmer, was willing to try to list for us the individuals who had come to her open house. She confessed to me that she was afraid that her irresponsibility had somehow led to Alicia's death. I got the feeling that Detective Goodenough had not done a particularly good job of convincing her otherwise. I reassured her that even if her programmer had been used, it had, at worst, made the murderer's job a little easier.

"If someone really wants to kill someone else," I told her, "he'll find a way. It would have been just as easy to break a window."

"But then the alarm would have gone off," Kat said.

I shook my head. "The alarm can't have been on, otherwise it would have gone off when the murderer opened the front door, even if he had used a key." I jotted down a note to ask Felix if Alicia normally turned the alarm on when she was home alone. If she did, then why had she left it off this time? Was she expecting someone?

As Marilyn did her best to remember the various realtors who had come to her open house, and whether or not they had brought clients with them, I took careful notes. None of the names sounded familiar, and while Kat knew some of the agents, she couldn't link them to Alicia in any way. Marilyn told me that there were a few people who had wandered in off the street, and that while she couldn't, of course, remember their names, she was fairly certain they'd signed in. So those individuals, at least, would be on the list Detective Goodenough had taken from her. That is, if they'd given their real names.

Once we'd exhausted the conversation about the open house, I spent a frustrating half hour trying delicately to figure out whether Marilyn was hiding anything. None of my gently put questions resulted in any kind of lead. Marilyn seemed genuinely never to have met Alicia Felix, not to know her, not to have had anything to do with the case in any way. Except that it was her programmer than had allowed the murderer access to the house.

Twenty-six

ALand I spent the next few days working on other cases, doing routine skip traces. I refused to set foot in the office until Julio was absolutely finished finding rat corpses, and Al had reluctantly admitted that the place was still plagued by the odor of dead vermin.

"I don't know where the hell they could be," he said. "In the walls, maybe? Anyway, Julio's going to poke some holes in the sheet rock and then repaint the whole damn garage."

"Good," I said. "He needs the work, and your garage could do with a renovation."

We were operating out of my kitchen, and his car. We didn't normally bother with skip traces—while they were once the bread and butter of private investigative services, nowadays most companies are aware of online tracing services and don't bother paying investigative fees to find the welshers and absconders that plague their businesses. We were doing these as a favor for a friend of Al's who had set up a semi-shady limited partnership scheme, only to find that the bulk of his investors had disappeared as soon as the economy had turned the least bit ugly. I tried to tell Al that the guy was probably paying us to avoid getting his own legs shot off by the people we were trying to find, but my partner ignored me. At any rate, none of the dozen disbarred lawyers and unlicensed physicians we tracked down seemed particularly dangerous. Just scrambling for cash, and not particularly honest.

The weekend found me absolutely gleeful at the *prospect* of time with the children, and out of Al's Suburban. That is, until Ruby began her by-now tedious refrain.

"I don't understand, why do I have to wait until I'm twelve to get my ears pierced?" she said.

"Because you have to be old enough to take care of the holes yourself. And that will be when you're twelve."

"But I'm old enough now! Both Isabel and Sophie got their ears pierced! All they had to do was clean the holes with special stuff and keep twirling their earrings. I can do that. I'm not a baby."

How could I explain to my child that the thought of a needle being jammed through her little white lobes, those pads of sweet flesh as precious to me as every other tiny, innocent part of her adorable little body, just made my heart rush to my mouth? We own our children's bodies when they're small. We created those little pearl toes, those dimpled elbows, those rounded cheeks. Our children belong to us as much—no *more*—than they belong to themselves. I reached around Ruby's waist and dragged her onto what lap I had left. She wriggled out of my arms, unintentionally jabbing me in the belly.

"Ouch!" I said.

"I don't feel like sitting on your lap."

"Okay," I said, my feelings hurt. Then, I looked at her. She was standing in a way that was unfamiliar to me. Her hip jutted out at an angle, and she had the toe of one sneaker balanced on the other foot. Her arms were crossed in front of her chest and she looked almost comically furious. She wanted to grow up, and I wasn't letting her. Then I thought of horrible little Madison and the other diet girls, and how scary that had all come to seem to me, in the wake of the tide of anorexia and bulimia that seemed to be washing over everything in my life. I was so afraid for Ruby, and so desperate for her to stay close to me so that I could protect her from all that.

"You know what, Ruby?" I said. "Let's go get your ears pierced."

Her shrieks of joy were so loud they made her little sister in my belly kick me in the ribs. Hard.

OUR first stop was the mall. None of the jewelry stores did ear-piercing, but we found a gift shop that advertised the service in the window. We waited at the register while the sales girl talked into her cell phone.

"He is like such a complete pig, and I like totally told him so. I instant messaged him, and I'm like, if you think I'm gonna just sit here while you boff her—"

"Excuse me!" I said loudly.

The salesgirl looked up at me from under her stiff, blond bangs. "What?"

"We need some help," I said.

"Mama?" Ruby said. "What does 'boff' mean?"

The girl laughed and said into her phone, "O'migod, I gotta go. I'll call you back in like a minute."

"Mama!" Ruby insisted.

"Nothing, honey. It's teenager talk." Then I turned to the girl. "We're interested in having her ears pierced."

"Cool!" she said, ducking under the counter and coming out to stand by us. "I just learned how to do that the other day. C'mon."

She led us to the front of the store where a little stool was set up in the window. She pointed at a row of stud earrings and told Ruby to pick out a pair.

"I've just got to remember how to do this," she said, picking up a white piercing gun. "Oops!" she shrieked, howling with laughter as a gold stud flew out of the gun and landed on the floor. "I guess someone loaded it already."

Ruby pointed out a pair of blue glass earrings, and the sales girl bit her lipsticked lip, leaving teeth marks in the heavy gloss. "Um, when's your birthday, because those are for December," she said.

"It doesn't matter," I told her.

"Well, like it totally does. I mean, she can't have like someone else's birthstone."

Ruby's lip began to tremble, giving lie to the notion that she was old enough to be doing this in the first place.

"Just give her the blue ones," I said.

"Okay, whatever," the sales girl said, and then, as if entirely unaware of our presence, reached a talon-nail up to her forehead and picked at a shiny pimple. I watched horrified as the zit popped under her finger. She glanced at the smear of puss on her nail and then wiped it casually on her jeans.

"You know what?" I said. "I've changed my mind. Come on, Ruby." I grabbed my daughter by the arm and dragged her out of the store. By the time we hit the parking lot, she was hysterical.

"Stop crying!" I said, opening the car door and lifting her

inside. "Stop crying, Ruby. We'll get your ears pierced. I promise. Just not there. That place was disgusting"

"Well then, where?" she snuffled.

"I don't know."

She looked as if she was about to being sobbing again.

"Ruby!" I warned. "Enough."

She sniffed dramatically, and we pulled out of the parking lot. We drove down Beverly Boulevard in silence, and then suddenly Ruby said, "How about there?"

She was pointing at a storefront brightly painted with geometric designs that looked vaguely tribal. A huge, green neon signed flashed the words "Body Piercing." Two young men were leaning up against the wall of the building, their skateboards tipped up against their legs, their dreadlocks blowing in the gentle breeze.

I was about to say no, when a thought occurred to me. Who better to entrust with my baby's precious lobes than someone whose business encompassed body parts far more sensitive and susceptible to infection?

I was probably not the first mother of two to hop out of her Volvo station wagon and into the waiting area of Tribal Memory Tat and Hole Works, but I doubt that they'd seen much of my kind of woman. The gaping mouths on the long line of bepierced and betatted young people waiting patiently on the paint-spattered vinyl couch and stools made that abundantly clear. Ruby and I crossed the cement floor with trepidation, both because we were nervous, and because the floor was decorated with a painting of the huge portrait of a Maori warrior in full face-paint, and it felt kind of weird to be stomping across his protruding tongue.

"Can I help you?" the young man behind the counter asked politely. He was young and part Asian, with long black hair caught up in a bun on top of his head. His ears were pierced with large, round, steel plugs that measured at least one inch in diameter, causing his lobes to hang low and distended against his cheeks. Each of his eyebrows sported a dozen rings of various sizes. I couldn't see under his clothes, but I was willing to bet that getting through a metal detector would have involved some nearly pornographic maneuvering.

"Exactly how sanitary are your facilities?" I said, ignoring the fact that I sounded like my Bubbe, who used to travel everywhere with a purse-sized bottle of Formula 409 with which she freely sprayed down park benches, bus seats, and even the chairs in restaurants.

"Good question," he said, and then he proceeded to outline for me the various cleansing tools he used. He showed me the prepackaged needles, each individually wrapped and sealed. He described the technique he used to sterilize the earrings, and then promised that he wore gloves throughout the procedure.

His professional thoroughness won my heart. Ruby's belonged to him the moment he showed her the gold hoops with the little mother-of-pearl beads he planned to use in her ears.

"Doesn't she have to have studs at first?" I asked.

"Nope," he said. "We find these work much better."

The procedure wasn't painless, but Squeak (that was what he told Ruby to call him) was true to his word. He washed his hands thoroughly, he changed gloves every time he touched something that hadn't been sterilized, and he took a good five minutes meticulously evening out the dots he drew on Ruby's ears. He assured me that if she ever wanted any more piercings in her ears, or if she ever planned on getting plugs like his own, there would be plenty of room in her lobes. I somehow managed to refrain from shouting, "Over my dead body!" The actual piercing was done with a long, black needle, and Ruby managed it with nary a tear, although her arms, wrapped tightly around my neck, seemed to be shaking. It's possible, though, that the trembling was my own.

The line of young men and women we had jumped (Squeak had asked them if they minded, and they had all assured us that they didn't) burst into applause when we walked out of the curtained piercing room. Ruby blushed and showed off her little hoops.

"Ooh!" a tall, blond girl of about eighteen exclaimed. "Mother-of-pearl! That's just what I want in my nipple!"

Twenty-seven

THAT Monday I took the list of Board of Realtor members, as well as the names Marilyn had remembered, over to Felix's house. Detective Goodenough arrived moments after I did.

"Ms. Applebaum," he said, not sounding at all surprised to see me. I was waiting in the living room for Farzad to get Felix, and the maid had let the detective in.

"How is the investigation proceeding?" I asked him. "Finding out about the tampering with the programmer will certainly help, I imagine."

He narrowed his eyes at me, and then nodded. "You're friends with the younger Mrs. Lahidji."

"Yes, I am."

We waited in silence until Felix and Farzad walked into the room. The men were obviously surprised to see the detective. They had been expecting only me. Goodenough pulled a long list of names out of his briefcase. In addition to the names of the members of the Board of Realtors that I had also brought, he had others that must have been from the sign-up sheet. After a quick glance at me, to which I replied with a nod, Felix and Farzad agreed to look over the names. The four of us passed over them, one at time, using Felix's Palm Pilot to see if anything hit. Nothing did. And neither did any of the names strike either man as familiar. I wasn't surprised. After we were done, the detective piled his papers together and slipped them back into his case.

"Do you think I could get a copy of the list?" I asked.

He smiled thinly and shook his head. "How's that certification coming, Ms. Applebaum?" he asked, instead of replying to my request.

I opened my mouth but could think of no searing reply.

He stood up. "I'll see myself out. If you think of anything new, you'll call me," he stated, rather than asked.

After he'd gone, Felix excused himself.

"I've got a lunch meeting at Barney's. I haven't met with the buyers there in ages, and I want to give them a sneak peek at the new line."

"So you're working again?"

He passed his hand over the stubble on his head. "I guess so. I mean, I have to get back sometime, don't I? Too many people depend on me." He didn't look at Farzad, but I did. The younger man had his lips pursed in a tiny frown.

After he left the room, I turned to Farzad. "It's good he's working, don't you think?"

"It's about time," the slight man said, kicking off his slippers and tucking his feet up under him. "So, you haven't found out anything, have you?"

"Not much, I'm afraid."

"So much for your house."

I winced and examined his face, hoping to see reflected

there at least some humor. He still wore his almost petulant moue. I felt a sinking in my stomach. There was just no way he would allow me to buy Felix's house unless this case came to some kind of satisfactory conclusion.

"You're still billing us, too, aren't you?" Farzad said.

"If you aren't satisfied, or if you think the bill is too high, you won't have to pay it." Now, that wasn't generally Al's and my policy, but neither did we usually force our services on people whose homes we hoped to buy.

Farzad acknowledged my statement as if it were no more than his due.

"So, who do *you* think killed Alicia?" I asked him.

"That detective thinks it was just a random sex-crime," he said.

"Did he tell you that?"

The little man shook his head. "No, but that's what he thinks. I'm sure of it."

"And what do *you* think?" I asked again.

He leaned his chin in his hands and cocked his head coquettishly. "What does it matter what I think? Aren't you the private eye? Maybe you think I did it?"

"Did you?" I asked in a pleasant tone of voice.

He raised his eyebrows in mock surprise. Then he said, "No, no of course not. Don't get me wrong, sometimes I felt like killing the woman. I mean, not really. But you know how it is. She was exasperating. She wasn't an easy person to share Felix with."

"Was that what it felt like? Sharing your boyfriend?"

"She lived with us, didn't she? And she worked for Felix. Alicia was always around, and she was a presence, if you know what I mean. She wasn't someone you could ignore."

I nodded. "That must have made moving to Palm Springs pretty attractive."

He smiled. "Absolutely. Of course that wasn't the only reason, and we still want to go. But getting away from her was definitely part of it. For me, at least."

I shifted tacks. "Farzad, why wasn't the alarm on the night Alicia was killed?"

He wrinkled his brow. "Well, it wouldn't have been, would it? We never used it when we were home, only when we went out. And even then Alicia was pretty bad about turning it on. Anyway, if there's nothing else . . ." He rose to his feet both suddenly and languidly, like a cat. "Let me see you out."

I was about to object, but there really wasn't anything more I could ask Farzad. Perhaps he had killed her. He certainly had motive. But he, like Felix, had been in Palm Springs. They would have to have conspired to kill her together, and to provide one another with an alibi, and that just didn't make any sense.

As I drove cross-town to my prenatal appointment, I ran through the list of suspects in my mind. There was Charlie Hoynes, and Dakota. And his ex-wife. There was Felix and Farzad. Nahid Lahidji, Julia Brennan. None of them seemed any more or less likely than the others. So who had killed Alicia, and why? Was it just some crazed psychopath, after all?

Just then, my cell phone rang. It was Kat. "You're not going to believe this," she said.

"What?"

"Marilyn found her programmer."

"She what?"

"She found her programmer. It was in the glove compartment of her car the whole time. She only thought it was in her purse. She hadn't driven the car, so she didn't see it."

"How did she suddenly find it?"

"She went into labor yesterday, and her husband was on the other side of town at a meeting. Her mother-in-law drove her to the hospital in Marilyn's car. Marilyn opened the glove compartment to look for some tapes to take into the delivery room with her."

What did this mean? If Marilyn's programmer hadn't been stolen, how had her number been used? Someone must have programmed her number into a different programmer. But who? And why?

"Did she tell all this to the detective?"

"I'm sure," Kat said. "Her babies are fine, by the way. Still in the NICU, but she says they'll be out in a few days."

"That's wonderful. Um, Kat?"

"Yes?"

"How are you feeling?"

There was silence on the other end of the line. "Okay, I guess."

That morning, before I'd gone out, I'd done a little Web surfing. I hadn't been sure whether I was going to talk to Kat about what I'd found out, but now that I had her on the phone, I couldn't bear not to. "Sweetie," I said. "I hope you don't think this is presumptuous of me, but I got a few names for you."

"Names?" she said warily.

"Of therapists. People who specialize in bulimia among women our age."

"I had a therapist."

"Did you like her?"

She didn't reply.

"Do you want me to give you the names?"

After a few seconds of silence, she said, "Okay."

"I'll email them to you."

"Okay."

"I hope you don't think I'm butting in to something that's none of my business."

"No. No," she said listlessly.

"Kat, you know you can call me. Anytime. Day or night. If you feel like doing something, or if you just want to talk."

"I know."

"Have you gone back to a meeting?"

"I was thinking about it."

"Maybe you should go to one. Is there one tonight?"

"There's one on Saturday, at Cedars."

"How about you bring Ashkon to my house, he can hang out with Isaac and Ruby, have a sleepover, even. And you can go to the meeting. You won't even have to tell Reza if you don't want to."

I wasn't sure whether or not she'd accept my offer, and I was tremendously relieved when she did.

I walked into the doctor's office, mulling over what Kat had told me about Marilyn's programmer, and nearly fell over with surprise. Peter was sitting, waiting for me, reading a copy of *Baby* magazine.

"Hey!" I said. My eyes nearly filled with tears at the unexpected sight.

"Hey, yourself."

I sat down next to him and grabbed his hand in my own. I squeezed, tightly. "What are you doing here?"

"Finding out all sorts of interesting things. Did you know that you're not supposed to be eating tunafish sandwiches while you're pregnant?"

"Really? Why not?"

"Mercury poisoning. Tuna is full of mercury. Which causes birth defects and learning disabilities."

When the nurse came to get me, she found Peter on his

knees between my legs, doing his best to administer a Stanford/Binet to my belly button.

Of all the appointments for Peter to join me for, he had to be there when my doctor read me the riot act about my weight.

"Twenty-five to thirty-five pounds," she said. "That's what we recommend."

I smiled a sickly smile.

"Juliet, you've already put on close to fifty pounds. And you're nowhere near done."

I nodded. "I know. Scary, isn't it?"

She shook her head. "Your blood sugar is perfect, so that's a good thing. Are we scheduling a c-section, given that you've had two? Recent studies do indicate a heightened risk of uterine rupture in post-caesarian trials of labor, particularly multiple caesarians."

It took me all of a second to decide. "Yes, let's schedule it."

"Good choice. Given that, the size of the baby isn't as important as if you were planning on a natural birth. But still. You are gaining weight faster than we would like."

I looked over the doctor's shoulder in time to catch Peter snickering into his hand. I freed a foot from the stirrup and aimed a kick at his groin. He jumped out of reach.

"I want you to watch what you eat," the doctor said, helping me sit up.

And watch, I did. I watched the milkshake and the French fries all the way from my plate to my lips. In my defense, I will say that it was Peter's idea that we go to Swingers for lunch after the appointment. I couldn't be expected to satisfy myself with some limp salad while he downed a burger, could I?

I had just turned down, with considerable ceremony, a

refill on my milkshake when Peter's cell phone rang. He answered it and murmured into the receiver for a minute. When he hung up, his face was pale.

"You're not going to believe this," he said.

"What?"

"That was Jake."

"Jake your agent?"

"Yeah."

"And?"

"Charlie Hoynes's daughter is dead."

"His daughter? You mean Halley?"

"Jake was on his way to the funeral, and he remembered that Hoynes and I had just got together. He called to make sure we knew about it."

I thought of Hoynes's wife, and her obvious desperation on the day we'd spoken. "Oh, No. That's awful. Did she die in the hospital? Was it the anorexia?"

Peter nodded. "I guess she starved herself to death."

The French fries and ice cream roiled in my stomach, and I put a hand over my mouth and ran to the ladies room.

Twenty-eight

PETER did not want to go to the funeral. He was right; we barely knew Hoynes, had never met his poor daughter, and my motivation for insisting we attend was entirely suspect. Nonetheless, within half an hour we'd gone home, changed our clothes, and were on our way out to the cemetery. I called the kids' schools from the car and arranged for Ruby and Isaac to stay late in their after-school programs.

The service had already started when we arrived at the chapel on the cemetery grounds, but it had clearly not been going on long. A thin woman with limp brown hair hanging shapelessly over her ears led the assembled congregation in a hymn that I'd never heard before. Something about sheep and water and Isaiah. She wore traditional priestly vestments, but draped with a shawl made out of some kind of African Kinte cloth. I'm not particularly good at distinguishing among the various Christian clergy, but the formality of her robes, combined with the consciously inclusive nature of her language and clothing, led me to infer that it might be an Episcopal service.

The hymn singing went on long enough for me to peruse the crowd. There was something familiar about it—something that seemed less than funereal, and it took me a while to put my finger on it. Finally, it hit me. But for the somberness of the tone, the room had the feel of a bat mitzvah. People were dressed in regulation black, but that had long since become the color of choice at every life-ceremony, from weddings to brises to bar mitzvahs. There were a few people weeping, most noticeably Charlie Hoynes's ex-wife. What gave the proceedings their adolescent, nearly celebratory feel, however, were the rows of teenagers, strictly segregated by sex—the boys in bright, barely-worn suits, the girls in dresses either too childlike for their size, or too skimpy and revealing for the event. The children seemed genuinely upset; all of the girls, and even one or two of the boys, were crying. I couldn't help but notice, however, that most of the children kept one eye on their compatriots to make sure their tears were carefully modulated to that of every other girl, no more nor less dramatic, their grief neither more nor less apparent.

After the service, I made Peter join the procession of cars out to the gravesite. I refrained, however, from forcing him to take one of the white roses handed out by the black-gloved attendants. We stood at the rear of the crowd, while the Episcopal priest murmured a few additional prayers. Halley Hoynes's mother was seated on a white wooden chair at the edge of the grave, and as the line of people began to pass by her, dropping their rose on top of the polished, golden wooden casket as it was lowered slowly into the black, loamy earth, she began to wail. Her cries were soft at first, high pitched and impossible to understand. Soon, though, her voice grew louder and clearer. She was keening the words 'my baby' over and over again. Hoynes sat a few feet away from her, Dakota at his side. He stared grimly into the rectangular hole, his face flushed, his lips clamped shut. Dakota wore a pair of oversized, black sunglasses and lipstick that shone dark and almost purple against her pallid cheeks. She too stared straight ahead, ignoring the cries that had now grown to shrieks. The procession passed, flower by flower, in front of Halley's wailing mother.

Finally, just when I felt that I, who knew the poor woman not at all, might be forced to approach her to offer some kind of a comfort, another woman, small, round, dressed in a grey coat, crouched next to the grieving mother and pressed her damp face to her own doughy cheeks. The little woman cried, too, but silently, and something about her noiseless grief seemed to still her friend's howling. They rocked together at the edge of the grave, until the last flower was tossed on the casket, and the priest had come to offer her arm.

As we made our way back down the narrow paths to our cars, the priest announced that the family would like us to join them at Barbara Hoynes's home in Brentwood. I pulled out my pad and jotted down the address. Peter glared at me.

"We're not going," he said.

"Yeah, we are."

"Why?"

I pulled open my car door and motioned for him to get in. I didn't want anyone else to hear this argument. "I don't know. Because Alicia Felix was murdered just a few weeks ago, and now Halley Hoynes is dead, and I just have a feeling about it all."

Peter slammed the car into reverse and began to back slowly down the hill. "How can you possibly have a feeling? That's ridiculous. Shameless. Charlie's daughter died of anorexia. What could that possibly have to do with Alicia's murder?"

"Alicia was anorexic, too!"

He shook his head at me. "And so is half of Los Angeles. So what?"

I sighed and, slipping off my shoes, lifted my swollen feet onto the dashboard, making sure to tuck my skirt under me so as not to flash any of the other mourners. "You know what Al always says about coincidences."

Peter shook his head impatiently. "Juliet, we don't know the woman. We never met her daughter. How can we just show up at her house? It's absurd. Anyway, aren't you afraid she'll recognize you?"

"There were at least a hundred people at this service. Do you honestly think anyone will notice us there?"

"You're not exactly small enough to fade into the wood-work, honey. And with my luck, Hoynes will trap me in some corner, and I'll end up committing to writing his wretched movie, just because I feel sorry for him!"

"Don't be absurd. His daughter is dead. The last thing Hoynes is going to want to do is talk business."

But of course that's exactly what Hoynes did want. As soon as we walked into the living room of the ostentatious plantation-style McMansion off Mulholland Drive, Hoynes grabbed Peter and dragged him off to talk business. Thank God Jake caught sight of the two of them and insinuated himself into their tête-à-tête, otherwise Peter's career would surely have foundered on the rocky shoals of a vampire abortion comedy.

Once I realized that my husband was safe in the hands of

his agent, I felt free to wander the edges of the crowd, eaves-
dropping. It was essentially a typical Hollywood scene, although there were more overdeveloped young women in
tight funeral wear than I'd seen before at the kind of parties
Peter and I attended. I supposed that these were Charlie's
actresses, all there to prove their allegiance and hope it
would be remembered when it came time to cast the next
television show or movie.

Barbara Hoynes's friends looked like they had wandered in
off the set of an entirely different picture. They were much
older, in their late forties or early fifties, as was she. Many of
them were typically thin and elegant, but the woman who
had comforted her at the graveside was not the only one who
looked like a regular person. There were one or two other
women who, like Barbara herself, looked their ages. Barbara
sat in an armchair in front of the empty fireplace, her face by
now more or less composed. It was obvious even sitting down
that she was a tall woman, and one who had once been shapely
but had now grown more stately and imposing. She had a
broad shelf of a bosom and a wide, flat face interlaced with a
fine webbing of wrinkles around her mouth and eyes. Unlike
her husband's current girlfriends, she had clearly avoided the
plastic surgeon's knife, although perhaps the size of her breasts
indicated a long-ago familiarity with the shape-altering formula so prevalent among the younger women in the room.

I was doing my best not to look like I was staring at Halley's mother, when I felt a hand on my arm.

"Hi," Dakota said. She was still wearing her sunglasses.

"Hi."

"This is a nightmare."

"It's very sad."

Dakota ran a trembling hand through her hair. "I just
can't believe it. That stupid girl."

I glanced at her, surprised. Most of us try not to express those kinds of sentiments, even if we do feel them.

Dakota took a huge gulp of the drink she held in her hands, grimaced, and sucked in air. "I just can't believe it," she said again.

"I'm sure it's a terrible shock."

"Halley was just so *stupid*. I mean, to end up killing herself?" She took another swallow, sucking the last bit of alcohol out of the plastic tumbler. She crunched an ice cube between her teeth and then swayed, grabbing my arm with her hand. It was only then that I realized how drunk she was. "If that bitch finds out about the pills, I am going to be so screwed," she mumbled.

I held my breath, willing her to continue.

"That's all I need, is for Tracker's lunatic wife to figure out that I gave that crazy girl some of my pills." She put a hand over her eyes. "Get me another drink, okay?"

I propped her against the wall and crossed quickly to the bar, sniffing the glass she'd put in my hand. Gin. I motioned to the bartender to refill the drink. "Gin. Straight up," I said.

He glanced at my belly, but followed my instructions.

Dakota was still waiting for me, and I pressed the glass into her hands. She lifted to her lips and drained it in a single, huge gulp.

"Dakota," I said softly. "What kind of pills did you give Halley?"

She wiped her mouth on the back of her hand, leaving a smear of red lipstick like a bloodstain. "Just normal pills. Speed, you know. But, like, natural."

"Ephedrine?" I asked.

"Natural ephedrine. It works great." Then, without another word, she stumbled off.

I heard a disgusted snort and turned to find the small,

heavy-set woman who had comforted Barbara when she had broken down at the graveside.

"Horrible woman," she said.

I nodded and extended my hand. "I'm Juliet Applebaum."

"Susan Kromm. Poor Barbara, to have to deal with that woman."

I nodded.

A man who was clearly her husband stepped up next to her. His head was a dome of mottled pink skin. He hadn't, thank goodness, attempted the dreaded comb-over, but the bedraggled length of the few strands of baby-fine hair remaining on his head led me to believe that he might be considering it. He put his hand on the small of his wife's back and she leaned into him.

"This is so hard," she whispered.

"I know, dear," he said, reaching a trembling finger to wipe a tear from her plump cheek.

The moment was so intimate that it made me feel uncomfortable to be part of it. Just then, though, my attention was distracted by a stifled giggle. Crowded around a grand piano, not too far from Barbara, was gathered a group of teenage girls. Three of them sat thigh by thigh on the piano bench, and the others leaned against the heavy black sides of the instrument. The girls were whispering to one another, and every once in a while one of them giggled, and was immediately hushed by her peers. What was remarkable about the girls, or perhaps what was unremarkable about them, was their size. There were all, to a one, tiny. Tall or short, their waists could easily have been spanned by my hands. They had long legs, revealed by miniskirts, on which their knees bulged round and bony, separating fleshless thigh from sticklike calf. Individually, they might have seemed skinny, perhaps a bit unusually so, but together, in a group, they looked like nothing so much as a well-dressed, carefully made-up group of concentration camp survivors.

I was not the only one whose attention was riveted on the girls. Barbara Hoynes's eyes kept returning to them as though drawn by an irresistible force. One by one her guests approached her, murmuring their condolences. Each time she shook the proffered hand, nodded her thanks, and then looked back at the collection of bony limbs huddled around her piano. At last, her attention seemed diverted once and for all. Charlie, who had finally released Peter from his grip, crossed the room toward his ex-wife. He held Dakota's hand in his, and she swayed against him. He came to a stop in front of Barbara's chair and cleared his throat ostentatiously.

"My dear—" he began, but Barbara cut him off.

"Not now. Just shut up, Charlie."

The room grew absolutely silent. It was so quiet that one could almost hear the ticking of a hundred watches on a hundred wrists.

"Just shut up, Charlie. Please." Her voice was thick with pain and suppressed rage.

"Our poor little girl," Hoynes said, his face growing red, his eyes filling with tears. His grief seemed tried-on, like an ill-fitting outfit from the back of a studio's costume warehouse. And yet it was most likely real, wasn't it? He had lost his daughter. His only child.

Barbara's composure broke, and she began to scream. "You pig. You son of a bitch. You killed her. You and your gaunt and wasted girlfriends. She knew what you liked. She knew what you wanted, and she starved herself to try to be that for you. Look at that . . . that *stick* you're with! Look at her! That's what killed your daughter. You're what killed my Halley!"

She stabbed her finger at Dakota, and lunged at her. The younger woman leapt back, tripping over her feet, Hoynes's hand the only thing that kept her from tumbling to the floor in a pile of twig limbs and falsely inflated breasts.

The crowd of people had stopped even pretending to look away or be busy with their own conversations. Even Susan Kromm seemed frozen by shock and horror. Suddenly, the grieving mother turned toward the group of girls who had claimed her attention before her ex-husband's approach.

"And you!" she shouted. "What is wrong with all of you? You watch your friends die, one after the other, and it makes no impression on you at all. Are you trying to kill yourselves? Is that it? Will you only be happy when every last one of you is dead?"

The girls at first seemed to shrink into themselves, then one of the three on the piano bench rose on shaky legs and ran from the room. Within seconds, the others followed. Barbara collapsed back in her chair and began to weep. The sound of her tears seemed to liberate the frozen crowd. Susan Kromm rushed up to her, along with a few other women. They crowded around her chair, stroking her hair and back. The others in the room began at first to whisper to one another, but quickly their voices rose to a low hum, and the tinkling of glasses and silverware resumed.

Peter caught my eye from across the room, his eyebrows wiggling frantically. My husband wanted out of there. I shook my head at him and held up a finger. I needed just another minute or two.

I walked out of the living room, through the front hall, searching for the girls. I found them outside, sitting on the wide low steps leading up the front porch. I opened the door and let myself out. As soon as they saw me, their voices hushed.

"Hi," I said.

There were five of them, gawky, skinny girls with identical long, straight hair and pale skin. None of them responded to my greeting.

"That was pretty awful, wasn't it?" I said.

A girl with brown hair and a mouth full of teal blue braces nodded, shivering dramatically and hugging herself with wrapped arms. "God," she said.

"She acts like it's our fault," another girl whispered. This one was the prettiest of the group, although her perfect features were marred by a rash of angry pimples across her chin and forehead.

The other girls nodded. A tiny girl with close-set eyes, wearing a pale-pink childlike jumper over a Peter Pan blouse said, "She's got it so backwards. I like almost told her, Halley was the one who taught *me* how to do a fifty calorie fast. She was like my mentor!"

"Really?" I said, sitting down next to them on the step.

The girl immediately seemed to regret her words.

One of her friends rolled her eyes, and then said, in a cloying, rehearsed voice, "Halley had a terrible problem."

"Did she?" I asked. Then, watching the girls out of the corner of my eye, I said in a soft voice, "Well, I wish I had that problem."

They grew still, staring at me.

"I mean," I continued. "Look at me. I'm so fat."

"Aren't you, like, pregnant?" the girl with the braces asked.

"Yeah," I said. "But I'm so *huge*. I'll never get back to the way I'm *supposed* to look. Not by normal means. I wish I could figure out what to do about it."

The pretty girl leaned toward me, her blond hair falling

over her pale grey eyes. "It's just a question of control," she said.

"What do you mean?"

"I mean, the only reason you look like that is because you aren't *controlling* yourself. I totally understand. I mean, look at me." She poked one boney thigh. "I'm a total gross pig, but this is nothing compared to what I looked like six months ago. You've just got to assert some control."

The girl in the pink jumper nodded her head vigorously. "You know, support really helps. I mean, the world is full of people who just want you to be as fat and disgusting as they are. You have to try to find other people to help you. To inspire you."

"Like you guys found each other?" I said.

They nodded.

"Where did you all meet?"

They glanced at one another, an unspoken debate going on. I smiled encouragingly, and finally the girl with the braces said, "We met online. In a Pro-Ana chat room."

Twenty-nine

THE story the girls told me sounded like some kind of sick joke, an urban legend passed along in whispers from one hysterical parent to another. They were, however, in dead earnest. These girls were, the five of them, Anas. Actually, the girl in pink was an Ana and a Mia, but the others seemed to look down on her indecisiveness. She would occasionally allow food to pass her lips, so long as she promptly forced herself to purge. Theirs was a purer devotion; like the girl they had gathered to mourn, they preferred never to eat at all.

Anas, they told me, viewed their anorexia not as a disease that must be cured, but rather as something to nurture and celebrate.

"Look," the girl with the braces told me. "We're not stupid. I mean, I think every single one of us is on the honor roll." They others all nodded. "We know anorexia is a mental illness," she said. "It's just that we prefer to suffer from it than to look . . ." Here she paused, and it was quite clear what she meant. Than to look like me.

One of the girls, a tall, stoop-shouldered creature with a sharp nose and a small mouth crowded with teeth, piped up, "We don't try to, what's the word? Make other people join us, or anything."

"Proselytize," I said.

She nodded. "Right. We don't do that. In fact, there isn't a single Ana website that doesn't say right off that it's not a place to come to try to learn how to be anorexic, it's just there to help and support people who already are."

"But not support like 'help cure,'" the pretty blond with the bad skin interjected. "There's always some idiot coming on the sites to flame us and tell us we're crazy and we need therapy and all that. We shut them down pretty quick."

The girl with the braces nodded. "I mean, *hello*. We're *all* in therapy. We're in like more therapy than anyone in the free world!"

The girls giggled.

"Why are you in therapy?" I asked. "Why bother, if you don't want to stop being anorexic?"

The girl in pink waved one tiny hand at the door behind us. "Why do you think?" she said. "Our parents. They make us go."

I nodded. "Halley was in the hospital, wasn't she? When she died?"

At the mention of what was clearly a dreaded place, a palpable shudder ran through the group. I turned to the last girl, the only one who hadn't spoken yet. She looked like a slightly mousier version of her blond friend. Her hair was dirty blond, and she wasn't as pretty, although her skin was clearer. It was brilliantly clear, in fact. So pale and white that I could see the blue of her veins pulsing in the hollows of her forehead. "Have you ever been the hospital?"

"Yes," she said in a small voice. "I was there with Halley. That's why I look like this." She wrapped her arms around herself, trying to shrink her already minuscule body into something even smaller and more invisible.

"Like what?" I asked gently.

"You know. Fat."

The girl with the braces leaned across and hugged her friend. "It's okay Tawna. It's not your fault."

I did, I thought, a good job of wiping the astonishment from my face. Was this child serious? She looked like she weighed no more than Ruby, even though she was a few inches taller than I. Did she really think she was *fat*? And did the others *agree* with her?

"They don't let you out until you reach a certain weight," the girl in pink explained to me. "It's awful. They watch you at every meal; they even force-feed you. You get weighed every day, and they won't discharge you until you reach what-ever weight they decide is enough."

"What was their goal weight for you, Tawna?" I asked.

She shook her head silently, as if the number were too depressing even to express aloud.

I let the question hang in the air for a moment, and then I asked the others, "So what happened to Halley, do you know? How did she die?"

Tawna shook her head, a queer glow lighting her luminous skin. "She was amazing," she whispered.

"What do you mean?"

The other girls all leaned in to hear. I wasn't sure if this story was being told for the first time, or if it was simply one so compelling that they were eager to hear it again and again.

"Halley was regal. Like a queen. No, better than a queen. Like a goddess. The doctors would come with their weight charts, and she would stare them down. She'd sit at meals and not even touch her food. Not even move it around on her plate. She just sat there with her hands in her lap, staring at the nurses, daring them to try to force-feed her."

"Wow," breathed the girl with the braces.

"The night she died, it was like a presence went through the ward. I could feel her passing through us, saying goodbye. You know, giving us some of her power. I know it sounds crazy, but I think she just willed her own heart to stop, I really do."

"If anybody could do that, it was Halley," the blond said.

They all nodded, sighing in appreciation of their friend's supreme control.

"Halley always said that was how Dina died. That she killed herself without killing herself, you know? She just willed herself dead," Tawna said.

"Dina?" I asked.

"Dina Kromm. She's another girl from the website," Tawna said. "She died a few months ago."

No wonder Susan Kromm had been so distraught. Halley's funeral must have reminded her of her own daughter's.

"Dina was a Mia *and* an Ana, like me," the girl in pink said, with pride.

"Not really," the girl with braces scowled. "She was a Mia like a hundred years ago. In junior high. By the time she died she was pure Ana." She said this with pride.

"Do you know lots of girls who end up killing themselves?" I asked.

"Not really," Tawna said. "I mean, you meet them in the hospital; it's kind of unavoidable because that's where they end up. And sometimes people from the websites just kind of disappear, and you aren't sure why. But we knew Dina and Halley, because we're all from LA."

"Do you get together often, in person?"

"No, not really," Tawna said. "We talk every day, but online. We instant message, or post to the boards. It's too hard to get to each other's houses. I mean, Rachel lives in the Valley, in like Calabasas, right?"

The girl in pink, Rachel, nodded. "I think Dina and Halley used to see more of each other, because they were both from Brentwood. But they didn't go to school together or anything. They met on the websites, just like we all did."

Our conversation was interrupted by the tinkling of a cell phone. "That's my ring," the girl with the braces said. She pulled out her phone and glanced at the caller ID screen. She answered the phone, saying, "What?" in a long-suffering tone. She looked at the blond girl. "It's my mom. Twyla, you ready to go?"

Twyla nodded. As if on cue, the other girls pulled out their phones and dialed their parents to come pick them up. I was dismissed. As I watched them drive away, I wondered if Alicia had introduced Halley to her Pro-Ana life. What had the supposedly recovered anorexic said to her boyfriend's daughter about this terrifying cyber-world? Had Halley spoken to Dakota about it, perhaps? Their relationship had been terrible, by all accounts, but Dakota had admitted giving Halley diet pills. Maybe they had shared the online world, as well.

Thirty

"GODDAMN it, Ruby!" I shouted. "Finish your food!"

She clamped her lips together and pushed the plate of noodles away.

"Ruby!"

"I hate it," she said through gritted teeth. "I hate it."

"You do *not!* It's beef and macaroni, just like Grandma Wyeth makes. Eat it!"

"I hate it when the noodles and the meat are touching! It's gross!"

"They have to touch; that's the whole point. It is not gross. You like this. You're the reason Daddy made it, because you like it so much at Grandma's house. Now eat it!"

"No!" she bellowed, throwing herself to her feet.

I grabbed her as she was running out the kitchen door and dragged her kicking and screaming back to the table.

"Juliet!" Peter said loudly.

I looked up at him.

"Honey," he said gently. "It's okay. She doesn't have to eat it. Leave her alone."

Suddenly, I saw myself through his eyes, my hair hanging in my eyes, my forehead sweaty, my face red with the effort of holding my squirming daughter.

"Oh God," I whispered, dropping Ruby. She collapsed into her chair, crying. "I'm sorry, Ruby," I said, and then I burst into tears myself. I ran out of the room and threw myself onto my bed.

I buried my face in my pillow and cradled my belly in my hands. Here was another girl, another chance for me to screw up, to create a person who so loathed herself and her body that she would rather die than look like a normal woman. Than look like me.

The bed shifted and I felt a warm hand stroking my hair. I leaned into Peter's leg, pressing my face against the slick softness of his ancient jeans. I squeezed my eyes shut. He kissed me on the back of the neck.

"Shades of Margie Applebaum, huh?" he said.

I opened my eyes. "My mother used to make me sit at the table all night until I cleaned my plate."

"Did that work?"

I nodded. "Usually. By the time the TV went on I'd gag whatever it was down. I didn't want to miss *Three's Company*."

He laughed.

I sat up and leaned against his chest. "Once, I remember she made this disgusting carrot thing. Like some kind of vegetable stew. Tsimmes, I guess. I must have sat in front of it for hours. I tried to eat it, I really did, but every time it got close to my lips, I would feel like I had to throw up. I couldn't do it."

"So what happened?" He pulled me close to him and kissed my neck again.

"My dad tiptoed into the kitchen and gobbled it up for me. He didn't say anything; he just stood over my plate and ate it as fast as he could. I don't think my mom ever knew what happened."

"Why didn't he just throw it out?"

"Because she would have found it in the trash and killed us both."

Peter laughed. I began to, as well, but then my eyes filled with tears.

"It's okay, sweetie. It really is. Ruby will get over it. And you apologized."

I nodded, wiping the tears from my eyes. I reached over him and, taking a tissue, blew my nose loudly. "What's she doing?"

"Eating a peanut butter sandwich in front of the TV."

"And Isaac?"

"Him, too."

"But he doesn't even like peanut butter!"

Peter smiled. "You know how it is; if Ruby's allowed to have a peanut butter sandwich in front of the television, then Isaac's going to want one, too, even if he has to choke it down."

I sighed. "Food. I just can't bear it. Why is it so *fraught?* Why don't we just eat what we want, until we're full, and that's it? Why is it such a *thing?*"

He squeezed me tighter. "I don't know, baby. But it's not as bad as you think it is. You're just freaking out because you spent too much time talking to those crazy girls today. Most people aren't like them. They're not normal."

"I know," I said.

He gave me a last kiss on the cheek and said, "I'm going to go clean up the kitchen. Why don't you relax. Read a book. Do your email. I'll put the kids to bed tonight."

I nodded and rolled over on to my side. I was debating a hot bath when the phone rang. It was Al.

"So, did you find out anything at the funeral?" he asked.

I groaned. The last thing I felt like doing was describing my conversation with the skeletal girls. "His ex-wife hated Alicia, that's for sure. I mean, not just her, specifically. She blamed her daughter's death on her husband's obsession with skinny women."

"Hmm. She's a pretty obvious suspect. I imagine Good-enough has questioned her already."

"I suppose so," I said. I told him about Dakota. "Maybe Alicia found out about the pills, and Dakota killed her to keep her from talking about it."

"But don't you think that would have been a pretty drastic reaction? I mean, maybe now it's a motive for murder, what with Halley dead. But Halley was still alive when Alicia was killed."

"You're right." I sighed.

"What's wrong with you?"

"What do you mean?"

"You sound strange. Is it the baby?"

"No, no. I'm fine. Just tired."

"Tell you what," he said. "I've got nothing going on to-morrow. You take the day off and relax, and I'll spend the day checking on all the possibles. Not the grieving parents, but the others. That friend of Alicia's. The waitress? Dakota the pill pusher. The Board of Realtors folks. I'll feel around one last time, and if I don't find anything, we'll call it a day on this case, okay?"

"You think we should give up?"

His voice softened. "I think this is one of those crimes better left to the professionals, kiddo. It was probably a B&E gone wrong. We're not going to find anything out, and

I'm betting Detective Goodenough won't, either. Someday the creep will do it again, and maybe he'll get cocky and leave more of a trail."

I knew he was right. I had allowed myself to get distracted with the Hollywood types, the anorexic girls. But I knew as well as he did that this was just one of those random, horrible crimes that never get solved. Didn't I? Then I remembered Brodsky.

"But if we don't solve this crime, we're not going to get hired by Brodsky, and our entire business is going to go under!" I groaned.

"There's nothing we can do about that."

I felt the prick of tears in my eyes, and swallowed, hard. Damn those pregnancy hormones. "I won't get my house, either. No house, and no business. Great."

"Look, Juliet. That's what this business is like. Sometimes we catch the guy, sometimes we don't."

I sighed. "I know."

"There's just nothing we can do about it."

"I know that, too."

"Get some rest," he said, and then he hung up.

I lay in bed for a while, listening to Peter do the dishes, and then the sounds of the children splashing in the bathtub. Ruby was instructing Isaac on what his role would be in the mermaid game they were about to play. That's always the way it is with them. They spend hours planning their games, deciding who will do what, who will say what, but they rarely get around to the actual game. It's the setup, the preparation, that's the fun, apparently.

After a little while, Peter called to me.

"Marcel wants his mother!" he said.

Like a modern-day, Batman-loving version of Proust, Isaac couldn't go to sleep without a kiss and what he called a "lie with me." As I lay cuddling my boy, who never seemed as small and baby-like as when dressed in his footy-pajamas, lying in his too-large expanse of bed, his face flushed from the bath and his fine hair still wet, I wondered what adult experience would trigger memories of these times with me. What would be his *madeleine?* The scent of Mr. Bubble? The taste of chocolate chip Teddy Bear grahams? The sensation of nestling his face against a woman's breast?

Lying next to Isaac made me feel infinitely calmer and less hopeless. When his breathing had grown deep and soft, I carefully heaved myself out of his bed and wandered down the hall to kiss his sister good night. She was in her own bed, surrounded by stuffed animals. I kissed her lightly on the forehead, turned off her light, and went to find her father.

Peter was stretched out on the sofa, a comic book catalogue in his hand.

"Feeling better?" he asked.

I nodded and sat down next to him. "Nothing like a few Isaac and Ruby hugs to improve my mood. Especially when someone else has gotten them cleaned up and into bed." I took his laptop off the coffee table. "Mind if I use this?"

I hadn't really meant to do it. Truthfully, I was feeling done with the case, sick of Alicia, sick of her problems, sick of the skinny girls. Yet, for some reason I found myself launching a search engine and inputting the words "Pro-Ana." The sites were every bit as horrifying as I had imagined they would be. They were all maintained by the girls themselves. Some were pretty basic, weblogs with a diary entries about progress losing weight, poems about their alienation from the world, complaints about their parents. Others were remarkably sophisticated. These often had entire archives of "trigger" photographs—pictures of particularly skinny Hollywood actresses and models, and occasionally pictures of the girls themselves.

At one point Peter looked over my shoulder. "Oh, *gross,*" he groaned. Peter, a man whose imagination includes cannibals with strips of flesh hanging from their teeth, couldn't bear to look at the photographs.

I followed a link to a message board. In page after page, girls wrote each other begging for advice on how to lose weight, asking for support in dealing with their parents, complaining about how awful they looked and felt—not because they were so thin, but because at eighty or ninety pounds, they were 'pigs.' I found a series of postings of girls joining forces to support each other through fasts. Every once in a while there would be a desperate message from a girl who felt herself succumbing to the urge to break the fast. The others would email frantically, encouraging her to be strong, sending her trigger photographs, sometimes even giving her their home phone numbers to call for more immediate support. These group fasts lasted a week, or ten days.

Most girls had a signature line that it took me a few minutes to figure out. Finally, I got it. They would sign their names, or their online nicknames, and then the initials "CW," "HWE," "LWE," "GW," followed by numbers. Each girl was letting the others know the most salient facts about her—her current weight, her highest weight ever, her lowest weight ever, and her goal weight. It was the last number that I found most disturbing. Not a single girl quoted a number over 100, and many listed seventy or eighty pounds as their goal. Some even hoped one day to break sixty-five. A few of the girls had the most chilling notation of all. At the end of their lists of weights they wrote the initials "UG," ultimate goal. And then the single word 'death.'

Finally, sickened and ultimately bored with the sameness of the pathology on exhibit, I clicked back over to the search engine and input Halley Hoynes's name. She didn't have a site of her own, but she had been a very active poster on a number of the bigger Pro-Ana sites. The last message I found from her was a desperate rant about how she was being forced to go into the hospital. She begged the girls to think of her and send her strength. There was a flurry of supportive postings, including a promise to pray for God to help her "keep the sick fat away."

I clicked to a page maintained by a girl who called herself Thin-Lizzie. On her links page, I scrolled through page after page of weblogs and chatroom sites. More of the same. At the bottom of the last page was a link marked "pics." I clicked on it and found the image that would lead me, finally, to Alicia Felix's murderer.

In the middle of the page of photographs was one of a woman with long blond hair, facing away from the camera. Her emaciated torso glowed white against the black background. I had seen that photograph before, in the album Dr. Calma's nurse had shown me. It was Alicia.

I clicked on the photograph and was led to Alicia Felix's Pro-Ana website. Her name was not, of course, anywhere on the site. Her photographs, however, were everywhere. In addition to the one from Dr. Calma's album, there were dozens of others, each showing off her gaunt body from a different perspective, and carefully hiding her face. The website was not merely a photo essay, however. Alicia provided more of the same kind of information and sick support that the other girls did on their pages, but there was something special about hers. The banner across the top of the page read

"Successfully and Beautifully Ana for Twenty Years!" Her message was quite simple. She had done it, and they could, too.

Alicia called herself Ana-Belle, and described herself as a television and film actress "whom you all would recognize immediately." One long essay called "The Perils of Plump," detailed her difficulties finding roles when her body size exceeded her goal weight. She did not list her credits, but she did make repeated references to actors, directors, and producers who had cast her because of her "perfect Ana body." One of the names she mentioned was Charlie Hoynes.

Alicia's, like the other sites, had links pages, inspirational photographs, diet tips, and 100-calorie-a-day foodplans. She also provided information for Mias, whom she described as "our bingeing sisters." She encouraged them to end a binge with milk or ice cream, because those dairy products came up easily. She cautioned them to brush their teeth frequently, lest they lose the enamel on their teeth and their teeth themselves begin to loosen in the bone. She also warned against "busy-body dentists" who might recognize the warning signs of bulimia. She suggested that Mias try to find older dentists because they wouldn't be as clued into the contemporary issues like eating disorders.

The most chilling section was a stark white page with a quotation at the top—"Scorn the Flesh and Love the Bone." It was a step-by-step instruction manual for surviving a hospital stay without gaining weight. Alicia told the girls what to say to make the physicians believe they were making progress in therapy. She told them to resist at first, but slowly to pretend to be coming around. Alicia told the girls to thank the therapists and nurses, to cry frequently in group therapy sessions, to warn other girls against the dangers of starvation. "The idea," Alicia wrote, "is to snow them with your words and your tears, so they don't even notice that you haven't eaten anything."

Alicia also gave specific information on how to plump up for weigh-ins. She suggested the girls drink large amounts of water, not so much as to make the nurses suspect they were bingeing on water, but enough to add pounds for the scale. She told the girls that in some cases their water consumption would be strictly monitored, and that some hospitals even turned off the sinks in bathrooms to prevent the girls from drinking to hide their weight loss. She suggested the toilet tanks. "That water is clean—it's not from the toilet itself—and there's enough water in your average tank to get you up to weight. Remember, even a few ounces will put the doctors on your side."

Alicia provided specific fat-burning exercises the girls could do in their beds in the middle of the night. Finally, she exhorted them to help one another. "Send a hospitalized friend some laxatives," she wrote. Unfortunately, she said, doctors had grown wise to the trick of sewing pills into the bodies of stuffed animals, but stick deodorant containers were a good place to smuggle pills.

There was more, much more, but by now I was too appalled to read on.

Alicia Felix was, quite clearly, the doyenne of the Pro-Ana universe. She was a role-model—a source of information and inspiration to these pathetic girls. She was, I could not help but feel, a monster, preying on their worst insecurities. Why had she done it? I wondered. What had it given her? Power? A sense of control? Or was she some kind of twisted altruist, wanting to share the skills she had acquired over a lifetime of anorexia?

I thought of Barbara Hoynes's rage earlier in the day, at

her daughter's funeral. How much angrier would she have been had she known exactly what Alicia was up to? Or perhaps she *had* known. Perhaps that was why she screamed at her ex-husband, blaming him and his girlfriends for their daughter's death. Perhaps that's what she had meant when she told me of Alicia's pernicious influence on her daughter.

Thirty-one

THE next morning, when I opened the door to pick up the newspaper, I found a terrifying man on our front stoop. He was huge, well over six feet tall, with a shaved head, a smashed, prize-fighter's nose, and a tattoo of a death's head climbing up from his neck over his left cheek. I gasped, as did he. He looked as scared to see me as I was to see him. He was clutching a letter in his hand, and had obviously been about to drop it in the mail-slot in the door when I opened the door.

"Who are you?" I said.

He pushed the letter toward me, but I backed away from his hand.

"Take it," he said, seeming to regain his composure. "Take it!"

"No," I said, grabbing the door behind me. I tried to slam it, but he wrenched the door out of my hands. That's when I screamed. Within seconds, Peter was tearing down the steps behind me.

"Take the letter!" the man said, just as Peter skidded to a stop next to me.

"Larry?" Peter said.

"Oh my God!" the scary guy said, staring at my husband. "Mr. Wyeth?"

"Call me Peter, please. What's up Larry? What are you doing here?"

"You know this guy?" I said.

"Sure I do," Peter said. "Larry played a corpse on the last Cannibal movie. Didn't you, Larry?"

The man was smiling now. "I sure did. A one-legged corpse. I'm hoping to get a shot at a speaking part in the sequel."

I raised my hands. "What's going on here?"

"Oh man," Larry groaned. "Look, I had no idea who you were. I mean, that you were Mr. Wyeth's wife and all. I was just doing a favor for a friend. I wasn't going to hurt you or anything. I was just supposed to drop this off." He turned to Peter. "Swear to God, man. I wasn't going to hurt your wife."

I snatched the letter out of his hand and tore open the envelope. In magic marker, on a sheet of plain white paper, it said, "Keep quiet about Dakota Swain, or else." I raised my eyes to those of the massive man standing in front of my door. "You have got to be kidding," I said.

He blushed. "I'm sorry, man. Dakota just asked me to deliver it. I don't even know what it says."

"Okay, well. Consider it delivered."

"You're not mad?" he said to Peter.

My husband looked at me, and I shook my head.

"Don't worry about it," Peter replied.

"Cool," Larry said. "Well, bye."

"Bye."

He took off down the steps and jumped into the cab of a pick-up truck that had been pulled up onto our front lawn, crushing the grass. He leaned his head out the window. "Dakota's cool!" he called. "She's just all freaked out because that kid died and all."

I slammed the door shut and leaned against it.

"What the hell?" Peter asked.

I shook my head.

"Are you going to call the cops?"

"I don't know."

"Because Larry's a real sweetheart."

"Right."

"He just looks scary." Peter took my hand and began leading me up the steps. "Do you think it's a real threat?"

"I doubt it," I said. "She's just terrified I'll tell Hoynes about the pills, and then he won't give her the part."

"Maybe you should call the cops. I mean, you can't be sure she's not dangerous," Peter said. Once burned, twice shy, but that's another story.

"I'll figure it out later. There's something I need to do first, this morning."

When Jews are mourning, we sit *shiva*. We sit in our homes, welcome guests, share food, and simply experience our grief for a period of seven days. I knew that Episcopalians had no similar formal ritual, but I was hoping that Barbara Hoynes would be home—I couldn't imagine that a mother would go anywhere on the day after burying her daughter. Still, I didn't expect to find Barbara Hoynes as I did, alone in her lavish home, wearing a bathrobe over her pajamas, rubbing sleep from her eyes.

"I'm so sorry." I said when she answered the door. "I woke you."

She leaned against the doorjamb. "Can I help you?" she mumbled in a voice thickened by sleep, or grief, or a combination of both.

I reminded her who I was.

She stared at me, wordlessly. Her hair was matted down on one side, caught in a single barrette that swung free as she shook her head.

"I'm so sorry to bother you, Ms. Hoynes, especially so soon after your daughter's death. I know how you felt about Alicia. I know it's asking a lot, but I hope you might consider talking to me, just for a few minutes."

"What time is it?" the woman asked.

I looked at my watch. "11:15," I said.

She shook her head. "I've been asleep for thirteen hours."

My eyes widened, but I merely said, "Well, that's to be expected, given everything."

She sighed. "It's to be expected given the three *Ambien* I took last night."

I nodded sympathetically. "I would have done the same. The nights must be unbearable."

She nodded. "They never end." She leaned back in the doorway. "Come in," she said, to my surprise.

She led me through the darkened rooms to the kitchen. She motioned to a chair, and then stood in the middle of the room, looking vaguely around her.

"Here," I said. "You sit down. Can I make you a cup of coffee, or tea?"

She collapsed into the chair and nodded. "Coffee. Over there." She pointed at a complicated piece of equipment that looked more like a flight simulator than an espresso machine. I did my best, trying to imitate the baristas from whom I bought coffee every day. I didn't do too badly, until it came time to steam the milk.

"Don't bother," Barbara said, holding out her hand for the cup. I splashed some cold milk in mine and sat down next to her.

"When we spoke last time, you told me that Alicia was a bad influence on your daughter. Did Alicia Felix actively encourage Halley to become anorexic? Was that how she got the disease?"

Barbara took a careful sip of her coffee and then set the cup down on the table with a trembling hand. "I wish I could blame that on Alicia, but Halley has had an eating disorder for years. Since she was a little girl. Alicia didn't make Halley anorexic. I did that all by myself."

"No," I murmured. "You can't blame yourself."

"Can't I?" Barbara said, staring at her hands. "Halley was always a chubby little girl. The first time I had her on a diet was when she was two. I sent her to summer camps for over-weight children from the time she was seven until she was twelve. Suddenly, she didn't need them any more. She was thin. It took a couple of years before I realized that she wasn't just healthy and slim; she was actually too thin. It took even longer for me to figure out that she was sick. So you see, as much as I wish I could, I can't blame Alicia. I can only blame myself."

I didn't know what to say. Instead, I just patted her hand.

Finally, I said, "Halley spent a lot of time on those Pro-Ana websites, didn't she?"

Barbara nodded, and then suddenly sobbed. She rubbed roughly at her eyes. "They all do. All those girls. *That* I blame on Alicia Felix. That I can lay squarely at her feet. She's the one who got Halley started on those." She beat her hands against the tabletop, and I jumped. "I was so stupid and naïve. At first I believed Halley when she told me that her father's girlfriend was helping her, that she'd got her involved in an online support group. I even got a DSL line so Halley could get online more quickly. I actually thought it was like some kind of group therapy. I was such an idiot."

"How did you find out what the sites really were? Did you track Halley's Internet usage?"

She shook her head. "I wish I had. But I was too trusting. It never occurred to me that anything like that whole Pro-Ana thing could even exist. I didn't find out about it until it was too late, until Halley was so far into it that I couldn't save her." She was crying freely now, wiping at her nose and mouth with the back of her fist. I looked around the room and, not finding any tissues, reached for a dishtowel that was hanging from the handle of the oven I gave it to her, and she wiped away the mucus that was dripping from her nose.

"How did you find out what was really going on?" I asked.

"Alicia's best friend, Dina Kromm. Her mother told me."

"Dina? The girl who died?"

Barbara nodded. "After her death, Susan and Duane went through Dina's computer. She'd bookmarked the Pro-Ana sites. They came to me and told me about them. They even showed them to me. That's how we found out about Alicia."

"They showed you her website?"

She blew her nose again. "They wanted me to join them on a campaign to get the sites shut down, or at least barred from the larger search engines. We were going through the sites, reading them. Alicia's is anonymous, but there were the pictures. She hid her face, but I could tell from her body that she was one of Charlie's girls. They all look the same. Massive breasts, blond hair. Skinny. And Alicia mentions Charlie's noxious TV show on the site. I knew right away it had to be Alicia. Halley said that Alicia had led her to the online support groups, and here was a site mentioning Charlie. It was too much of a coincidence. It had to be her."

"Did you confront your husband with what you'd found out?"

"I tried to, but he refused to take my calls. He never would, that despicable creep. He always made me go through his lawyer when I wanted to talk to him."

"Did you confront Halley about it?"

She nodded. "Right then, in front of Duane and Susan. I thought that given what happened to Dina, Halley would tell us the truth. And she did, in a way."

"In a way?"

"I called her downstairs and showed her the site. I remember I was screaming. I asked her if *this* was what she meant by support groups. I asked her if this was her father's girlfriend."

"What did she say?"

Barbara knotted her hands together, her knuckles white against her chapped, red fingers. "She screamed right back at me. She gave me this ridiculous nonsense about anorexia being a life-choice not a disease. She said Alicia was her idol, that she was beautiful. That all the girls worshipped her. That . . . that . . ." her voice broke. She continued in a whisper. "She said she wished Alicia was her mother."

I leaned across the table and put my arm around her. Her body shook with sobs.

We sat like that for a moment, and then she said, "I told Halley she couldn't see Alicia anymore. I called Charlie's lawyer; I called his office. But he wouldn't speak to me. I was going to take him to court. I was going to get a restraining order against Alicia, and maybe even try to stop Halley's un- supervised visitation with him. At least get rid of those overnights. Then Alicia was killed. And you know what? I was happy. I really was. Because she could never hurt Halley again. It never occurred to me that it was already too late."

Barbara sat up in her chair, shaking away my arm. I leaned back and looked at her. She took a shaky breath. "You probably want to know if I killed her, don't you?"

I did, but I doubted she'd tell me if she had.

"The day she died was Halley's first day in the hospital. I spent the whole day there with her. They let me sleep with her for the first night until they moved her to the ward. I almost wish it had been me who killed Alicia Felix, but it wasn't."

Thirty-two

I got the address of the Kromms and then left Barbara alone in her house. I didn't want to. The idea of a mother grieving in a place empty but for memories of her child was nearly more than I could bear. Barbara was there, forced to stare at the beautifully framed photographs of her child, compelled to walk by the room with its pastel sheets and poster of Buffy the Vampire Slayer, the stacks of CDs by Fiona Apple and Alanis Morissette, the outgrown stuffed animals and American Girl dolls gathering dust on the shelves, the iMac covered in stickers with its Grrl Power mouse pad. Halley's room might have looked nothing like I imagined. The silence in the house, however, I knew would be exactly like that of my worst fears. The silence of a disappeared child is like no other.

I picked Ruby up from school, leaving Isaac for his father. I needed some time with my girl, and I figured Peter and Isaac could amuse themselves with Legos and superheroes for a little while. Ruby and I had tea in her favorite café in Santa Monica, then we went on a drive through the Canyon. It was while we were winding through the narrow streets, counting Jacaranda trees, that I realized we were only a few blocks from where Halley's friend Dina had lived. I rechecked the address and telephone number that Barbara Hoynes had given me, and then turned to Ruby.

"Hey, chickadee. Do you mind if we make a stop?"

She was chewing on the neck of her T-shirt. She spat out the fabric. "A work stop?"

"Don't chew your clothes. Yes, a work stop. But a short one."

She flicked out her tongue, catching the stretched out, damp bit of shirt in her mouth. "Okay," she said.

"Don't chew your clothes."

"It's all chewed up, already."

The blue cotton was crumpled and wadded, full of tiny holes made by her teeth. There was no point in trying to save it.

Dina's parents, Duane and Susan Kromm, lived in a stucco house set back from the road and nestled in a flower garden. It didn't look any larger than my apartment, but given the neighborhood, probably cost well over two million dollars.

Susan Kromm answered the door. "Can I help you?" she said in a soft, sweet voice.

She glanced down at Ruby. "Hello," she said.

"Hi," Ruby said.

"I'm Juliet Applebaum," I said. "We met at Halley's funeral?"

She smiled uncertainly.

"I hope you don't mind us dropping by like this. I know this is a painful time for you. But Barbara Hoynes gave me your name and address. I'm investigating what happened to Alicia Felix."

Susan Kromm's face paled, and she bit her lip. "Why are you here? I mean, we didn't know the woman. We never met her."

"I understand. I was hoping to talk to you a bit about the Pro-Ana websites. Barbara told me that you and your husband were involved in a campaign to have them shut down."

Susan nodded.

"Do you mind if we come in?" I asked.

She looked at Ruby.

"Ruby will amuse herself," I reassured the woman. "I have some paper and a pen in my purse."

Still looking unwilling, and suspicious, Susan motioned us inside. "Does she watch television?" she asked.

"Yes, I do!" Ruby replied.

Ruby and I followed Susan into her kitchen. There was a small sitting area on one end of the room. She snapped on the TV, changed the channel, and handed Ruby the remote. "It's on Cartoon Disney, honey. Don't change it without asking your mom, okay?"

"Okay," Ruby said.

"Would you like a cookie? I have Girl Scout cookies." She turned to me. "They got delivered a few days ago. Dina must have ordered them from one of the neighbor girls." The older woman's cheeks twitched as she tried to hold back tears. "She ordered my favorite, Thin Mints, and her dad's, Tagalongs. She never would have eaten them herself, but she liked to see us eat. I used to think she just liked to see us enjoying our food. Now I think it had more to do with feeling better than us, because she could resist a cookie, and neither Duane nor I could."

I laid a comforting hang on her arm. "I'm fine," she said, swallowing hard. She bustled around her kitchen, laying a small pile of cookies on a plate for Ruby, and pouring a glass of milk to go with them.

"What do you say?" I said, when Ruby had accepted the proffered plate and glass.

"Thank you," my daughter mumbled, her face already smeared with chocolate. "Is this nonfat milk?"

"Ruby!"

"What?"

"Yes, honey. It's nonfat. Is that okay?" Susan said.

Ruby nodded. "Good. Nonfat is the best."

I resisted the urge to spank her. It wouldn't have done any good. I satisfied myself with watching her gobble the cookies. Milk or no, she was getting plenty of good old fashioned fat into her body.

"I'm so sorry about that," I said, as Susan and I sat down at the kitchen table on the far side of the room.

"Oh, no. Please don't apologize. It's fine," Susan said. She put another plate of cookies in front of me, and I popped a Thin Mint into my mouth before considering how I was going to question the woman with my mouth full of food.

"She was a terrible person, that Alicia," Susan said.

I nodded.

"Those hospital 'tips?' Did you see those?"

"Yes," I said.

"That's what killed Dina. And Halley, too."

Tears had begun to spill down her cheeks.

"What happened to Dina?" I asked gently.

She wiped her eyes with a pale pink tissue she pulled from a box with a crocheted cover. "She drank the water in the toilet tank in her hospital room. Trying to fake weight gain. She was so weak from starvation that her kidneys couldn't handle the strain. They shut down, and then her heart just stopped." Susan's voice was so quiet it was almost inaudible.

"And you think she learned how to do that from Alicia's website?"

"I know she did. And it wasn't just the site. That woman would instant message her. Email her. Encourage her. She killed my little girl. Alicia Felix killed my daughter. You can't know what that feels like. You just can't."

At the same moment, we looked over at Ruby who was trying to see how many cookies she could cram, unchewed, into her mouth. Susan reached out a trembling hand and gripped mine, tightly. "Hold on to her. As tight as you can," she whispered.

"I will. I will."

We sat there for what felt like hours, but was probably not more than a moment or two. We were silent, until we heard the front door open, and a voice called out, "Susan? Sue?"

"In here, Duane," she called back.

Duane Kromm came back into the room, stopping when he saw Ruby. "Hello there," he said.

"Hi," she replied. Then, for no reason that I can think of, as my daughter is not known for her willingness to share anything, especially not cookies, Ruby held the plate out toward Dina's father. "Want one?"

"Don't mind if I do," he said, taking a Tagalong.

"They're best if you just pop them in," Ruby said. "Don't chew until it's all in your mouth."

Duane followed her instructions carefully. He swallowed, and then smiled at Ruby, his teeth covered in chocolate. "You're absolutely right. That's the way to eat them."

She nodded seriously, and then she turned her attention back to the television.

He crossed the room and extended his hand. "Duane Kromm," he said.

Susan said, "This is Juliet . . . er . . ."

"Applebaum," I said. "We met at Halley's funeral."

"She's investigating the murder of Alicia Felix," Susan said.

The smile faded from Duane's face, and he sat down heavily in the chair next to his wife.

"I was hoping you could tell me a little bit about your campaign to shut down the Pro-Ana sites," I said.

Duane and Susan looked at each other. Finally, she said, "We . . . we haven't really gotten very far."

"No?" I said, surprised.

"We've been busy, with work and all."

"Work?"

She nodded. Her face was flushed.

"What do you do?"

"We work in real estate. I mean, Duane's a realtor. I don't sell much anymore. I sit on the Board of Realtors."

I stared at her, comprehension hitting me suddenly. I opened my mouth, but no words came out. Finally, I said, "Why did you choose Marilyn Farley's programmer, Susan?"

Duane stared at me. His lips were bright pink, and a bead of saliva sat in the center of the lower one.

At that moment, Ruby giggled, and I realized what I had done. I had brought my little girl into the home of a murderer. I stood up slowly. "Ruby, come here," I said.

Her head snapped up. She could hear the fear in my voice.

Duane also stood.

"No!" Susan moaned.

I began to back up in Ruby's direction. I held my hand out to her.

Duane took a step toward me, and I flinched.

"Stop," Susan said. "Duane, stop."

He looked back at her, his entire face, even his head, flushed bright red. "She knows," he said.

"The little girl. Look at her little girl." Susan's voice was shrill, and tears had begun to course down her cheeks.

Her husband looked at Ruby, who had stood up, her face smeared in chocolate, her lower lip trembling.

"Mommy," she whispered. I crossed the room and scooped her up into my arms.

"He won't hurt you," Susan said. "He won't."

I looked at her husband. He collapsed into a chair and put his head in his hands.

"It doesn't matter. It doesn't matter anymore," he said.

His wife rushed to his side and wrapped her arms around him. Suddenly, he looked up at me. "Susan wasn't involved. She only changed the programmer to protect me," he said. "I used her programmer to get in the door of the house. When I told her what I'd done, she took the programmer down to the Board office right away, in the middle of the night, and used the computer to reprogram it. She just picked the number randomly. We were lucky Alicia was alone in the house. We made it back in plenty of time to put the programmer back in and erase the other numbers."

"Hush, Duane. Hush," Susan whispered, reaching her hand to her husband's lips.

He shook free of her. "There's no point. She knows I killed that woman." He turned to me. "I stabbed her, and I'm not sorry. She killed our little girl."

Susan, her voice ragged with weeping, said, "What are you going to do? Call the police?"

My breath was caught in my chest, and I squeezed Ruby close to me. How was I going to get my little girl out of this house, safely away from him?

He shook his head, very slightly. "I'm not going to hurt you," he said. "Or your beautiful little girl."

"What are you going to do?" I asked, willing my voice not to tremble.

"It would be better for me if I turned myself in, wouldn't it?"

"Yes," I said.

He sighed. "Okay then."

Thirty-three

I called Felix and Farzad as soon as I knew for sure that Duane Kromm was under arrest. I had, in fact, watched from my car, Ruby strapped into the booster seat she was fast outgrowing, as Detective Goodenough pulled up to the Kromm's house, accompanied by a police cruiser with two uniformed officers. I had called the detective directly, not really expecting that he would carry out the arrest himself. He had, though. It had been his hand on Duane's shoulder, steering the older man out the door and into the back seat of the cruiser. The handcuffs had seemed unnecessary to me, although of course I knew that they were standard procedure.

My conversation with Farzad, who had answered the telephone, had been brief. I outlined quickly what had happened, and I promised to come by the next day to give him more details.

When I arrived the next morning at their house, I found

Detective Goodenough there before me. He was out of mufti, dressed in a pair of jeans and a thin silk T-shirt rather than his usual suit and tie. The maid led me into the living room, where the three men sat drinking small cups of Farzad's excellent coffee. I felt, for a moment, like I was interrupting something.

"Detective Goodenough was . . . uh . . . good enough to come by on his day off to tell us about the arrest," Felix said, smiling at his pun.

I waited to see what the detective would say. Would he acknowledge my role in the arrest, or would he assume credit himself?

The tall man raised a cinnamon-colored eyebrow at me and said, "I was just recounting the tale of your excellent detective work, Ms. Applebaum. You'll be a force to reckon with if you ever get yourself certified."

I lowered myself into the remaining empty armchair. "Thank you," I said.

"I still don't really understand it," Felix said, leaning forward in his chair. "I mean, I can't believe the man would blame poor Alicia for his daughter's death, just because of those websites. It seems so crazy."

I slid my eyes over to Farzad. He sipped delicately at his coffee. I got the feeling that he understood full well why Duane had felt a murderous rage toward Alicia Felix. I certainly did. Detective Goodenough didn't respond to Felix, and it seemed to me that he, too, comprehended the motive for the murder. Felix's inability to do so probably stemmed from the fact that he loved his sister too much to imagine her as a kind of Pied Piper of anorexia, playing the girls to their grim deaths.

"Will there be a trial, do you think?" Farzad asked.

I looked over at Goodenough, who seemed inclined to let

me answer for him. "I don't know," I said. "Probably not, given that he turned himself in. I think the prosecution will likely offer a deal to avoid a trial. A jury is likely to feel . . ." and here I paused.

We were all silent for a moment, and then Felix said, "Sympathy. That's what you were going to say, isn't it? The jury will have sympathy for that man."

I leaned forward and placed what I hoped was a comforting hand on his knee. "Perhaps. Not because of anything about Alicia, but rather because Duane was a grieving father." But of course it was because of the kind of woman Alicia was. Any defense lawyer worth his or her salt would make sure the jury knew exactly what she had done, the damage she had wrought.

Felix sighed heavily. "So if there's no trial, then what? How long will he go to jail?"

I let the detective handle that.

"We'll be pushing for murder two," he said. "The defense will probably ask for voluntary manslaughter. We'll see how it pans out. I promise you, Felix, I'll be calling the DA, putting pressure on for the maximum."

Felix nodded at the other man. I glanced over at Farzad who was chewing on his lower lip. Perhaps he felt, as I did, that there was not much to be gained, in the larger scheme of things, by putting Duane Kromm in jail for decades. I knew, however, that neither of us would ever say as much to Felix.

"Do you think you'll be moving to Palm Springs, now?" I asked.

Farzad smiled and cast a sly eye in my direction. "Juliet wants to know if we'll keep up our side of the bargain."

"What bargain?" Felix asked.

I looked down at my hands resting on my belly. At that

moment, the baby kicked me, hard, right in the ribs, and I grunted. "Sorry," I said. "Baby's kicking."

"What bargain?" Felix asked again.

"You know Juliet wants to buy the house. That's why she was here in the first place. I told her that if she found out who killed Alicia, we'd give her first shot at making an offer."

"You did not!" Felix said.

"I did indeed," he said.

Felix glared at me. "And is that why you helped us?"

Shame kept me from looking into his eyes. "I helped you because I wanted to find out what happened to your sister. And because you hired me. And, well, yes it's true, because I wanted the house. But of course you're under no obligation. Obviously."

Goodenough interrupted us. "Without Ms. Applebaum's assistance, we may never have found the killer. It certainly would have taken us significantly longer. And who knows if we would have been able to obtain a full confession."

I looked at him, gratefully.

Felix jerked to his feet. "I'm sorry. I'm just . . . this is all so hard to deal with . . ." He stumbled out of the room. I leaned my head in my hands, embarrassed at the hash I'd made of the conversation.

"Juliet," Farzad said gently. I raised my eyes to his. "Give him time. He's angry now, but not at you."

"I know. I'm sorry," I said.

"I'll call Nahid."

"No, really. I mean, let's just leave that alone for now, okay?"

He nodded. "And your bill?"

I smiled thinly. "That I have," I said reaching into my bag.

Thirty-four

"YOU have got to get rid of this wallpaper," Stacy said, her head cocked to one side, and her hands on her hips.

It really was awful. Flocked gold roses on a background of red velvet. It wasn't however, as disturbing as the mirrored ceiling in the master bedroom. "We can't. It's original. Ramon Navarro apparently designed it himself. Or at least that's what Nahid said. Still, even with the wallpaper, it's a pretty great house, don't you think?"

At that moment, Kat walked through the French doors into the living room. "I don't know what that inspector was talking about. That's no fifty thousand dollars in dry rot damage."

"Thank God!" I exclaimed. What with covering over the fish pond in the kitchen and repairing the railings in all the various balconies overlooking the first floor from the second, there wasn't going to be much money left for structural repairs.

"That's going to cost you at least one hundred and fifty thousand dollars. Definitely. They've eaten through the foundation, for heaven's sake! I've never seen that before." Kat continued.

I groaned.

"Is Peter really going to use the dungeon as his office?" Stacy asked. "It's so gloomy and depressing down there."

"Uh, Stacy? Peter? Gloomy and depressing?"

"Right. Right. It's perfect for him. Is it true that it has iron handcuff holders pounded into the walls?"

"That's nothing," Kat said. "There's an old wooden saw-horse down there. I can't even imagine what Ramon was getting up to on that."

"If he really did own the house," I said.

"Oh, he owned it," Kat said. "Not even Nahid would lie about that. I'm just not sure he ever lived here. He might have rented it to some other weird silent movie star friend of his."

"Or else kept it for one of his mistresses," Stacy said.

I looked down to the crook of my arm where Sadie rested, quiet for once. Moving with a newborn is not something I recommend to anyone. Between nursing and napping, I wasn't spending much time unpacking. The bulk of the work was falling to Peter and the kids. That meant that we were still living out of boxes two weeks after moving in, and probably would be for the next couple of months. Every time one of the children needed a clean pair of jeans or wanted to locate a missing toy they would upend a box and leave the contents scattered on the floor. So far I still wasn't able to bend over and pick anything up, but I was hoping to feel better any day.

Felix hadn't, in the end, sold us his house. Nahid Lahidji had put it on the open market and had started a bidding war the likes of which the LA real estate market hadn't seen in months. Apparently, I wasn't the only person not put off by the home's grisly history. Truth be told, by the time Duane Kromm was arrested for Alicia Felix's murder, I wasn't entirely sure I wanted any more to do with that beautiful house. There were a few images I knew I'd never get out of my mind. One was Alicia in the bathtub, her skeletal body torn and stiff. The other was one I hadn't seen but only imagined—that same woman, hunched over a computer, weaving her malignant web to ensnare those wretched girls.

Felix had done me a more important favor, however. He had called Harvey Brodsky. I'm not sure what he told him, but it was enough to convince the man to offer us a contract. From now on, Al and I would be providing investigative services to Brodsky's high-profile clients. The man had advanced us enough money to hire an exterminator, put Julio on salary as a part-time receptionist (with strict instructions to stay away from the computers . . . at least until we could convince his probation officer otherwise), and even, wonder of wonders, pay ourselves a little.

Kat had also come through in the end. The house she found for us was nowhere near as impeccably done as Felix's house; in fact it was pretty much a crumbling pile, but it was certainly fabulous. It hadn't been touched since 1926, when Ramon Navarro had it built, which meant it had its original tile bathrooms, moldings and built-ins, and Maxwell Parish–style murals sprinkled throughout the house. It also had its original electricity, plumbing, and roof, but someday we'd have the money to fix all that. The fixtures were all a kind of Hollywood Gothic wrought iron and ornate, with the occasional ghoul's head popping out of nowhere on a chandelier or sconce.

Peter had fallen in love with the house at first sight. The

dungeon was definitely his favorite room, but the ballroom on the first floor was a close second. He was already full of plans to redo the cracked black and white parquet floor himself. I wasn't planning on holding my breath. The room was vast enough for the kids to ride their bikes in on rainy days. The whole house was huge, in fact. There were bedrooms galore, although many of them were oddly shaped and tucked under the eaves, or accessible only through a bathroom, or a closet. It was a strange house, which, as Ruby pointed out, was entirely appropriate, given that her family was pretty strange, as least when compared to those of the other kids in school. I took issue with that, vociferously. Peter's an odd bird, sure, but I consider myself absolutely and completely normal. More or less.

I could tell that the house was going to suck up every spare cent we ever earned, but somehow that didn't bother me much. Perhaps because I had no time to be worried. Miss Sadie had made her surprise appearance a good two weeks before my scheduled c-section date. We'd planned on being moved in in plenty of time to welcome her home. Instead, the movers had loaded dozens of newborn diapers into their boxes, and I'd limped my way up the jacaranda- and jasmine-flanked front path with the baby in my arms. It didn't really matter that I didn't have the nursery set up for her; Sadie refused to sleep in her brother's old crib. The only place she'd close her eyes was our bed. That wasn't that unusual; both the other kids had spent a few weeks sleeping with us. The problem was that Ruby and Isaac had decided that what was good enough for the baby was good enough for them, and we had yet to spend a night without three extra sets of toes digging into our sides, and pushing us to the far ends of the bed. I was grateful that Mr. Navarro's old bedstead was still in the master bedroom. I wasn't sure where I was going so find a new mattress to replace the musty, sagging one—they don't make them in that size anymore, if they ever did. He'd probably had to special order the king and a half we were currently inhabiting with varying levels of comfort from a special company that catered especially to silent movie Lotharios. I hoped they were still in business.

"How are you feeling?" Stacy asked Kat.

Kat smiled. "Okay. Ready to give birth."

"When are you due?"

"In a couple of weeks. Although I don't think I can last that long. It's going to be castor oil for me in a few days."

I smiled at Kat. For all her desperation to be done with the pregnancy, she looked better than she had in weeks. She had started seeing a new therapist, and was working on coming to peace with the various elements in her life that had conspired to reinvigorate her bulimia. She had decided not to go back to work for Nahid after her maternity leave, but to spend at least a few years home with her kids. Reza, to my surprise, had not only supported her decision, but had defended it to his mother. Kat had finally come clean with him about her problem, and they were working on it together. I wasn't naïve enough to think all was solved for Kat, and that now she would be fine forever. Alicia Felix's case had taught me just how tenacious and persistent a foe an eating disorder is. But Kat had a good chance of being all right, especially if we all made sure to be there for her. And I wasn't going anywhere.

The baby woke in my arms and began to cry. I sat down on a wooden crate that contained the pieces of the Appalachian rocking chair Lilly had sent to me as a baby present. Peter had sworn he would assemble the thing before the baby was weaned, but in the meantime the box made for an adequate nursing chair. I lifted my shirt, and Sadie flung herself at my breast, grunting and snuffling like a miniature water buffalo. I sighed as I felt the tingling of my milk letting down and stroked her velvet cheek with my finger. I knew that one day this little girl, like her sister, would start to think about how she looked and what she ate. Right now, though, I was filling up her body, plumping up her flesh, building her bones and brain. Life is a meager business, sometimes. There are lean times, shortages, tough winters, barren patches. It was my job, my duty and pleasure, to see that she started out suitably, and blessed to be, fat.